A Rose for Jenny

CAROLE GIFT PAGE

A JANET THOMA BOOK

THOMAS NELSON PUBLISHERS
Nashville

Published in Nashville, Tennessee, by Thomas Nelson, Inc.

Library of Congress Cataloging-in-Publication Data

Page, Carole Gift.
  A rose for jenny / Carole Gift Page.
    p.   cm. — (Heartland memories; bk. 5)
  ISBN 0-7852-7671-6
  I. Title. II. Series: Page, Carole Gift. Heartland memories; bk. 5.

Printed in the United States of America

1 2 3 4 5 6 QPV 04 03 02 01 00 99

To my children with all my love—
Heather Gift Page;
Kimberle Carole Bunch and her husband, Jay;
and David Aldon Page and his wife, Lisa.

She was going away. She didn't know where. She didn't know when. She just knew she had to go. Had known it somewhere in her skin and marrow since the day she was born. A day God must have looked down on her with dark, scowling eyes—she being born with a dead father, an unwed mother, and an aunt and uncle pretending to raise her as their own.

She was a child of whims, everyone's whim but her own. Belonging to everyone and no one all at once. Moved back and forth between the big, drafty Victorian houses on Honeysuckle Lane and Maypole Drive like a summer boarder, as if folks couldn't quite decide whose kin she was. That's how it had been throughout her full eighteen years.

As a child she had learned to recognize the knowing looks behind her neighbors' polite smiles as they inquired, "How's our little Miss Jenny today? And how's your mama? And your auntie?" The insinuation being, which family is the poor little tyke abiding with this week?

The truth was, she was hardly sure herself. She was like the wind, shifting and changing, coming and going, impossible to clasp in your hands. She knew this much. She was Jenny Herrick until her mama married Robert Wayne, but she would have, *should have* been Jenny Reed if her mama had married her papa and he hadn't died before she was born.

For most of her life, the particulars of Jenny's birth had remained shrouded in mystery—her father dying at Pearl Harbor, her mother giving her away. Her kin—the Reeds, the Herricks, and the Waynes—were as closemouthed as tombs about her heritage. It had taken most of Jenny's life to put the cryptic pieces together, like an immense jigsaw puzzle she was forced to assemble in secret. As if she were the one to be ashamed instead of those who had sired and raised her.

But during her growing-up years she'd reached a woeful conclusion. With so many pieces missing, the puzzle of her life would never be complete and Jenny Wayne would never feel like a whole person who truly belonged. Even now at eighteen, she'd go anywhere in the world to find that feeling of belonging; she'd do anything to know where she was meant to be. She figured it had to be somewhere besides Willowbrook, somewhere where she didn't feel so out of place, like an ugly old domino in a fancy game of chess.

Now, at last, it was time to discover what worlds lay beyond Willowbrook. It had to exist—that place she was born for . . . and someone she was made for who would love her best of all. It couldn't be a fairy tale. The need was too real inside her. She would find what she was looking for. After all, this was her high school graduation day, and the universe was waiting. After tonight, nothing would ever be the same again.

"I go out walkin' . . . after midnight . . ."

Jenny stirred, her mind snapping back to the moment, reality flooding in—her grandmother's antiquated bedroom smelling faintly of musk and lavender sachet. Jenny stood at the dormer window, staring into nowhere, her slender frame swaying instinctively to the plaintive Patsy Cline tune coming from the television set. Jenny's mind had been spinning away like a spindle of yarn in a frisky cat's mouth. Had Grandma Betty noticed? In her mysterious, eccentric ways, could she read Jenny's mind and guess she was going away? Jenny whirled around, her hands on the windowsill, her shoulder blades against the cool glass.

With relief she saw that Grandma Betty was sitting in her rocker as always, her skeletal form lost in the folds of her loose housedress, her raven-brown eyes fixed on the flickering black and white images on the screen. Her bony fingers kneaded the tufted arms of the chair; it could have been her usual nervous fidgeting or maybe she was keeping time with the music. Jenny couldn't be sure.

But, thank heavens, everything was as ordinary as ever. Jenny's extravagant plans remained her special secret to savor and enjoy. Grandma Betty, more the renegade than Jenny ever thought of being, was still watching *American Bandstand,* oblivious of all the daring ideas stirring in Jenny's mind. And Patsy Cline was crooning the final notes of "Walking After Midnight," her husky voice as haunting and smoldering as a wisp of smoke in the night.

At last Betty looked up and caught Jenny watching her. In her dry, raspy, take-charge voice, she said, "Come here, child. Sit a spell. Watch the show with me."

It took Jenny a minute to find her voice. "I—I can't, Grams."

"You always watch with me."

"I know, but not this time." Jenny hated saying no to her grandmother. The sad, irascible old woman had a way of wrapping Jenny around her little finger, even now, with Jenny a grown woman ready to strike out and make her own mark in the world.

"I said, sit down," said Betty in a way no one would dare refuse. Sometimes the elderly woman's demands were impossible to meet, like the awkward times she insisted Jenny send Betty's dead husband, Tom, upstairs to her room for a chat. Or, like yesterday, when she ordered Jenny's mother, Catherine, and Jenny's stepfather, Robert Wayne, out of her house because they had offended her sensibilities in some way.

Of course, it was all too easy to offend Grandma Betty. Alcohol had plundered her mind, skewing her view of the world, and what alcohol hadn't done, mental illness had accomplished, so that simply conversing with her was always an adventure. No one knew, going in, whether she was in her right mind this time or in some distant realm of the imagination no one else could enter.

Since birth, Jenny had been her grandmother's favorite. She and Grams were like peas from the same pod. While the rest of the family juggled a thousand and one duties and demands, Grams always had time for Jenny. She made Jenny feel as if there was nothing on earth she'd rather be doing than sitting with her granddaughter, chatting or watching their favorite television shows. And, of course, Jenny could get away with things with Grams that no one else in the household dared to try.

Like saying no to her.

"I can't watch television now, Grandma Betty," Jenny told her in a quiet, firm voice. "I have to get ready. This is my graduation day."

Betty looked up at her, her dark eyes glazing, the lines in her angular, crepe-paper face sagging in dismay. Her gray-brown hair stuck out from her head in all directions, as if a bird's nest were perched on her cranium. She might have looked comical to some, but not to Jenny, who felt only a pang of sadness and a smidgen of guilt. Usually Jenny took the time before school each morning to brush her grandmother's hair, but today, with all her graduation plans, she'd forgotten.

"I guess I can stay a minute," Jenny said, going over to the bureau for the silver-handled hairbrush. She slipped over to her grandmother's chair and gently brushed Betty's thick, unruly hair back from her wrinkled face.

"Watch the show, child," Betty said again, pointing to the television screen. In his bright, buoyant voice, Dick Clark was introducing the next performer. Jenny could imagine him turning his handsome, smiling face to the camera and announcing Jenny Wayne, the popular new singer with her song already climbing the charts. She could taste the desire inside her, worse than hunger or thirst. Someday. Someday she'd be on *Bandstand* and everyone would be applauding her.

"Look, Jenny, look!" Betty sat forward, her bony fingers gripping

Jenny's wrist, her shoulders hunched, her neck stretching like a whooping crane's. "I like that man. Look, Jenny. He looks like my Tom when he was young. Do you suppose he's my Tom?"

"No, Grandma. Your Tom's in heaven with Jesus."

"Oh." Betty released Jenny's wrist and sat back, her shoulders slumping, and allowed Jenny to brush her hair. After a minute she said, "Will you take me to see Tom?"

"I can't, Grandma."

"You take me, Jenny. Old Tom doesn't like waiting."

"I'm graduating tonight, Grams."

Betty's lined mouth settled into a pout. "Stay home with me."

"I can't. I'm getting my diploma." Just saying the words made her breathless with excitement. "And Danny and I are singing a duet at the ceremony. It's a special honor, Grandma. Half of Willowbrook will be there."

"I'll go too," said Betty, hoisting herself unsteadily out of the rocker. Her spindly arms and legs trembled as her slight frame wobbled inside her baggy housedress. She was so thin, Jenny noted, a strong breeze could carry her away.

Jenny gently urged her back into the chair. "You can't go, Grams. I wish you could, but you've been ailing and need your rest." Actually, Jenny had tried to persuade her family to let Grams go, but their decision was final; no one wanted Betty making a scene at the graduation ceremony. Jenny pressed her cheek against her grandmother's forehead. "I promise, Grams, Danny and I will come back and sing our duet just for you, okay?"

Betty's bristly brows arched in puzzlement. "Danny?"

"You know. My cousin. Pastor Marshall's son. He's graduating too."

"Oh, yes. Danny," she said vaguely.

Danny wasn't actually Jenny's cousin, not by blood anyway, but the relationship was too complicated to explain to Betty. Jenny wasn't sure how much her grandmother even remembered about her husband

Tom's other family—the mistress and two children he had kept secret for years. Jenny had never really known her grandfather, but it was common knowledge that Tom Herrick's infidelities were what had driven Betty to drink in the first place.

Perhaps, in some ironic way, God had been merciful in blurring Betty's memory. She apparently remembered only the good things about her husband; she never mentioned his second family, even though, over the years, the two families had managed to accept Tom's ignominious legacy and had grown into one multifarious clan.

It was Tom's daughter, Bethany Rose, who had married the local minister, Todd Marshall, after his wife died of tuberculosis. Bethany had even adopted Todd's son, Danny, making Danny Jenny's cousin in a roundabout fashion. But Danny was more, so much more. He was Jenny's dearest friend in the whole world.

"Is he a nice boy?" Betty was asking.

Jenny started, her mind flying back to her grandmother's quaint bedroom with its floral-print wallpaper and antique mahogany furniture. The air, heavy with musk and lavender and other pungent smells— cedar chips, menthol, mothballs—was suddenly too close. She felt a bit feverish, light-headed. Maybe it was summer coming too early, or more likely—if she admitted it—thoughts of Danny made her cheeks flush with a pleased, self-conscious warmth. "I'm sorry, Grams. What did you say?"

"This boy. Danny. Is he a good boy?"

"Oh, yes. Very nice. He wants to sing and make music just like I do. Maybe we'll join a band together someday soon. You've met him before, Grams."

"Is that him there on the television?"

"No, but he's very handsome. Tall and strong. And he has dark brown hair combed back in duck tails. Like Elvis. And he has the dreamiest blue-green eyes that look right into you, like he knows you better than you know yourself."

"Like my Tom used to look at me."

"Yes, Grams. Just like your Tom." Jenny felt her excitement rising. "And Danny—he has such a wonderful voice. Like Dean Martin's. Only he doesn't sing like him—all croony and soft. Danny likes a beat. He's crazy about gospel and rhythm and blues."

"Like Elvis," said Betty.

Jenny stifled a laugh. "Don't tell Mama that. She's still hopelessly in love with Sinatra and the Dorsey brothers. She thinks Elvis is sinful."

Betty looked around, twisting her frail shoulders. "Where is Catherine? Where is my daughter?"

"She's in Chicago," said Jenny, a dark edge of concern stealing into her voice. She hadn't wanted her mother making the trip so close to her graduation, but she'd gone anyway. "She's at a reception for a new exhibit of her paintings at the Art Institute. Remember? I showed you the article in the newspaper. But she's coming home. She promised. She's coming in on the train this afternoon. Papa Robert is picking her up at the depot. They should be home any time now."

"Catherine's coming home?" echoed Betty distractedly.

"Yes, Grandma. She promised she wouldn't miss my high school graduation for anything."

Her grandmother reached out knobby fingers and touched Jenny's face. "You look like my Catherine. Only prettier."

"Thanks, Grandma." Jenny knew she had her mother's thick auburn hair and her green eyes and freckles, but most folks said she had her father's aristocratic good looks. Whenever Grandmother Anna reminisced about her son, Chilton, she'd say, "Jenny, that boy of mine—your father—was the handsomest lad this state of Indiana ever saw. Had the look of royalty about him, he did. We lost a precious treasure when we lost Chip."

Jenny always felt waves of tearful emotions when she gazed at the photos taken at the Willowbrook depot of Chilton Reed going off to war. He looked incredibly handsome and invincible, standing proud and confident in his jaunty, white sailor outfit.

Jenny had long ago convinced herself she and her father looked alike, although maybe she only imagined the resemblance because she wanted to believe—had to believe—she carried something of him in her genes.

Jenny realized Grandma Betty was still looking up expectantly, waiting, not comprehending that Jenny had to forego their television watching tonight.

"Listen, Grams, I've got to run and get ready for the ceremony, but I'll see you—" Jenny heard the telephone ring downstairs. She headed out the door, blowing a kiss back at her grandmother. "I'll see you before we leave, Grams."

She raced downstairs to the parlor and answered the phone on the fifth ring with a breathless, "Hello?"

"Jenny? It's me, Mama."

Jenny toed the fringe on the oriental carpet. "Mama? Are you at the depot? Papa Robert should be there picking you up. Don't you see him?"

"I'm not at the depot, honey."

"Not at the depot? Then where?"

"Sweetheart, I'm still in Chicago."

"Chicago?" Jenny sank down on the Queen Anne chair. The ripple of concern she'd felt earlier was blossoming into panic, disbelief. "You can't be. Your train is supposed to be here by now."

"I know, honey. I'm so sorry. I missed the train."

The panic exploded now. "Missed the train? You couldn't!"

"I got tied up at the Institute, honey. The reception went longer than I expected. Listen, I really tried to make it. I caught a taxi, but you know how bad Chicago's cross-town traffic can be. Wouldn't you know, I missed the train by five minutes."

Jenny fought back a nauseous feeling in the pit of her stomach.

"Then take another train, Mama. Maybe if you hurry—"

"No, Jenny. I already checked. The next train won't arrive in Willowbrook until midnight."

Hot tears welled in Jenny's eyes. "But my graduation—!"

"I know, honey. I'm sick about it. I really wanted to be there for all the pomp and circumstance—and you being an honor student and singing and all. You don't know how bad I feel."

"You've got to be here, Mama," Jenny sobbed. "You promised."

An edge of annoyance crept into her mother's voice. "There's nothing I can do, Jenny. You'll just have to accept it. You're old enough to know we can't always have the things we want in this life."

"No, Mama! You've got to hear me sing. Danny and me. We're singing, 'Climb Every Mountain.' Your favorite song. It won't be the same without you."

"You can sing for me when I get home."

"No! It won't be the same."

"Jenny, this is long distance. I'm running out of change. I'll be home as soon as I can. I promise. Call the depot and have them page Robert and tell him what happened, okay?"

Jenny sniffed noisily. "Hurry, Mama."

"You'll have to help your sister get ready. Make her wear her green taffeta dress, no matter how much she protests."

"Laura's not here. She rode to the station with Papa. She's wearing the pink striped dress Grandmother Anna made her."

"That's too short. Make her wear the green one."

Jenny wanted to say she didn't care whether her ten-year-old sister wore the green dress or her birthday suit, but she held her tongue. This wasn't the time to set her mother off.

"Did you hear me, Jenny?"

She swallowed a sob. "Yes, Mama."

Her mother's voice softened. "I'm sorry it turned out this way, honey. But you'll have Robert and Laura there, and your aunt and uncle. Annie and Knowl wouldn't miss seeing you graduate for the world."

"I know, Mama." Jenny started to say, *They keep their word*, but she knew it would only infuriate her mother to remind her that Annie and Knowl had been there for her since the day she was born. Annie had her own family now and a successful career as an author, but she was still standing in for Jenny's mother. Was it because she considered Jenny a charity case or because Annie had raised Jenny for the first two years of her life and still felt like Jenny's mother?

Even now, as Jenny returned the receiver to its cradle, she thought darkly, *Annie's my real mother. Not you, Mama. It'll always be Annie.*

2

Robert was there, and her sister, Laura, and Aunt Annie and Uncle Knowl, and a dozen other relatives and friends, but Mama didn't make it for the graduation ceremony. She was on a train somewhere between Chicago and Willowbrook, due to arrive at midnight. Jenny knew this fact in her mind, but as she crossed the stage to receive her diploma, her eyes scanned the audience, desperately searching for the face of her mother.

But Mama was never there when it counted.

Her mother missed the graduation party too. It wasn't a party exactly, not in the frivolous sense, but more like a reception. A bit formal and stuffy for Jenny's tastes. Uncle Knowl chatted with anyone who would listen about politics and the upcoming presidential election. Once the editor of the *Willowbrook News,* Knowl still kept close tabs on local and national events. And when he wasn't talking politics, Aunt Annie was answering questions about her next book and when it would be published. Annie was a celebrity of sorts, especially for a small town like Willowbrook. She had once had a book on the *New York Times* Bestseller List—*Pacific Dawn*, a fictional account of Pearl Harbor, inspired by Annie's brother Chip, Jenny's father, who died on the *USS Arizona*. Jenny had tried reading the novel several times, but every time she came to the part about the *Arizona* going down and the sailors dying in the flaming, oil-soaked sea, her tears always made the words blur, so she had finally given up.

Folks who weren't talking politics or literature were swapping the latest gossip about people who weren't at the party, and Jenny found that most insufferable of all. If she and Danny had had their way, they would have gone to the senior dance at the glamorous Willowbrook Hotel downtown. That's where nearly every other graduate was spending the evening.

But the two of them were stuck here at Danny's house, where his father had insisted on hosting the reception. Danny's house was actually the parsonage, an old two-story Victorian the church had renovated. Nice, but nothing fancy. The furniture was careworn and covered with doilies and ceramic vases like the furniture in Grandmother Betty's room at home. The parsonage rooms felt old; they had seen decades of history and accommodated dozens of families through the years.

Without her mother here, Jenny felt even less enthusiastic about celebrating her graduation at the parsonage. From the beginning, the reception had been more a matter of accommodating the wishes of her parents and Danny's, as if they were the ones graduating.

More than anything she wished she were at the hotel, where the music would be loud and the beat frantic and exciting. A local group, the Mad Caps, was performing. It was a group for which Danny had auditioned, but it hadn't worked out. They kept putting him off, saying "we'll let you know; we'll get back with you," but they never did. That's why Danny kept talking about starting his own group; he'd show them. He'd show everyone; he'd get a group and go to town, and make everyone sit up and take notice. Someday he'd be as big as Elvis, and Jenny would be another Brenda Lee, singing her heart out for the world.

But at the parsonage tonight their secret hopes and dreams were tucked away as they chatted dutifully with her Papa Robert and with Danny's stepmother Bethany Rose and his father, the Reverend Todd Marshall. "Purdue!" boomed the reverend in a voice that could have been the voice of God. "That's where Danny belongs. Or, if he has a mind for traveling, he can try one of the big schools back East. Right, Danny?"

Danny shrugged, privately rolling his eyes at Jenny. They had both decided college wasn't for them. Not this year. Not when they had other, more exciting roads to travel.

Bethany Rose, who still looked young enough to be a college student herself, tossed back her long auburn hair and looped her slender arm around the reverend's. With her natural, freckled beauty, she looked more like Catherine—her half-sister, Jenny's mama—than either of them were willing to admit. "Todd, darling," Bethany said in a silky smooth voice, "I think Danny will decide about college when he's good and ready, and not a moment before."

"I know that's what you keep saying, sweetheart, but time is of the essence," the reverend said with forced patience. "Danny's got to decide before the best schools have filled their enrollment quotas for the fall semester. Surely most of Danny's classmates applied to the colleges of their choice months ago."

Bethany was silent. So was Danny. Jenny knew Danny's parents had had this discussion often in recent months, always reaching the same peevish stalemate. Danny always remained outwardly detached, letting them hash it out. Jenny knew he had no intention of starting college in the fall, but his folks didn't want to hear it. Especially his dad.

The reverend, a handsome, polished man who carried himself with immense dignity, was an older, heavier version of Danny. With his robust frame and natural good looks, Danny's father looked more like a matinee idol than a minister. But he was as stern and uncompromising as any preacher Jenny had ever met. If you asked Danny, his father was too rigid and unrelenting. All too often, Danny and the reverend were like oil and water; they didn't mix, and when they tried, there was an inevitable explosion.

"Well, Jenny hasn't decided about college either," said Papa Robert, tactfully trying to ease the tension, "and that's okay."

A grateful smile flickered on Jenny's lips. Her stepfather often made a point of being in her corner, sometimes even when it meant taking sides against his wife. A tall, exuberant, square-shouldered man who had always seemed larger than life, Papa Robert was in business with Uncle Knowl. They owned Herrick House Publishers, and it consumed their thoughts, their time, their very lives. But somehow they still managed to find a little time for their families.

"I'll be happy if Jenny studies for a year or two here at home," Robert was saying. "Now that Willowbrook is a full-fledged university and not just a junior college, her mother and I are hoping she'll stay on here and study."

"Yes, it's a fine school," Bethany Rose agreed.

"You're right. I've got nothing against Willowbrook University. But still . . ." The pastor's words drifted off.

During the lull that followed, Jenny and Danny excused themselves and, stifling giggles, made their way over to the refreshment table. Other friends and relatives were here at the party, too, and should be greeted, but Jenny wasn't in the mood to converse with them tonight. So, at the first opportunity, she slipped off by herself, nursing a glass of warm lemonade. The night was so sultry, the ice cubes melted the minute they hit the tepid liquid. Even with all the windows open and a faint breeze stirring the chintz curtains, Jenny could feel the perspiration on her skin dampening her formfitting white linen dress.

Jenny's private reverie was short-lived as Deacon and Mrs. Schindler, longtime pillars of the community in physical stature as well as social standing, ambled over and offered their congratulations. Mrs. Schindler, as stout as her husband was bald, inquired politely, "Where's your mother, Jennifer, dear? We haven't seen her all evening."

Jenny averted her gaze. "Mama wasn't able to come."

Mrs. Schindler's enormous bosom heaved in feigned astonishment. "You mean she missed your graduation ceremony entirely?"

Jenny nodded. She could feel her chin puckering, but she refused to let anyone see how deeply the tendrils of hurt ran.

"Is she ill?" asked Mrs. Schindler with exaggerated concern.

"No, ma'am, she's not ill. She's . . . out of town."

"Goodness gracious!" Mrs. Schindler touched her hanky to a corner of her gaping mouth. "Why would your mother go out of town when her daughter's graduating?"

For the umpteenth time that evening, Jenny explained about her mother's art show and how she had missed the early train out of Chicago and would be arriving at the depot at midnight. Just when Jenny thought she would have to endure Mrs. Schindler's consoling overtures all night, Papa Robert came striding over, one eye on his wrist watch, and said, "Jenny, don't let me forget about picking up your mama. You know she can't wait to get home to you, and it would be a shame to leave her sitting at the train station waiting this time of night."

"Oh, that would be a dreadful thing," Mrs. Schindler agreed.

Danny came to Jenny's rescue too. Looking dashingly handsome, if a bit uneasy, in his new black suit, he brought Jenny a paper plate with a slice of chocolate cake. Then he offered Mrs. Schindler his arm and said gallantly, "May I escort you over to the refreshment table for some cake? It's going fast."

Mrs. Schindler broke into an appreciative smile. "Oh, my dear young man, thank you. You're every bit as kind as your father. Maybe someday you'll be a minister too."

Danny smiled politely, but under his breath Jenny heard him say, "Never in a million years!" Several moments later Danny returned to Jenny's side and whispered, "I can't take this anymore. Let's get out of here. Sneak over to the dance."

"We can't. They'd catch us for sure."

Danny clasped her hand in his, interlocking their fingers. "Then let's go out on the porch and sit on the swing. No one can find fault with that."

She nodded. Hand in hand they zigzagged through the warm crowd and stole out the front door to the rambling porch. At last they could inhale the fresh night air, smelling of newly mown grass and sweet wild flowers. But no breeze was stirring now; the air was close and heavy, palpable as a shroud. Danny sat down on the old oak swing and pulled Jenny down beside him. They rocked with a slow, steady rhythm, the swing's rusty creaking moan breaking the dark silence.

Bits of lamplight spilled through the window sending narrow streamers of gold through the slats of the venetian blinds; the pale light etched the contours of Danny's face with a burnished glow. "I'm glad to get out of there," he said quietly. "Nobody cares about us graduating. All they can talk about are politics and the news. The U-2 incident. Senator John Kennedy running against Ike."

"That's better than all the local gossip—who's drinking too much or running around or going bankrupt. I hate all the talk," said Jenny. "It has nothing to do with us. What difference does it make who wins the election? Or who's running around on his wife?"

Danny slipped his arm companionably around her shoulder. "Actually, I guess I don't mind all the election talk. I like Kennedy. I hope he wins."

"Don't tell my Grandmother Anna. She likes Ike."

Danny smiled. "Ike's okay too. Tell her I said so."

"Ha! I'm staying out of it." Jenny could feel the nubby fabric of Danny's suit jacket rubbing against her bare arm, scratchy, but not unpleasant. She savored his closeness, the lemony scent of his aftershave mingling with the perspiration on his tanned skin. She hoped he would kiss her, then as quickly felt a twinge of panic. They had walked the edge between friendship and romance for so long, being ever so careful not to step over the line, both afraid of the direction their relationship would take if they acknowledged they wanted to be more than friends. Or maybe Jenny only imagined that Danny felt the same stirring of passion, the hunger for physical closeness, when they were together.

They sat in silence, his fingertips stroking her arm, but his mind was obviously somewhere else, far away. She watched the fireflies blink and wink in the darkness like golden stars, shooting this way and that, magical, free to explore the heavens. *Why couldn't people be like that,* she wondered, *free to fly where they wished, to test the world, to soar and sail the night winds?* She and Danny had just graduated; all the speeches had been filled with lofty talk about the future, about the boundless possibilities open to them. "The world is yours," the principal had said. "Step out and seize the opportunities spread out before you."

Danny looked at her, his eyes shadowed. "I don't feel any different. Do you?"

"Different?"

"We're graduates. Adults."

"Maybe it takes time to sink in. I feel the same. Excited. But let down too. Now what, Danny? What happens now?"

He removed his arm from her shoulder and sat forward, rubbing his hands together. "I don't know, Jen. But I can't stay here."

She stared at him, trying to read his expression, but his profile was as unreadable as granite. "You mean, here, your house? Or Willow-brook?"

"Both. This parsonage, this town. I'm suffocating. I can't fit in. Can't be what they want anymore."

"Our folks think things are all set. I'm going to Willowbrook University. You're going to Purdue."

"Our parents can talk all they want. But they can't make the decision for us." He reached over and took her hand. "That's not what you want, is it? Our future mapped out for us by our parents?"

She chuckled dryly. "You know better. I'd love to run off and join a band and make a record and be famous and all that. I think about it all the time. Only wishing doesn't make it happen."

"You don't know what can happen unless you try."

She looked at him, traced the solid curve of his chin. No one understood the deep yearnings of her heart better than Danny. They both felt the same gnawing hunger to create a new life for themselves. "Try? Try what? I wouldn't even know where to begin."

He squeezed her hand gently, yet deliberately, one finger at a time. "We've talked about it long enough. Let's do it."

"Do what?"

"The two of us, go off together and join a band. Will you go with me, Jen?"

Jenny felt a ripple of excitement raise goose bumps on her skin, a heady sensation mingled with caution and disbelief. "What would we do? Just pack up and go?"

"Maybe. Why not?"

"Don't tease me, Danny. We could really go off and join a band?"

"If things worked out right."

"What things?"

"Just things."

"Tell me."

"If I do, you have to promise not to breathe a word to anyone, especially not to your gossipy little sister."

Jenny lowered her voice to a whisper. "I won't. Besides, I don't tell her anything. You know that."

Danny interlocked his fingers with hers again, snugly, possessively. "Okay, here's the thing. I know a guy, a buddy of mine. He graduated a few years back. He has his own band, and he might be looking for some new members."

"New members? Like who?"

"I don't know. He's always looking for a new drummer or singer or whatever. There's always a big turnover in the music business. Guys join bands. Then they drop out."

"How do you know all this?"

"I wrote him. Told him we want to join up. I'm just waiting to hear."

"But he wouldn't want both of us, would he? What chance is there he'd want both of us, Danny? I don't want you to go without me."

"I wouldn't. I swear. He'd have to take both of us." He pressed her hand against his cheek. She could feel the faint stubble of his beard against the back of her hand. "Would you go, Jenny? Are you saying you'd go with me? We've been saying we'd strike out on our own after graduation. We've talked about going away for months now."

"I know, but it was just talk. A dream. Something we'd do some-day after graduation." She shook her head in confusion. "Now it's here. Real. Possible. We just pack up and leave home, just like that. But how do we know things will work out? How do we know we can trust this guy? Who is he anyway? What's his name?"

"You don't know him. Callan Swan. I don't think he's cut a record yet; his stuff isn't on the radio."

"Then why would you want to go with him? How do you know he's not a loser?"

Danny's voice took on a defensive edge. "He's no loser! He's doing great. He's lined up gigs all over the Midwest. County and state fairs from here to Louisiana. It's just a matter of time before a record com-pany discovers him. He's got a great sound, Jen. You'll love him."

She licked her lips. Her mouth felt dry just at the thought of trav-eling around with a band she didn't know and singing at county fairs in places she'd never been. "You really think we could do it, Danny?"

"Why not? We're great together. Someday, once we get some expe-rience under our belt, we'll start our own band."

She leaned against him and he circled her shoulder with his arm again, drawing her close. She liked the feeling of being enveloped in his protective warmth, like the shelter of a cave during a storm. "I don't know, Danny. I want to go. But it's scary—just to pack up and go on the road. Like swinging on a trapeze without a net."

"You'd be safe, Jen. I'd take good care of you. I wouldn't let you out of my sight for a minute." He paused. "You do feel safe with me, don't you?"

"Sure I do. We're best friends, right?" She relaxed her head against his shoulder and he nuzzled her hair with his chin.

"Best friends always," he whispered. His voice grew husky as he added with emphasis, "You can trust me, Jen. I respect you."

"I know you do."

"I wouldn't expect anything from you—you know what I mean. This isn't a line like some guys dish out—"

"I know, Danny."

"Just to see if they can get a girl to make out or something." His voice trailed off, but his fingers grew fidgety on her arm. He tapped her skin rhythmically, as if he were playing a tune with a quick, erratic beat.

"When will you hear from your friend?" she asked softly.

He shrugged. "Anytime. This week. Next. Who knows?"

"Then we have to wait?" she asked with disappointment. "We have to hang in limbo, not knowing?"

"What else can we do?"

"Maybe he'll never call. Maybe he doesn't need anybody. Maybe it's all just a dream. We'll never get away from Willowbrook, and we'll have to go to college to keep our parents happy."

"It's not a dream. We have to get away," said Danny stonily. "One way or another."

"Our families . . . they'll never let us go."

"We won't ask them. We'll just go."

She chewed her lower lip. "I've thought about what it would be like, just running off. But I don't know, Danny. I don't think I—"

"What's to keep us here, Jen? Tell me that. How close are either one of us to our families? Think about it."

Jenny winced. Danny had a point. Her own mother had missed her graduation.

"If you think about it, Jen, neither of us has a normal family like on television. *Ozzie and Harriet. Father Knows Best*. You never knew your real father—"

"How could I?" she countered. "He died before I was born."

"Exactly. That's what I'm saying. We were both illegitimate."

"Don't say that!" She hated the word, hated the very idea that she was a mistake, her mother's poor misbegotten child. But Danny was right. That was one thing they had in common. They were both born out of wedlock.

"You know how it was for me," said Danny gruffly. "I never met my father until I was eight years old. He didn't even know about me until my mom got sick with TB and went looking for him. There was my mom dying and him wanting to be my dad, like he could make up for all that lost time."

"At least you finally got to know your father. I'll never know mine."

"I know. That's tough."

"Grandma Anna talks about my daddy sometimes. But Mama never does. With Mama, it's as if he never lived at all." Her voice caught. "I'll never know what he was like, or how he felt about things, or what he wanted to do with his life—"

Danny's thoughts were already racing on. "And as far as mothers are concerned," he went on thickly, "we both missed out there too. My mother was too sick with tuberculosis to raise me. She farmed me out to relatives. Then when she finally found my father, she died and Bethany became my stepmother. She's nice enough, but—"

"Bethany loves you, Danny. I know she does."

"Yeah, I know, but she's still not my real mom. She's so young, sometimes she seems more like a big sister. And, tell you the truth, I've got more common sense than she does. She acts like a child sometimes."

A breeze stirred and Jenny felt a slight chill, even with the heat still making the air heavy and moist. "But she tries to be a good mom."

"Your mother tries too," said Danny.

"Does she?" Jenny challenged raggedly. "Then why is she off at some art reception in Chicago instead of here with me on the most important night of my life?"

"She tried to get here, Jen."

"Did she?" Under her breath, Jenny added, "It doesn't matter. Annie's more like my real mother than Catherine. Annie wanted me when I was born. I would have been happier with Annie. I knew she loved me."

"Catherine loves you too, Jen. You know she does."

"Yeah, I suppose so, in her own way. But not like Annie. She'll never be like Annie."

"They're two different people. Annie's good at taking care of folks and making them feel loved. Your mom—she had a hard life growing up. You know how hard she had it, Jen, with your grandmother being alcoholic and your grandfather running around on your grandmother."

"I know I shouldn't blame Mama for not being a good mother. But what you feel is what you feel."

They drifted into silence for a while, allowing themselves to be lulled by the chirrup of crickets and the wing-fluttering drone of big brown moths around the rusty porch light. Jenny felt her taut nerves unwind and the rising night breeze cool her skin. She felt better; even her anger against her mother was dissipating in the night air.

A few minutes later the stillness was shattered by a shrill, breathy voice from inside—Jenny's younger sister, Laura. "Jenny, what's you doing on the porch, sitting there in the dark with Danny?"

"It's not dark," Jenny shot back. "The porch light is on."

"Not so's you can see anything. You two stealing kisses?"

"You know better than that," said Jenny. "Go back inside, smarty pants."

Laura opened the screen door a few inches and let it bang shut. "I'm telling Mama you sat on the porch all night. You skipped out on your own party."

"Did not! I'm right here. That's more than I can say for Mama."

From inside, Laura pressed her face against the old screen, so that her features took on a comical distortion. She wasn't a pretty girl. Folks noted that she looked like a miniature version of Papa Robert, who was certainly a handsome man. But his distinctive features didn't sit well on Laura's small, ten-year-old face. Still, maybe she'd surprise everyone and outgrow the awkwardness and become a beauty like Mama.

"You always say mean things about Mama," she told Jenny accusingly. "Why can't you be nice to her?"

Jenny's full lips settled into a pout. "Leave me alone, little sister, or I'll box your ears."

"You do and I'll tell Daddy. I'll—"

From the hallway, a lyrical female voice interrupted. "Jenny, Laura, what's going on here?"

Danny pulled away abruptly, removing his arm from Jenny's shoulder as Laura said, "Nothing, Aunt Annie. I'm just telling Jenny and Danny to come inside, like you said."

Annie stepped out onto the porch—a tall, graceful woman with shiny brown hair and an extraordinary face—not beautiful exactly, but warm and memorable, especially her large, darkly lashed eyes. "My goodness, Laura," Annie said with a wry half-smile, "I didn't hear you utter one word I told you. I said to tell Jenny we missed her; the party wasn't complete without her."

"That's what I said," insisted Laura with a little whine in her voice. "Something like that anyways."

Annie walked over to the porch railing and circled the sturdy, round pillar with one arm. "No wonder you two are out here," she said, taking a deep breath. "It's wonderful out here, the air sweet with lilacs and roses, the breeze cool and refreshing. I just might tell folks to bring the party out here, the house is so stifling."

"That's not necessary," said Danny, standing up and smoothing his pant legs. "Jenny and I were just coming inside."

"Well, that's just fine," said Annie pleasantly, "because I know how much it means to Todd to share this evening with his son. He's so proud of you, Danny."

They all filed dutifully back into the house, but the way Annie had handled it, Jenny almost believed it had been her own idea. Annie had that way about her, making people feel better about themselves, even if they were doing something wrong. She was amazing. If it had been her mother telling her to come back inside, the whole thing would have deteriorated into a shouting match, and they wouldn't have been on speaking terms for the rest of the evening. Not that it mattered. Her mother wasn't here, and by the time her train came in, the party would be long over.

Inside, the house felt hot as an oven. No air to breathe. Too many warm bodies mingling, talking, laughing, the walls too close, the window screens seemingly holding back the wispy streamers of fresh, lilac-scented air. Jenny had half a mind to go back outside.

"Want something to eat?" asked Danny, eyeing the bountiful feast spread out on the dining room table—Bethany's homemade potato salad and baked beans and a mountain of ham-salad sandwiches in little white triangles with the crusts cut off.

"I'll have a sandwich," said Jenny, knowing Danny was itching to load up his plate with goodies. "And some more of that lemonade, if there's any more ice."

While Danny headed for the table, Jenny drifted around the parlor, catching bits and pieces of conversations. Her Uncle Knowl and her stepfather were still talking about world affairs. You could count on the two of them to dissect and analyze the daily headlines until they were blue in the face and everyone around them was bored to distraction. It struck Jenny. *If only they spent as much time concentrating on the people in their own houses* . . .

Knowl was saying, "Ike hasn't got the foggiest notion how he's going to resolve this fiasco with Khrushchev. We've admitted the U-2 was on a spy mission. Where do we go from here? The Commies have us right where they want us."

Robert nodded and rubbed his chin thoughtfully, his thick brows furrowed over deep brown eyes. "It's a shame, that's all I can say. This Powers fellow—"

"Francis Gary Powers—"

"Right. He's as good as hanged."

Knowl nodded. "The Russians say they'll put him on trial. You know how they work. Shoot first, ask questions later."

"There must be something Eisenhower can do, short of apologizing."

"Well, the way I see it, the president's standing around with egg on his face, especially with Khrushchev canceling the Paris summit conference—"

"And canceling his invitation to Ike to visit the USSR. For a Cold War, things are heating up pretty fast."

Jenny listened for a moment, certain the men were too absorbed in their conversation to notice her. As she was about to move on, Robert caught a glimpse of her. He pulled her over and gave her a fatherly hug. "How's my girl?" he whispered. "Enjoying the party?"

She smiled and brushed a kiss on his cheek, then drifted on. He returned to his conversation with Knowl without missing a beat.

Oh, well. She didn't want to stand around listening to her stepfather and uncle carrying on about world crises tonight; she had enough crises of her own.

A gaggle of church ladies stood near the punch bowl, gossiping and erupting periodically in sudden, boisterous laughter as they sipped their punch and devoured the goodies. Jenny hovered near the edge of their little coterie and listened. Mrs. Periwinkle, the organist, was telling Mrs. Ledbetter about her gallstone operation. With every gory, stomach-turning detail, Mrs. Periwinkle was assailed by a chorus of voices declaring, "That's nothing, Madge. Listen to what happened to me!"

Mrs. Periwinkle stopped her epic tale long enough to bestow an ingratiating smile on Jenny. "Well, here's the graduation girl," she cooed. "You and Danny were simply marvelous, my dear. What superb voices God has given the two of you. You must do something with your music."

"We plan to, Mrs. Periwinkle." Jenny considered confiding that she and Danny planned to join a band, but Mrs. Periwinkle would probably faint dead away. "We'll likely be studying music in college," she said instead. At least, that's what their parents had planned for them.

"That's wonderful that you're going on to college," said Mrs. Ledbetter in a voice dripping with syrup. She reached out and pinched Jenny's cheek and winked. "Just think, I've known you since you were small as a grasshopper, and here you are going off to college. I bet you'll be a grand singer just like your Aunt Alice Marie."

"By the way," said Mrs. Periwinkle, "where is your Aunt Alice Marie these days? We haven't heard much about her since she married that traveling preacher—Helmut, was it?—a few years back."

"Helmut Schwarz. But he goes by Helm."

"Yes, of course. Didn't I hear they moved overseas?"

"Yes, ma'am. They're living in Israel with his father."

"I think I did hear that. Is Alice Marie still singing?"

"Yes. And she has two children now, a boy and a girl."

Mrs. Ledbetter smiled widely. "I never imagined Alice Marie the motherly type."

"She's a wonderful mother. She and Uncle Helm are doing some missionary work, too, wherever they can," said Jenny. "She writes home sometimes. She's very happy."

"Well, that's wonderful," said Mrs. Periwinkle. "And we wish just as much happiness for you, too, Jenny, dear. You have a lot to live up to, you know, coming from such an accomplished family."

"Yes, ma'am."

"My gracious, Jenny, just think of the talent," exclaimed Mrs. Ledbetter. "Your mother an acclaimed artist, your Aunt Annie a celebrated author, and your Aunt Alice Marie a famous singer. Not to mention how successful your stepfather and uncle have been with their publishing house. You must be very proud to be a member of such an illustrious family."

Jenny forced a polite nod, her stomach churning with smoldering indignation. She had heard such speeches a hundred times over the years from as many people, and every time she felt—not pride—but a burgeoning sense of inadequacy. No matter how hard she tried, she would never measure up, never accomplish what her forebears had done. Surely she was foolish even to try.

Danny returned just in time to rescue her, carrying paper plates heaped with sandwiches and salads. Jenny took her plate gratefully— took both plates, in fact—while Danny went back for the lemonades. They went to the staircase and sat down on the carpeted steps; it was the only seat left in the house. Jenny balanced her plate in one hand and with the other discreetly pulled her slim linen skirt down over her knees. Her hose were sticking uncomfortably to her legs, and the hooks on her garter belt were digging into her thighs. What she wouldn't give to be at home in her room where she could strip down to her underwear and stretch out on the feather bed and let the cool breeze from the open window ripple over her.

"We've got to make plans, Jenny," Danny was saying with an air of conspiracy.

"Plans?"

"Like I said, we can join this guy Callan Swan's band. Go on the road. It'll be more than you ever dreamed."

Jenny's heart pounded with a mixture of excitement and anxiety. "You keep saying it, Danny, but how do you know he'll hire us? Maybe he doesn't need anybody."

"I told you. I wrote him. He says he's got openings. It won't be a piece of cake. It'll mean living out of cheap hotel rooms and traveling from town to town in a rattletrap bus. But it's a start, Jen. What do you say? Are you with me?"

She was silent for a long moment, thinking about her family, her home, her heritage. Could she walk away from everything she'd ever known to take a chance on something as flimsy and elusive as a dream? She would be risking her future, perhaps her very life. Was it worth it? With a decisive sigh, she wound her arm around Danny's and squeezed his hand tightly. "Sure, Danny. I'm with you. Whatever you say. Where else would I be, except with you?"

3

The midnight train was running a half hour late. For nearly an hour Jenny and Papa Robert stood on the sagging station platform waiting for her mother. They waited in silence, breathing in the warm air heavy with diesel oil and the lingering coal-black smoke from countless sooty, grinding engines.

Every night for as long as she could remember, Jenny had lain in her bed in the darkness listening to the midnight train rumbling through Willowbrook on its lonely journey from Chicago to Indianapolis. Its long, mournful whistle always sent chills up her spine. It was like something alive and breathing, its lonesome cry riding the night wind, letting the world know it was out there. And yet its eerie phantom moan summoned images of a ghost train riding the edge of some netherworld existing only in her imagination.

Every time that hollow, haunting wail came echoing through the inky stillness, her skin prickled and her ears strained to listen. The ghost train was coming for her—had to be—its blackened locomotive roaring and puffing, its creaky boxcars and sleek passenger cars vibrating over the iron tracks like a dark, shiny snake zigzagging through a marshy field.

At last the train thundered in like a dark, looming prehistoric behemoth set on devouring the very earth under its roaring wheels. The platform shuddered and the wind whipped to a frenzy; the deafening noise rang shrill as a siren in Jenny's ears. She caught her breath and tried to hold back her excitement. If she let herself feel excited, her anger at Mama might dissipate, and she wasn't ready to let go of her resentment over Mama missing her graduation. But the presence of the monstrous, belching, shuddering train erased every emotion except excitement.

Jenny imagined herself on that very train traveling to a grand city like Chicago, sitting in a velvety seat looking out the window as the world passed by. The very idea stole her breath and fired her imagination. Oh, to be going somewhere! Somewhere exotic and glamorous and fascinating. And to have a purpose for going!

I'm ready to go anywhere the train will take me, as long as it carries me far away from Willowbrook!

Not that Willowbrook was an unpleasant place to live. It was a typical provincial Indiana town with cobbled streets weaving through old neighborhoods of faded Victorian estates and new neighborhoods of boxy, look-alike houses erected after the war. Willowbrook was fine if your life was already settled and your future determined. But it was no place for a girl who had just graduated and was ready to explore a glorious, unimaginable world of tempting possibilities.

Papa Robert shook her arm. "Jen, watch for your mother."

She turned her gaze to the passengers emerging one by one, aided by the conductor as they descended the steep, narrow steps.

After several passengers had disembarked, Jenny spotted the familiar figure of her mother—a shapely woman in a green linen suit, her pillbox hat nestled in a cloud of flaming red hair. Even at forty-one, her mother looked stunning.

Catherine spotted them as quickly as they saw her and began waving as she hastened toward them; she was carrying an overnight bag and a bouquet of red roses. She rushed into Robert's arms for a quick embrace, then entwined her arms around Jenny. "Oh, sweetheart, it's so good to be home," she sighed, then thrust the roses at Jenny. "These are for you, darling. They were selling them at this little shop in Chicago, next to the station. A peace offering. For missing your graduation. Am I forgiven?"

Jenny shrank back, unwilling to accept the bouquet. If she took the flowers, her mother would consider herself forgiven and the matter closed. Jenny wasn't ready to let it drop that easily. The pain and disappointment were still too keen, and, more dismaying, her mother showed little sense of remorse.

"The roses are beautiful, aren't they, Jen?" Robert coaxed, urging the tissue-wrapped bundle into her hands. He would do anything to avoid a painful scene between his wife and stepdaughter, but his intrusion only fueled her anger. This was too big a deal to be dismissed; she refused to let her anger be assuaged by a silly bouquet purchased on the run. It was only an afterthought. A whim. A sorry excuse for an unforgivable infraction of the heart. There was nothing hard-won in a handful of store-bought flowers.

Her mother's bright, vivid expression darkened, her smile fading into a frown. "I'm sorry, honey. You know how much I wanted to be here for your graduation. I blame these trains. You can never count on them. And the Chicago traffic was ghastly. I'm ready to write a letter of complaint, but I don't know who on earth I'd send it to." She reached out and ran her long, smooth fingers along Jenny's flushed cheek. "You're not going to hold this against me, are you?"

Jenny felt her eyes filling, but she vowed not to cry.

"I bet it was beautiful," her mother went on, her expression softening. "I bet you looked beautiful in your cap and gown. The loveliest girl in the place. I hope you took scads of pictures."

"We did," Robert assured her. He took Catherine's overnight bag and circled her waist with his arm. "Come on. Let's get home before the sun comes up."

Catherine linked one arm around Robert and the other around Jenny. The three of them made a wobbly trio as they crossed the uneven platform to the brick station house. A lightning flash of memory seared

Jenny's mind with an indelible image—Jenny as a small child being pulled onto an east-bound train by her mother as her Aunt Annie stood waving a tearful goodbye.

Jenny remembered little of that event except for a floppy, brown teddy bear she clutched for dear life—and the shattering sensation that she was being torn from her precious Annie, the only mother she had ever known. She was too young to comprehend that her mother was whisking her off to New York City and that it would be years before she saw Annie again. Somewhere in a dusky crevice of her heart, that sobbing child still resented the woman who had wrenched her from Annie's arms.

Even tonight, as the threesome shambled arm in arm toward Robert's car, laughing at their own awkward gait, Jenny cast a sidelong glance at her mother and wondered, *Why did you take me from Annie when you never had time for me anyway?*

As Robert pulled away from the station, Catherine, the scent of her expensive perfume filling the automobile, glanced around from the front seat and said, "Now I want to hear all about your graduation, Jen. Every detail."

Jenny set her bouquet beside her and sank down in her seat, crossing her arms, lowering her head. "There's nothing to tell. They called my name and I walked across the stage and got my diploma. Your evening was probably more exciting than mine."

Jenny waited for her mother to insist that nothing could have been more exciting than seeing her daughter graduate. The hope was almost an ache in Jenny's chest.

Instead, Catherine said breathlessly, "Well, I must admit it has been an exciting day for me." She looked over at Robert, her voice taking on fresh animation. "Darling, you remember me telling you that a representative from the Museum of Modern Art was going to be at the reception?"

"You may have. I—"

"Well, he was there, Robert, all the way from New York, and—you won't believe this—he told me the Museum is interested in displaying some of my paintings in a special exhibit titled, 'Realism in Twentieth Century American Art.'"

"Sounds great, Cath."

"Can you imagine, Robert? They want to include my work. My paintings will be on display with the works of Charles Turner and Andrew Wyeth!" She laughed lightly.

As her mother rambled on, Jenny pulled a long-stem rose from her bouquet and began plucking the petals one by one and tossing them on the floor.

"I'm still reeling," Catherine rushed on. "Do you know how long I've worked for this day, Robert? Knowing my paintings are being taken seriously by art connoisseurs like—"

"That's wonderful, Cath, splendid," Robert interjected. "I'm proud of you, darling. And I'm sure Jenny's proud of you, too, aren't you, Jen?" Robert glanced back but didn't wait for Jenny to respond. He went on quickly with a cautionary tone. "We'll want to hear all about your extraordinary day, just as I'm sure you want to hear all about Jenny's evening. The ceremony was very moving, and you should have heard Jenny and Danny's duet. It was the most beautiful rendition of 'Climb Every Mountain.' You should have heard the applause they received."

There was a moment of awkward silence before Catherine blurted, "Of course, the duet! I'm sorry, sweetheart. I almost forgot about you and Danny singing. I'm sure it was extraordinary. You know how much I wanted to hear you. I hope the two of you will sing your song just for me sometime."

"We promised to sing it for Grandma Betty," Jenny said dully. "You can hear it then."

When she arrived home, Jenny went straight upstairs to her grandmother's darkened room. She tiptoed across the creaking floor, found a drinking glass, and carefully arranged her roses in the glass. She set the bouquet on the bedside table where her grandmother would see it when she woke in the morning.

Jenny stood by the bed and brushed Grandma Betty's ropy hair back from her peaceful face. "You wanted to be there tonight, Grams, didn't you?" she whispered. "At the ceremony and at my party? If only you weren't ailing. If only they'd let you come. I should have made them. I should have insisted. You wouldn't have made a scene. You were the one I wanted there most of all." Jenny leaned over and kissed her grandmother's cool forehead. "At least you can have my roses. You'll enjoy them more than I."

It was nearly 2:00 A.M. when Jenny finally climbed into bed and lay back, fluffing the feather pillow under her head. She stared up into the humid, airless darkness, her warm cotton nightgown already clinging to her skin. The windows were open, but the breeze was too faint to make it through the screens. The lace curtains hung limp and motionless, like exhausted ghosts, as bereft of spirit as Jenny herself. Where was the excitement she had felt as she crossed the platform and wrapped her fingers around the rolled parchment that testified of her achievement? She was a graduate, *magna cum laude*.

But her mother's absence and apparent lack of remorse overshadowed the graduation and Jenny's fleeting euphoria. All of her life she had held her tongue when her mother pranced off to still another art show or exhibition while missing the "Back to School" nights, the teacher conferences, student concerts, and plays. Jenny had learned early that when she came home from school eager to share the day's events, she would find her mother at her easel painting and only half listening to her daughter's earnest prattle.

After a while, when her mother asked distractedly, "How was your day?" Jenny would respond with an abbreviated, "It was fine" or "It was okay." She didn't volunteer more unless her mother set down her brush and turned from her canvas and prompted, "Well, what did you do? You must have done something. Tell me." But those times were all too few. Mostly, when their brief conversations ended, her mother looked relieved to get back to her painting.

The thought came to Jenny, *She'll be sorry when I'm gone*.

The idea took her breath away—the possibility that she would soon be leaving her home and family and Willowbrook behind. And why not? There were too many other exciting places in the world for a young, adventuresome woman to explore.

Jenny thought about those places now as another train whistle moaned its haunting melody through the early morning shadows. She pictured herself riding the train to Detroit or Columbus or Cincinnati or even some far-flung city like New York or Los Angeles. She would walk along wide, paved boulevards among towering skyscrapers and attend the opera and museums and concerts and plays. If she went to New York, she could audition for a Broadway musical and become a singer people would take seriously, a rising star, not just an ordinary teenage girl who sang hymns in the church choir.

She would do anything to stop being ordinary.

Anything to win the kind of acclaim her mother and Aunt Annie and Aunt Alice Marie knew. But Jenny couldn't paint like her mother, or write books like Aunt Annie, or sing on her own television show like Aunt Alice Marie. Even though people often told her she had a voice as lovely as Alice Marie's, Jenny was never sure whether they spoke sincerely or were just being kind. The truth was, the women in her family cast such long shadows, she could never find her own little patch of sunlight to bask in. At times it seemed hopeless. And excruciatingly painful. The Reed and Herrick women were so extraordinary that to be ordinary was to be a failure.

Let me be anything, Jenny thought, *but not ordinary!*

As far back as she remembered, she had dreamed of getting on a train and following the tracks wherever they took her. Once, when she was twelve, she decided to run away from home. Without a word to anyone, she started walking down the street away from her house. She walked for hours, until her chest ached and her feet were sore inside her cramped saddle shoes. She walked until she realized she had nowhere to go, so in dismay she turned around and walked back home. She expected a scolding, the tongue-lashing of her life, for causing everyone to worry. Maybe the police were already searching for her; certainly her mother had called Robert home from the publishing house and told him her daughter was missing. No doubt he would be out looking for her.

But when Jenny arrived home, she realized with a sharp pang of disappointment that no one had even noticed she was gone. Her mother was in her art studio at the back of the house working on a commission for the mayor of some big city, and Robert was still at work, no doubt editing the next great American novel.

The memory was as searing today as when she was twelve.

I still don't know who I am, she acknowledged silently. *I'm eighteen and a high school graduate, but I have no idea where my family leaves off and I begin. I'm everyone and no one. I have my mother's flaming red hair, my Aunt Alice Marie's soprano voice, and my Aunt Annie's introspective nature. I'm little pieces of everybody else, but where is the person I can recognize as me?*

There was one vital piece of the puzzle missing—her real father. Chilton Reed. Chip. Aunt Annie's older brother. Jenny was convinced if she could have known him—if he hadn't died at Pearl Harbor before she was born—she would know who she was supposed to be. Maybe she was just like him. People told her she looked like him. Maybe if he'd been here to raise her, she'd have a clearer picture of the person she was meant to be.

4

It was the first Monday of July, a warm, muggy day with heavy gray clouds hugging the horizon, ready to empty themselves on dusty hamlets and parched cornfields. Jenny had spent the morning cleaning house and doing laundry. She was hanging the last of the percale sheets over the backyard clothesline, as if in defiance of the threatening torrents, when Laura called her inside. "Danny's on the phone, and he sounds excited. Better come quick!"

Jenny dropped the clothespin bag in the grass and ran inside to the parlor, where her sister gave her a knowing little smile as she handed her the receiver. Laura stood rooted to the spot, arms folded, head cocked just so, obviously intending to listen to every word. Jenny scowled and nodded toward the door. "Scram, silly goose!" At last Laura got the hint and moseyed away, her chin jutting out in mute defiance. "I'm here, Danny," Jenny said when she was sure Laura was out of hearing distance. "What's up?"

"May I come over, Jen? I've got some great news," he confided. "I need to see you right away."

"Give me a half hour," she told him, brushing back a stray wisp of russet-red hair from her damp forehead. She hurried to the upstairs bathroom, turned the spigots on full blast, and splashed cool water on her face. She put on capri pants and a sleeveless, floral print blouse, tying the shirttails in a knot at her waist. She ran a brush through her long, burnished curls, bringing out the shine, and applied a smidgen of makeup—a touch of rouge on her cheekbones, violet eye shadow on her lids, and on her mouth, lipstick as vivid as crimson roses.

True to his word, Danny arrived exactly a half hour after his phone call. "Where can we talk?" he asked when she met him at the door. He was wearing pegged jeans and a T-shirt with the sleeves rolled to the shoulder, and his hair was slicked back like waves, so shiny black with pure lanolin you could almost see your reflection. His dad said he looked like a hood, a punk kid, and what was he trying to prove? Jenny had heard the two argue about it more than once. It was the thing Danny and his father quarreled over constantly these days.

Even now, she could hear Pastor Marshall in her head, challenging Danny, wanting to know if he was trying to mimic that raunchy, hip-swinging singer, Elvis Presley, because if he was he was doing a pretty good job of it, and no one would guess he was a decent, God-fearing kid, the preacher's son.

Jenny suspected that the reverend's tirades against Danny's appearance were exactly what drove Danny to imitate Elvis so compulsively. He looked at her now with heavy-lidded eyes that seemed to smolder, velvety green-suede eyes that could always prompt a tickle of pleasure in the pit of her stomach. "Well, Jen? Let's talk. Preferably somewhere where your folks and grandmother aren't hovering around, eavesdropping."

"We could take a walk," she suggested, stepping onto the sprawling, lattice-trimmed porch.

He looked at the dusky sky. "It's going to pour any minute now."

She nodded. She could smell the rain, feel a burr of electricity in the atmosphere. Storm clouds prowled the horizon like great shadowed beasts. "I don't mind getting wet, if you don't."

"You kidding? I'm not made of sugar. Let's go."

They walked down Maypole Drive past turn-of-the-century houses that were once elegant but now looked a bit seedy and shopworn with their antiquated gothic arches, faded cupolas, and weathered wrap-around porches looking garish with gingerbread trim. At the corner they turned onto Honeysuckle Lane—Jenny's favorite street, for it was in the dusty-rose mansion on the corner that she'd lived blissfully with Knowl and Annie before her mother came and took her away.

They stopped and Jenny gazed through the wrought iron fence at the ivy-covered Victorian mansion ensconced on its vast manicured lawn and surrounded by solemn oaks and weeping willows.

Danny looked at her. "You miss this old place, don't you?"

"More than I can say. Somehow it always stays the same."

It was true. The rest of the neighborhood showed its age, manifesting a shabby, archaic grandeur, but Annie's house never changed. In a way she couldn't express with words, Jenny had always felt cheated, not only of the parents she cherished, but of this home she adored as well.

She knew even as she gazed longingly at the house that Annie was there inside with her own children, showering them with the same bountiful love she had once bestowed on Jenny. Jenny couldn't help resenting thirteen-year-old Maggie and seven-year-old Jon Knowl; they had replaced Jenny in Knowl and Annie's hearts. She had gone from being their only child, deeply beloved, to their niece, fondly loved, who came to visit now and then.

Danny slipped his arm around Jenny's shoulder and drew her close. "Listen, Jen, it's okay to talk about how you feel. I'm here for you."

"It's nothing. I'm okay."

"Come on, Jen. I can see it in your face—the hurt, the sadness. Tell me about it."

She inhaled deeply. "I was just remembering. When I was a little girl I begged my mother to let me go over to Annie's to play. I cried. Threw tantrums. I was too young to understand why I had been uprooted so drastically. I didn't understand why I couldn't still live at Annie's house and be Annie's little girl."

"I bet that sent your mother into a frenzy."

"Pure, sharp-tongued fury." Jenny could hear her mother even now. How dare Jenny be so ungrateful and disrespectful to the mother who had given her life? What kind of spoiled, cheeky girl was she? Sometimes her mother would shout hysterically, "All right, if you want to go back and live with Annie, go ahead. Get out of here, Miss Smarty Pants. Just go!"

But, of course, Jenny never did, for Annie had her own family now; there was no longer room in Annie's heart or her home for Jenny. She leaned against Danny, resting her head against his shoulder. "After a while I stopped asking if I could go back to Annie's. I knew it would only send my mother into another fit of indignation."

"But Annie always loves to see you, you know that," said Danny, breaking into her brooding memories. "Annie's probably home right now. Do you want to go inside and see her?"

"No, not now," said Jenny. "She's always so busy with her writing and her own children."

"But she always has time for you, Jen."

Jenny gave him a look of defiance. "I said not now, Danny." Her tone softened. "I'll see her another time when I help her do research for one of her books. Besides, you said you wanted to talk to me—alone. Let's keep walking."

He reached for her hand and swung it casually as they fell into step along the uneven, weed-infested sidewalk. His touch sent a ripple of pleasure through her.

"Listen, Jen, what we've talked about for ages is finally coming true," he said with unmistakable excitement. "I heard from my buddy, Callan Swan, the guy with the band. You know. The Bell Tones. They're going to be performing at the county fair the end of the month through the first week of August. He says maybe we can join up with the band. He needs another guy on guitar and a couple of backup singers."

"Really? And he wants us?"

"Could be, if we're lucky. It's a sweet deal, Jen. Room and board and a cut of the profits. I know it probably won't be much, but . . ."

"It doesn't matter, as long as we're together."

"Right. It's a start. They've got their own bus, and if Callan gives the word, they'll take us with them when they leave Willowbrook."

Jenny shivered in spite of the muggy warmth. "You make it sound like it's all set. Like it's really going to happen."

"It is, Jen. Listen, we're not talking about some no-talent, lowlife band. We're talking the big time. Okay, maybe not the big time yet, but the Bell Tones have performed all over Indiana . . . and Michigan and Ohio too. They were even on the local bandstand show in Chicago a few weeks ago. It's just a matter of time before they're booked in Nashville and Philadelphia. Man alive, Cal even thinks he can get the group on *American Bandstand*, and once we're on *Bandstand*, you know somebody's going to want us to cut a record."

"But are you sure your friend Cal . . . are you sure he's not just all talk?"

"All talk? Come on, Jen. This guy's performed with some of the biggest names in the business—Fabian, Bobby Darin, the Big Bopper, Jerry Lee Lewis—"

Jenny fought a sickish, butterfly feeling in the pit of her stomach. "We're going to pack up and join a band, just like that? So soon? It's really going to happen?"

"We might never get a chance like this again, Jen. It's not every day a band has openings for both a guy and a girl. If Cal's backup singers hadn't run off and tied the knot—"

"Danny, that's not the point."

"Then what is? I thought this was what you wanted—the opportunity of a lifetime."

"It is, Danny." Her breathing felt shallow, her heart pumping fast. "But it's all happening so fast."

"Not fast enough for me," he said thickly. "I've counted the days until I could get out on my own, be my own boss and not have to answer anymore to my old man. Now we've got our big break, and all you can do is raise doubts. Are you backing out on me, Jen?"

"No, Danny, I promise I'm not. It's just—it was so easy to talk big about what we'd do and where we'd go when it was all a far-off dream. Now it's real. What will we tell our parents?"

"Nothing. We'll just go."

"But our parents would be worried sick if we just . . . disappeared."

"We'll phone them when we're on the road and tell them we're okay. We'll send postcards of the places we've been. It'll be okay, Jen. You trust me, don't you?"

She searched his smoky green eyes. "You know I do."

His hand tightened around her fingers, sending a sweet, tickling flutter up her arm. "The way I see it, all we really have is each other. And that's all we need, right?"

"Um—right." The ripple of pleasure turned to alarm. Why were her feelings for Danny so complicated, always a blend of joy and misgivings, of sweet excitement tied to a troubling knot of uneasiness? She felt a stiletto of cold wetness on her cheek and realized the rain had started; the sky was darkening and the wind rising, making a whispering sound in the trees. It was as if the weather were echoing the aching restlessness in her heart and setting the stage for the inevitable changes to come.

Would the future be as eerily foreboding as the massive storm clouds swirling overhead, relentlessly devouring the last faint streamers of sunlight? She shivered. Large raindrops spattered with a rhythmic rat-a-tat on the sidewalk. She liked the feel of cold rain on her face and pelting her hair.

She looked over at Danny. Large raindrops were festooned like tiny diamonds on his raven black hair. In the dusky, moving shadows of the storm, he looked exactly like Elvis before Elvis had to go in the army and shave off all his hair. Jenny had no doubt. With his looks and voice, Danny was destined to be a big star. Maybe, just maybe, she had a chance too. No matter who she hurt or how hard the road might be, no matter what, she had to try for it. She'd regret it for the rest of her life if she didn't.

"So what do we do now, Danny—while we're waiting for Cal and his band to come to town?"

"Nothing. Just go about our business and keep quiet. Can you do that, Jen? Go on like nothing's happening . . . and when it's time to go, just go?"

She looked at him for a long minute and knew she'd go to the ends of the earth for Danny. "I'll do it," she promised, her voice so soft, the sound was nearly lost in the distant rumble of thunder clouds.

Jenny, in a green knit shirt and denim shorts, sat reading in the cherry wood rocker by the window in the study at Annie's house on Honeysuckle Lane. Annie sat at the mahogany desk nearby, her fingers working the keys of her sturdy old Remington typewriter. She was wearing a white sleeveless blouse and peddle-pushers, her long chestnut hair pulled back in a pony tail. Annie always dressed casually when she wrote. Except for the fine network of lines around her eyes, she could have been twenty instead of forty.

Jenny had come over to help Annie with research for her latest book, a novel set during the Civil War. But even as she thumbed through a heavy volume about Atlanta during the 1860s, absently scanning the yellowed, tissue-thin pages, her mind was on something else. "Annie, what was my father like?"

"Your father?" Annie echoed, her expression softening as her fingers paused over the keys.

"Yes, my father. Your brother Chip."

Annie smiled wistfully. "I know who you mean."

"I guess it takes a minute to break away from the Civil War."

Annie nodded. "You know me so well. Sometimes I forget where my characters leave off and the real world begins. Thank goodness you're here to help keep me grounded in reality."

Jenny wasn't sure whether that was a compliment or not, but she would take it as one. She was glad to be the one Annie asked to help with her research. Jenny was always eager to go to the library and drag a stack of books over to Annie's house so they could pore over the thick historical tomes together. She loved helping out and feeling needed. These were the only times Jenny had Annie all to herself once again, as she had when she was a child. And Annie was always so effusive in her gratitude.

"Let's see. Your father?" Annie repeated, her voice breaking slightly as tears glistened at the corners of her eyes. "Oh, my goodness, he was a handsome young man. He had the blond good looks and strong, sturdy face of a Nordic warrior. All the girls liked him. And he was such a charmer. He had a way about him. You couldn't stay mad at him, even when he had just played an annoying practical joke—"

"Practical joke?"

"Oh, yes, he loved playing practical jokes." Annie laughed lightly, her tone almost whimsical. "I remember once Chip and Knowl made Catherine and me believe there was a great grizzly bear in the woods behind our house. Knowl had coaxed us girls into the woods, and then he disappeared. And suddenly we heard this huge, vicious roar. Cath and I were scared out of our wits. We started running and got lost, but that bear just seemed to follow us, roaring loudly enough to make the trees tremble. Or maybe we were the only ones trembling."

"Oh, Annie, I'd tremble too," said Jenny. "What did you do?"

"The only thing we could think to do. Cath and I climbed up on the lower limb of a tree and sat there hugging each other and crying. And would you believe? Your father and Knowl came bursting out of the forest laughing like banshees and waving a big old bull horn. They were our bears!"

"How mean! Did you get back at them?" asked Jenny breathlessly, feeling as if she herself had been running from the bears.

"Oh, yes. Cath and I chased Knowl and Chip all the way home. But I'll tell you a secret. We didn't really mind them teasing us, because I was already in love with Knowl and your mama was in love with Chip."

Jenny sighed dreamily. "It sounds like a fairy tale . . . best friends being in love with each other's brother."

Annie nodded, her face clouding. "I just wish Catherine could have had a happy ending with Chip like I did with Knowl." She put her fingertips to her lips and shook her head. "Oh, I'm sorry, Jenny. I didn't mean that Cath isn't happy. She has you and Robert and—"

"I know what you mean," Jenny assured her, but she wondered if there was more truth in Annie's words than she was willing to admit. They were both quiet for a moment. Then Jenny said with a tremor of emotion in her voice, "I wish I could have known my father."

Annie looked at her with an expression of swift, raw pain and said, "Oh, honey, so do I!"

Jenny flinched and looked away. She couldn't bear feeling the weight of Annie's pain on top of her own. She swallowed a sob. "At least you knew him. To me, he's only other people's memories and old-time pictures in a book."

"Well, he was very real . . . and so full of life," said Annie, gazing wistfully around the study. "Sometimes, as a little boy, he'd play in this very room. He'd bring his little cast-metal cars and trucks in here while our papa sat at his desk working. Chip would pretend the patterns in the rug were roads and he'd make the screechiest sounds for his cars as he ran them over the carpet. Sometimes Papa would get so exasperated, he'd say, 'Chilton Reed, you take those noisy cars outside or get their mufflers fixed. They're the loudest contraptions I ever heard!'"

Jenny laughed, but it was a bittersweet sensation. "Mama won't even talk to me about him," she said quietly. "I think it hurts her too much. She would rather pretend he never existed."

Annie's eyes glistened. "Your mother never got over your father dying before he could marry her and give you his name."

Jenny forced out the words. "Did he know I was coming?"

"No, but if he had known he would have loved you very much."

"It's not fair." Jenny swallowed a sob. "All I have of him is what people tell me, and that's not enough."

Annie studied Jenny with a curious half-smile. "If you really want to know what your father was like, look in the mirror. Some of your expressions are just like his, and your gestures too. The way you crinkle your eyes when you laugh, the way your chin dimples when you smile, even the way you turn your head just so when you're thinking hard about something. He's part of you, Jenny, even though you never knew him, and no one can take that from you."

Jenny looked instinctively toward the gilded mirror near the door. Did she look like Chip Reed? Share some of his very gestures and expressions? Whenever Grandmother Anna brought out the old photo albums with their thick black paper and yellowed pictures stuck on with little white tabs, Jenny would pore over the black-and-white images, trying to trace her own features in her father's blurred, smiling face. The idea warmed her. It was amazing how Annie always knew what to say to make her feel better.

"I wish I still lived here with you," she said impulsively, then realized by the distressed look on Annie's face that she had said the wrong thing. "I mean, I know you aren't my mother, but sometimes it feels like you are."

Annie slipped away from her typewriter and put a tender hand on Jenny's shoulder. "Honey, I try very hard not to let your mother feel that I'm trying to take her place. Otherwise, I—"

Jenny put her hand over Annie's. "I know. I shouldn't have said anything. I'm sorry."

"No, don't ever be sorry." Annie looked squarely in Jenny's eyes. "I love you. Nothing will ever change that."

"But you have your own family now," said Jenny, forcing a brightness into her voice she didn't feel. "I understand that."

"Then I hope you understand I will always be concerned about you. I still remember when you were my little girl playing with your painted wheelbarrow and riding on your rocking horse." A bittersweet smile played on Annie's lips. "And now I think about you being a grown-up young lady and having a life of your own, and I wonder what you'll be doing next year, and the year after that."

Jenny bit her lower lip. Did she dare tell Annie that she and Danny would be joining a band? Would Annie keep her secret? She could at least hint at the idea. "Who knows? Maybe in a year or two I'll be off singing in a band with Danny. What would you think of that, Annie?"

Annie's expression fell. She sat down in the Queen Anne chair across from Jenny, her gaze troubled. "I'd hate to see you get involved in something like that, honey. The music these days—it's not the wholesome music your Aunt Alice Marie used to sing. It's like something the devil dreamed up. The lyrics, the beat—it makes young people do terrible things. I can't imagine you and Danny involved in this whole ugly rock 'n' roll business."

"It's not all bad, Annie," Jenny protested. "There's a lot of good music playing now, and it's our own music, not the jazz or swing of your generation."

Annie chuckled. "Now I'm beginning to feel old." She crossed her arms loosely and drummed her fingers on her elbow. "You know, Jenny, I would love to see you use your music for the Lord. He gave you a beautiful voice to sing His praises."

Jenny glanced out the window, pretending she hadn't heard Annie's remarks. Her aunt was a wonderful woman whom Jenny dearly loved, but she could be a bit pious. In fact, it was a sore point at times between

Annie and Catherine. Annie had a way of making people feel she had a direct pipeline to God.

"Did you hear me, Jenny? Nothing on this earth will make you happier than singing God's praises."

Jenny picked up the research book she had been perusing earlier and opened it at random. Her face felt warm and her spirit restless. Growing up in such a religious family had never been easy. What chance did she have with Uncle Todd a minister, Uncle Helm an evangelist, and Uncle Knowl and her stepfather owners of a publishing house that sent Christian literature out all over the world?

Not that she had anything against God. She dutifully went to church every Sunday and sang in the choir and performed in evangelistic services whenever she was asked. But she had never managed to have a close relationship with God like Annie—and even her own mother—had.

"I'm sorry, Jenny. I've made you feel uncomfortable, haven't I?"

Jenny quickly shook her head. "No, Annie. It's not that. I'm just not religious like you and my mom. Everybody's different."

Annie sat forward and gazed intently at Jenny, her eyes shining with a bright, urgent fervor. "You're right, honey. God has a different way of working with each of His children. But somewhere inside of you is a hunger that needs filling. You can try everything in the world, but nothing will satisfy that hunger except Jesus' love."

Jenny gazed back at Annie, stoutly, unblinking. "A part of me is missing," she said solemnly. "But it's not God; it's my father. He's the empty place in me I can never fill."

*"We gotta go and never stop going till we get there . . .
Where we going, man? . . . I don't know, but we gotta
go . . ."*

Jenny and Danny were ensconced on her living room
couch, she fanning herself against the midsummer heat
while he read aloud from Jack Kerouac's Beat Generation novel, *On the Road.* Jenny's mind was wandering to thoughts of
an icy lemonade, but she didn't want to interrupt Danny. He liked Kerouac's rhythmic, reckless, freewheeling style; it was like poetry gone
wild, the words singing and dancing like jazz, bebop, and blues all in
one brazen literary escapade.

Kerouac had inspired half of the songs Danny had written, even
though Danny's father had forbidden him to keep the novel in his
house. It was the parsonage, after all, a house of God. No place for
the likes of Kerouac, whose works Pastor Marshall called "godless,
vulgar trash," which only prompted Danny to like them all the more.

Jenny had a feeling Danny liked Kerouac even more since they had
decided to go on the road; maybe he had visions of the two of them
experiencing Kerouac's exciting, outrageous adventures in their own
travels. Jenny wasn't sure she was up to such a mercurial lifestyle, but
whatever she and Danny faced, it had to be better than their placid,
painfully dull lives in Willowbrook. And one thing they both agreed
on: their music was their ticket to that magnificent, vast new world.

That's why Danny and Jenny had spent the afternoon—and nearly every afternoon for the past two weeks—rehearsing for their audition with Callan Swan's band. It was already July 13, Danny kept reminding her, and their audition was only two weeks away. They had to be at their best.

As Danny waxed eloquent with Kerouac's audacious ramblings, Jenny's eyes strayed across the room to the flickering black and white images of the television screen. The Democratic National Convention was on, the sound turned too low to hear. They had watched for a while but had grown tired of the endless speeches. Now Jenny sensed something was about to happen. She sat up and stopped fanning herself. "Danny, maybe we should listen."

He closed his book and set it on the pedestal table beside the couch, then crossed the room and turned up the volume. "Maybe they're finally going to get around to nominating somebody."

A wiry, plain-faced man with dark hair and dark-rimmed glasses was speaking in a booming, theatrical voice. "Ladies and gentlemen, to lead us to a fruitful America, to a peaceful world for mankind everywhere, is the great senator from the state of Massachusetts, John F. Kennedy!"

The applause was thunderous as Senator Kennedy strode to the podium. Danny sat forward and listened raptly. When Kennedy had finished speaking, Danny sat back against the cushion and cracked his knuckles. "Now that's a man I could vote for, Jen, if I was old enough to vote. I like what he has to say and the way he says it."

Jenny resumed fanning herself. "Grandmother Anna says if Mr. Kennedy ends up in the White House, we'll all be taking orders from the Pope."

"That's a lot of nonsense."

"Maybe, maybe not."

"Well, what would you say if I got into politics someday?" said Danny with an air of bravado.

"You? In politics? Never! Music is your life."

"But if I didn't have my music, I'd want to find another way to reach people and make them feel and see things the way I do."

She stifled a chuckle. "You could be the first singing president."

"The world's not ready for that yet." He playfully tossed a throw pillow at her. "Folks are still trying to get used to Elvis the Pelvis and good old rock 'n' roll."

She threw the pillow back at him. "Maybe you better leave before Mama and Papa Robert get home."

"They got a problem with me being here?"

She smiled slyly. "They don't like me having boys over when they're not home."

"Even me, your cousin?"

"My so-called cousin."

"Your Grandma Betty's here."

"In her room. In her own little world."

"So when will your folks get home?"

"Any minute now. They're just around the corner watching the convention with Annie and Knowl."

"They still don't suspect our plans, do they?"

She shook her head. "Mama would lock me in my room forever and Papa Robert would throw away the key."

Danny stood, picked up his Kerouac book, and shuffled toward the door. "Two weeks, Jen. We have to be ready for Callan and the Bell Tones in two weeks. If he likes us, we go with them."

Jenny felt a shiver along her spine. She had never wanted anything more in her life, and she had never felt more terrified.

Jenny loved the county fair—the sawdust and noise, the carnival tents, sideshows, livestock exhibitions, the crush of the crowds, the clanging bells and flashing lights, the sound of the calliope, the smell of caramel corn, and the taste of candied apples. But tonight she could concentrate on only one nerve-jarring fact: she and Danny would be auditioning for Callan Swan after his evening show.

They had arrived at the stadium early enough to get front-row seats. It was a warm evening with mosquitoes and fireflies out in equal numbers, and as the bleachers filled with cheering, foot-stomping humanity, the temperature soared as well. Jenny felt light-headed and besieged with jitters. What if Callan Swan didn't like them or didn't think they were talented enough to join his band? She and Danny had staked all their hopes and dreams on this single opportunity. What if she disappointed Danny? Or what if Callan wanted Danny but not her? Would Danny go off with the band and leave her behind?

It seemed forever before the spotlight focused on center stage, the drum roll sounded, and welcoming applause reverberated through the grandstand. Imagining herself there in the center of that glaring spotlight, Jenny was ready to bolt and run. Performing professionally was vastly different from singing in church or for the graduation ceremony. Was she really ready for the big time?

But as the Bell Tones launched into their first number, Jenny's insecurities and self-absorption turned into undisguised admiration. She had never seen them perform, but she realized immediately they were well worth the wait. They had a fresh, upbeat sound, original, easy to listen to—a smooth, seamless blend of rock 'n' roll, rhythm and blues, and country. They sang several original numbers that Jenny could easily imagine making the Top Ten charts. Danny hadn't mentioned that Callan Swan was a songwriter, as well as the lead singer and band leader; he was obviously a man of many talents.

The Bell Tones followed their original numbers with their own stylized version of several popular favorites—Jackie Wilson's "Lonely Teardrops," Pat Boone's "April Love," and Guy Mitchell's "Singing the Blues." Then they closed the show with a medley of songs made famous by Fabian, Neil Sedaka, and Bobby Rydell. They performed three encores before the audience would allow them to leave the stage.

After the show, Jenny and Danny made their way backstage, where a crew was already dismantling the set and band members were packing up their instruments. A black man in a black shirt and white straw hat with red and black trim looked up and flashed a generous smile as he packed up the drums. With his wide-set black eyes and smooth, blunt, cocoa-brown features, he wasn't exactly handsome, but his expression was quick, and fluid, and pleasantly animated. "You Danny DiCaprio?"

Danny nodded. He had already decided to go by his mother's maiden name, DiCaprio, instead of his father's name, Marshall.

"Then you looking for Callan Swan, over there." The black man gestured with a limber toss of his head.

Jenny followed Danny over to the upright piano where the band leader was putting sheet music in a leather satchel.

"Cal?" said Danny tentatively.

Callan Swan looked up with a disinterested half-smile—a tall, broad-shouldered man with a square jaw, heavy brows over piercing brown eyes, and a stunning black pompadour. "Oh, yeah, you're Danny, right? Here for the tryout?"

"Yeah. And this is Jenny Wayne. We're both trying out."

Callan stretched out a hand to Jenny, his eyes crinkling approvingly. She unthinkingly wiped her palm on her skirt before extending her hand. He grinned with amusement and held her hand firmly in his for what seemed forever. "Hi, Jenny. Glad you could make it."

"Thanks for letting us try out," she said, her voice cracking nervously. Heaven help her, she would never get through this audition!

Cal finally, reluctantly released her hand, but his eyes lingered on her. She shivered, feeling somehow naked, exposed. "So okay," said Callan, turning his attention back to Danny. "You two need some accompaniment?"

"No, I have my guitar," said Danny, patting the shiny black case he carried in his left hand. He gave Jenny a glance that said he had noticed Callan's obvious attentiveness to her. He got out his guitar and spent several moments tuning it while Jenny felt her throat grow dry. *Dear Lord, please don't let me make a fool of myself,* she prayed silently.

Callan sat back on the piano bench and casually folded his arms. "Okay, so let's hear what you two got."

"Right now? Right here?" she asked, as a beefy stagehand pushed a set divider—an artificial brick wall—past her on rollers that creaked and groaned mercilessly.

"Sure, right here," said Callan. "Where else? This isn't Carnegie Hall. It's the county fair, for crying out loud!"

Jenny's face grew warm with embarrassment. Danny edged close and squeezed her hand, giving her a look that said, *Let's do it! This is our big break. We can't blow it now!*

Jenny drew in a deep breath and licked her lips as Danny's fingers moved expertly over the strings, playing the introduction. They had practiced this a hundred times. *Just take it easy,* she told herself. *Give yourself to the music; let it flow from your soul.*

They sang one of Danny's songs—"Born to Love You," a romantic ballad he had written for Jenny; it showcased the perfect harmony in their voices. It was a soft sound, maybe too soft for Callan Swan and the Bell Tones, but it showed them at their best. After an adequate beginning, Jenny felt her voice grow strong. Yes, the notes were coming out solid and clean; she was riding the crest, sailing high, soaring effortlessly. A wave of euphoria helped her clear the high notes with room to spare.

When they had finished, Callan rubbed his jaw thoughtfully but said nothing. The black man clapped his hands slowly and nodded. The other band members continued packing up their gear.

Cal said, "What else you got?"

Danny strummed his guitar, introducing one of his songs with a faster tempo, a heavier beat. Jenny allowed herself to relax a little.

Her confidence was up; she and Danny were giving it their best. If Callan Swan didn't want them, someone else would.

This time, when they finished, the other band members were watching, listening, their expressions muted. But Jenny had a feeling they liked what they heard.

Callan stood up and shuffled over to Danny. "Not bad," he said. "You two got a nice sound. It's not our sound, but it's fresh and catchy. But you're both still a couple of kids, wet behind the ears. Inexperience can kill a band. If you can't pull your own weight, someone else has gotta do it for you. We need seasoned musicians who know the score. Know what I mean?"

"Are you saying you can't use us?" asked Danny, his voice thick with disappointment.

Cal made a so-so gesture with his hand. "No, I'm not saying that at all. It's just—well, I gotta be careful. If I get the wrong people in here, it changes the whole sound, and we've worked hard to perfect our sound. It's what folks expect of us."

"We'll give it everything we've got," said Danny.

"I'm sure you will, but only time will tell if you can really fit in with our band and play our sound."

"Are you saying . . . we're hired?" asked Danny.

Callan looked over at Jenny, then back at Danny. He crossed his arms again and drummed his fingers on his elbow. "Now let me get this straight. You two are together? She's your girl?"

Danny gave Jenny a searching look, as if to ask, "What do we say?" But she wasn't about to get Danny out of this one.

"You're asking if Jen's my girlfriend?" said Danny, stalling.

"Yeah," said Cal, sounding impatient. "A simple question, right?"

"Right," said Danny, too quickly. "I guess I forgot to tell you. Jen and I—we're cousins."

Cal's lips curled into a pleased, self-satisfied smile. "Cousins? Why didn't you say so?"

Danny stared down at the floor. "It didn't seem important."

"Not kissin' cousins, I hope," Cal teased.

"Just cousins," Danny repeated, looking miserable.

Cal's eyes traveled back to Jenny, moving slowly, appreciatively over her figure. She was wearing a modest cotton dress, but when Callan looked at her, she felt as if he saw right through her clothes. "I think you two are just what this band needs," Cal said with a cunning smile. "You'll be a real asset." As an afterthought he glanced at Danny and added, "Yes, a real asset. Both of you."

Jenny shivered. She felt as if Danny had just thrown her to the wolves. One wolf, in particular!

"The thing is," said Callan, "all I need right now are backup singers— a man and a woman. You two gotta be willing to take a back seat, to make the lead singer look good. You gotta sing what I tell you to sing, and otherwise keep your mouth shut and take orders. I run the show. Understand?"

"Yes, sir," said Danny.

Jenny wasn't so sure, but she nodded anyway. She couldn't mess this up for Danny, but didn't he see how this guy was looking at her, practically making a pass in front of everyone? Or was Jenny mistaken about the uncomfortable feeling Callan Swan gave her?

"Come on over here, guys," Cal told the other band members. "I want you to meet the rookies." Three white men and the black man sidled over, looking nonchalant, eyeing Jenny and Danny with cool detachment or mild curiosity.

"This is Gil Russo," said Cal. A tall, lanky youth ambled forward and nodded. "He's our lead guitar player. Comes from Detroit. Been with the band since we started three years ago." Gil had curly brown hair, dark half-moon eyes, and wide lips that flashed a contemptuous half-smile. "Welcome aboard," he drawled.

Danny shook his hand and Jenny murmured, "Hi."

Cal slipped a possessive arm around Jenny's shoulder and turned her toward a short man in a baseball cap, whose grin was as wide as his face. "This here is our drummer, Andy Loomis, from Indianapolis. He plays a wild guitar and sings okay too. Been with us a year now."

Andy reached out and clasped Jenny's hand, then Danny's. "Welcome to the party." Andy's round, pliable face with its ski-jump nose, apple cheeks, prominent teeth, and bright, mischievous eyes possessed a boyish, exaggerated quality, as if his features could be molded like putty into comical, bizarre expressions. Jenny liked Andy immediately; there was a guileless sincerity about him; whatever he was feeling would surely blaze across his face for all the world to see.

"And this is Lee Slocum," said Cal, as a lean man with a thin face and angular features offered his hand. "Lee's our driver, the only one the guys will trust behind the wheel. Lee's from Philadelphia, and he keeps promising to get us on *Bandstand*, but so far, no soap."

"One of these days we'll make it," said Lee, with a toothy, uneven grin. He had such a gaunt, mousy, beady-eyed look, Jenny half expected to see his whiskers twitch. His most prominent feature was his hair—the same Elvis-style pompadour Callan had, but on Lee it looked top heavy and whimsically absurd, dwarfing his already narrow face.

"Lee plays guitar and sings backup," said Callan. "He's got a falsetto to rival Buddy Holly's. You should hear him sing 'Peggy Sue.'"

"That's one of my favorites," said Jenny.

"Then I'll be sure to sing it for you one of these days," said Lee as he bowed with a little flourish and gallantly lifted Jenny's hand to his lips.

Jenny's face grew warm, but Lee's attentiveness didn't bother her half as much as Callan's casual arm around her shoulder.

"And this is the man who helps me keep the whole show running like clockwork," said Callan, thumping the black man's muscled back. "Emmett Sanders is from Chicago and plays piano, guitar, and drums. You name it, he does it. He makes us hum. He's my right-hand man and my left-hand man, all in one."

"You better believe it," said Emmett, clasping Danny's hand, then Jenny's. His hand was large and strong and his smile as quick and bright as lightning. Emmett moved and spoke with a confident, soft-spoken authority that Jenny liked. For a big man, he possessed the limber grace of a dancer.

"So that's our band," said Callan, his arm still loosely around Jenny's shoulder. "If you want to give us a try, we'll take you with us next week when we finish our gig here in Willowbrook. We'll give it a trial run for a couple of weeks and see how we do together. If it works, you got your-selves a steady job." He looked at Jenny, his long fingers lightly mas-saging her shoulder. "One thing, Jenny, . . . or do you go by Jennifer?"

"Jenny," she said quietly, yearning to slip out of Callan's overbear-ing grasp. "Or you can call me Jen."

"Jen it is." Cal bent his face close to hers, his breath warm, pun-gent with the smells of rum and tobacco. "Listen, Jen, you're going to be the only girl traveling with a bunch of noisy, messy, fun-loving guys. Think you can handle it?"

She wanted to shout, *Not on your life!* Instead, she managed a faint, "I—I'll try."

"It's not going to be like home, is it, fellas? Tell her what it's like on the road."

"Cheap motels and greasy spoons," said Lee.

"Riding a bus till your behind is numb," said Andy.

"Waking up in one town and falling asleep in another," said Gil, "and you never remember which town was which. After a while they all run together and you have no idea where on God's green earth you are. You just go where the bus takes you."

"If you don't have lots of gumption and guts," said Emmett with a wry, amused smile, "life on the road will turn you into a zombie or a lunatic. Maybe both."

"You still want to try it?" asked Callan, casting Danny a sly, defiant look.

Danny lifted his chin resolutely. "I'm game if Jenny is."

She swallowed a growing lump in her throat. "Sure, I'm game. This is what we've . . . been dreaming of."

"Okay. Then we'll see the two of you here a week from today. Pack light. A suitcase, overnight bag. That's it. We don't have a lot of room in the bus." Cal looked at Jenny. That look again. "Bring a couple of glitzy gowns, okay? Something slinky, with sequins and spangles, to show off your figure."

"Wait a minute," protested Danny. "You didn't say anything about wanting some sexy torch singer in a slinky dress."

"Danny's right. You said you just wanted a backup singer," Jenny stammered. "You're the lead. The spotlight should be on you, not me."

Cal winked meaningfully. "That was the original plan. But if you doll yourself up, sweetheart, maybe we'll get you out in the spotlight too. I bet we could sound real good together. That is, if I decide I want to share the spotlight." Cal looked over at Lee. "Who does Jenny remind you of? One of those actresses who sings? What's her name? You know, the girl-next-door type who still looks sexy as a vamp."

"Annette Funicello?" suggested Lee.

"Sandra Dee," said Gil.

"Okay, whoever," said Cal. "The point is, my pretty little Jenny Wayne, on stage you're going to look real good to the eyes, and that's something the Bell Tones can use."

Jenny felt a wave of anxiety rise in her chest. Worse than anxiety. Panic. She twisted out of Callan's grasp and nearly fled into Danny's arms. Danny looked momentarily flustered, his expression stricken, as if he weren't quite sure how Callan would react to Jenny's retreat from his arms. Obviously the last thing Danny wanted to do was aggravate Callan Swan.

Just as tears threatened behind Jenny's eyes, Emmett strolled over and spoke in a deep, soothing voice. "Miss Jenny, don't you let Callan

Swan get you all alarmed. You'll be doing just whatever you feels comfortable doing, okay? Cal's a big talker; only sometimes he don't listen to half of what he says. And neither do we."

Everyone chuckled, including Cal, to Jenny's relief. Maybe Callan Swan *was* all talk. Maybe he didn't mean anything at all by the way he wrapped his arm around her so possessively. Maybe he was just showing off for the guys, showing he was boss, a big man with the ladies.

Maybe Jenny had a whole lot to learn about the way musicians behaved on the road, and the way they looked at things, especially women. She would be foolish to expect traveling musicians to act like the boys at school or at church. Surely she wasn't going to let her own innocence and inborn prudishness prevent her from pursuing the chance of a lifetime!

Callan gave the empty stage a sweeping once-over, then reached over and clasped Danny's shoulder. "Looks like we're ready to get out of here. You and Jenny want to join us at the tavern around the corner for a little nightcap? My treat."

"No thanks," said Danny uneasily. "It's late. We'd better get home."

Callan shrugged. "Suit yourself. Enjoy the comforts of home while you got them."

"That's for sure," said Emmett, grinning, "because next week home will be an old rattletrap bus on a highway that never ends, and towns you wanna forget, with names you can never remember. It's like no life you ever knew before, in your nightmares or your dreams."

6

For a week Jenny lived suspended between two worlds— the past and the future. It was an eerie, surreal sensation, this period of waiting, silently biding her time, knowing the moments with her family were quickly dissolving. Soon all she would have of home were her memories.

She considered not going on the road with the band, but at the same time she stealthily packed her bag and prepared to go. She found herself seeing her family with a fresh appreciation, secretly studying their profiles in the evening lamplight or lingering with them at the dinner table just to chat. This warm, charitable feeling extended even to her mother, with whom she rarely saw eye to eye.

With the days flying by at breakneck speed, Jenny wanted to store up all the good memories she could gather, because already she sensed this adventure she was about to embark on would not deliver all the promises she hoped for. As much as she wanted her independence and a life and career of her own choosing, she realized the road ahead could be arduous, frightening, perhaps even filled with disappointments and heartaches. This sobering glimpse into an uncertain future prompted a deeper sense of responsibility toward those she was leaving behind.

Her family would be hurt; there was no getting around it. They would never understand how she and Danny could leave without telling them. And, certainly, they wouldn't approve of her new lifestyle, traveling the country with a rock 'n' roll band. She could almost hear Papa Robert sputtering, "Has that girl taken leave of her senses? She was raised in a Christian home, and now she's off flirting with the devil and singing his music!"

Was she? Was she sinning against God by running off and joining Callan Swan's band? It didn't feel like sinning, but her entire family would be convinced of it. They would tell her she had better get her life straightened out with God. But God was a little less real to Jenny than the father she never knew.

Both God and Chilton Reed had supposedly played an immense role in her life; both, in a sense, created her. But to this day both remained as elusive in her mind as smoke in the night, as the cloudy vapor on a window pane. Since childhood, Jenny's head had been filled with stories of God and stories of her father, and yet, now that she was an adult, the stories had no meaning, no substance beyond words that faded into whispers in the air. Where was God when she needed Him? Where was her father? They existed only in her imagination, in her secret yearnings and dreams. They had nothing to do with the flesh and blood woman named Jennifer Wayne.

So whether she was sinning by running away seemed of little relevance. Still, it grieved her to think of hurting her family. She had better be sure she wasn't going off on a whim, only to change her mind when the going got tough. Too much was at stake to risk making a mistake.

As the days dwindled away, Jenny's misgivings lingered even as her resolve deepened. No matter how many doubts swirled in her mind, she would go with Danny when the band left town on Sunday afternoon.

On Saturday evening, with only hours left before she would be leaving Willowbrook, Jenny stole upstairs to her room, removed her suitcase from her closet, and opened it on her bed. The rest of the family was downstairs preparing a huge family dinner to celebrate Jon Knowl's eighth birthday, so this was her chance; one last time to make sure she had everything she needed. Underwear, pajamas, shirts, jeans, dresses, toiletries, cosmetics. She looked around her room, mentally checking her closet and drawers. There were so many things she would have to leave behind, so many lovely outfits she had no room for.

She drifted over to her bureau and picked up the gold-framed photograph of her family beside the leather-bound Bible Annie had given her years ago. As she gazed at the picture, a pang of conscience wrenched her heart and a solid, sorrowful lump formed in her throat. They were all looking back at her, Mama and Robert and Laura— even she herself—smiling and carefree, as if she weren't about to desert her own kin. There wasn't room in her suitcase for the bulky frame, but she could take the picture. She carefully pulled the photograph out of the frame and slipped it into her Bible where it would be safe. She hugged the Bible against her chest for a long moment, then tucked it into her suitcase. There! Now, in a way, she was taking God and her family with her.

The bedroom door flew open suddenly and Laura burst inside, her pony tail bobbing, her saddle shoes scuffing the hardwood floor. "Jenny, Mama wants you downstairs right this minute!"

Before Jenny could reply, Laura sidled over to the bed and peered curiously at the suitcase. "What are you packing for? You going somewhere?"

Jenny slammed the suitcase shut, picked it up in her arms, and shoved it back into the closet. "Yeah, I'm going somewhere," she shot back. "To the moon!"

Laura's gaze remained riveted on the bulging suitcase. "What's in there? You're hiding something. What are you hiding?"

In one swift, exaggerated motion, Jenny shut the closet door, so hard it shuddered noisily. "I'm not hiding anything, small fry. Can't a girl have some privacy?"

"I'm telling Mama," squealed Laura, stamping her foot.

"Telling her what?" demanded Jenny, staring her sister down.

Laura stuck out her square jaw. Her small brown eyes snapped. "I'm telling her you're going on a trip somewhere; you're packing a suitcase and you won't let me see what's in it."

"I'm not packing anything. And I'm not going anywhere. I—I was just putting some clothes away I don't wear anymore."

This answer seemed to satisfy Laura momentarily. "Oh. Is that all? Well, who cares about your old clothes?"

"That's what I said. It's just ugly old stuff I'll probably throw away someday."

Laura shrugged and headed back toward the door, her full skirt swishing around her spindly calves. "Well, you better get downstairs right now. Mama's having a fit."

"A fit?"

"She's mad as a hornet."

"At me? What did I do?"

"You came upstairs and hid in your room when she needed your help with dinner. Everyone will be here any minute, and the kitchen looks like a cyclone hit it."

"I helped Mama earlier. I set the table. I peeled the potatoes and shelled the peas. What more does she want?"

"Go ask her yourself. She told me to come get you."

"Okay, squirt, I'll be right down. Scram now, will you?"

Laura's forehead puckered and her lower lip jutted out in a pout. "You're always so mean to me. Why are you so mean?"

Jenny felt a stab of regret. She didn't want this to be her sister's last memory of her. "Laura, wait. Come here."

Laura gave her a skeptical look but slowly inched over. "What?"

Jenny reached out and touched Laura's round, freckled face and tucked a wisp of umber-brown hair behind Laura's ear. "I'm sorry I got mad. You're not so bad for a kid sister."

Laura's brown eyes widened into saucers. "Really? Then you'll let me see inside the suitcase?"

Jenny laughed ruefully. "I didn't say that. It's just—I'm glad you're my sister."

Laura shrank back, puzzlement turning her beetling brows into question marks. "Me, too." She paused in the doorway. "If you give me half your dessert, I won't tell Mama how weird you're acting or what you're hiding in the closet."

Jenny grabbed up a lacy throw pillow from the bed and pitched it at Laura as she flounced out of the room. "Get out of here, Smarty-Pants, before I take back what I just said!"

When Jenny entered the kitchen moments later, her mother was stirring a pan of beef drippings and bemoaning the fact that the gravy was lumpy. Seeing Jenny, her already flushed face turned crimson. "Where'd you disappear to, young lady, right when I needed you most?"

"I was upstairs. I did everything you asked."

"Well, I wasn't through asking. You know how hectic it is trying to get a big dinner on the table. I've only got two hands, for heaven's sake!"

"I'm sorry. I didn't think—"

"That's the trouble, Jen! You never think. You'd rather loll around in your room daydreaming than help your poor mother get a meal on the table."

Jenny's anger flared, but she forced her voice to remain calm. "I thought I did help. I didn't know you had more for me to do."

"Well, look around, Jen. The potatoes need to be mashed and I burned the cheese sauce for the cauliflower. I left the roast in too long; it'll probably be as tough as shoe leather." Catherine ran her hands distractedly through her mussed carrot-red curls. "I should know better than to offer to fix a birthday dinner. I must be crazy. Why do I think I've got to keep up with Annie?"

"You don't, Mama. Why do you always think you do?"

"Because everything always comes so easy for her. Annie has her mother Anna to do all the cooking for them, so Annie can traipse off and write her books any time she pleases. Nobody does that for me when I'm trying to paint. What do I have? I have a loony mother sitting in her room watching television all day who doesn't know whether she's in Indiana or New Jersey or Timbuktu! I'm stuck with a crazy mother, and I'm getting just as crazy trying to get this lousy dinner on the table!"

Jenny stole over and put a tentative hand on her mother's arm. "I'm sorry, Mama. I'll do whatever you want. Just tell me."

Catherine's expression softened and her green eyes glistened momentarily with tenderness and regret. "I'm sorry, honey. You know me. I just hate putting on big dinners. Nothing ever goes right."

"Then why do you do it?"

She shrugged. "I've got to take my turn like everyone else. You'll understand someday. It's a family thing. Just wait. I bet you'll hate it as much as I do, but you'll do it just the same. You do what's expected of you to keep peace in the family. And you never breathe a word about how much you hate it. You just grit your teeth and smile and say it was no trouble at all."

Jenny shook her head. "I don't want to live that way."

"Who does? But if I complain and say what I really think, Annie and my dear brother Knowl and your Papa Robert will shake their heads and say I'm becoming just as ornery as Mama, and I'll die before I hear them say that."

Jenny rubbed her mother's arm lightly. "They would never say that, Mama."

"Then why do I hear them saying it in my head?"

"Maybe it's what you're afraid of, deep inside."

Catherine brushed off Jenny's touch and turned back to her gravy. "Oh, so now my daughter is the great Sigmund Freud himself. Trying to figure out what makes people tick. Well, you may be a high school graduate, daughter, but you've still got a lot to learn."

Jenny bit her lower lip to keep from hurling back an unkind remark. Tears smarted in her eyes. This was her last evening with her mother and they still couldn't get along. Why did it always turn out like this, the two of them clashing, always setting each other off, never saying the right things? Jenny turned to the stove, picked up the wire potato masher, and gingerly lifted the heavy iron lid on the potatoes. Spirals of steam escaped, burning her wrist. She uttered an exclamation of pain and let the lid clatter back on the huge kettle.

"Be careful," her mother scolded. "If you spill those potatoes, I'm calling everyone and telling them the dinner is ruined—and just stay home."

"The dinner's not ruined, Mama," said Jenny, a sob of emotion catching in her throat.

Her mother came over and seized her wrist. "You burned yourself."

"It's okay."

"It's already turning red. It could blister." She led Jenny over to the sink and turned on the spigot full blast. "Hold your arm under the cold water. If that doesn't help, put some ice on it."

"I'm fine, Mama. It's nothing."

"I said it could blister. You never know. Play it safe."

That evening, no one sitting around the dining room table partaking of that bountiful feast would have guessed that, an hour earlier, Catherine had been ready to pull her hair out and cancel the entire dinner. Without exception, the Herricks, the Marshalls, and the Waynes seemed to be relishing every morsel. At Jenny's insistence, even Grandma Betty had come downstairs and joined the party. She sat beside Jenny, twisting her linen napkin and looking a little befuddled by all the commotion, but Jenny kept whispering encouraging little asides to make her smile. "You look so nice in that dress, Grandma Betty . . . I'm so glad you felt up to having dinner with us tonight . . . Don't you just love Mama's roast beef?"

Everyone at the table complimented Mama on her cooking, even if she wasn't ready to believe a word of it. "The dinner is simply delicious, Cath," said Annie. "You've outdone yourself."

"The roast is a little dry," replied Cath.

"I love your mashed potatoes," said Bethany Rose, sitting between Danny and the reverend. "Mine are always lumpy. How do you make them so smooth and creamy?"

"Ask Jenny," said Cath. "She mashed the potatoes."

"And have you noticed how much Maggie and Jon Knowl love your creamed cauliflower?" said Knowl, scraping the bowl clean. "We can hardly get them to eat vegetables at home."

"I burned the cheese sauce and had to start over," said Catherine, rejecting every compliment like a duck repelling water.

"Well, whether you want to admit it or not," said Robert, "this is a wonderful dinner, Cath, darling, and I'm proud of you."

For the first time that evening Catherine dropped her defenses and gazed up gratefully at Robert. "You really liked it, sweetheart? Thanks, but it wasn't all that much trouble."

"Now, where's the cake?" exclaimed eight-year-old Jon Knowl, the spitting image of his father, right down to the large wire-rim spectacles on his button nose.

"Yes, where's the cake?" echoed Grandma Betty. "I want cake!"

"No one's having cake until we get the table cleared," said Catherine, reaching for the soiled plates.

Jenny jumped up. "Danny and I will clear the table, Mama. We'll do the dishes too, won't we, Danny?"

Danny looked up in surprise, then quickly recovered and said, "Sure, Mrs. Wayne. Jenny and I would love to do the dishes for you. Uh, while you go ahead and serve the cake."

"Well, thank you, Danny," said Catherine, flushing slightly. "You're becoming a very polite and helpful young man. Bethany Rose, you and Todd should be real proud of your son."

"We are," said Todd, giving Danny a look that said he sensed the boy was up to something. "Danny's a good boy, but usually not quite so eager to help out in the kitchen."

"I think he's just looking for a chance to spend a little time alone with Jenny," said Bethany Rose, giving Jenny a knowing smile.

Jenny rolled her eyes. "Will you all stop it? We're just good friends, that's all."

"Well, you two have certainly been spending enough time together lately rehearsing Danny's songs," said Todd, drumming his fingers on the linen tablecloth. He looked over at Knowl with an ironic smile. "I told Bethany that Danny should have had a summer job, but she wanted him to spend time on his music. You'd think the kids were performing at Carnegie Hall or something." Todd looked back at Danny. "What are you two practicing for anyway? It can't be church. Those weren't hymns I heard you singing."

"There's nothing wrong with my songs, Dad," protested Danny, his jaw tightening.

"I didn't say there was, son. I'm just wondering where you plan to sing songs that have such a strong, exuberant beat."

Danny's brows furrowed, shading the reproach in his eyes. "I don't know, Dad. But I'll think of somewhere."

"They're going to sing on Dick Clark's show," said Grandma Betty brightly. "*American Bandstand*. It's my favorite television show. Besides *Strike It Rich*."

"*American Bandstand*? That teenage dance program?" said Todd with a hint of amusement. "Now I've heard everything."

"Don't pay any attention to my mother," whispered Catherine. "She doesn't know what she's saying."

"It may be idle talk," said Todd, his tone sobering, "but that show is the last place on earth I would ever want my son singing."

"Is that so, Dad?" said Danny hotly. "Well, maybe someday I will sing on *Bandstand*. I'd give anything to have that chance."

The reverend countered with his own solemn retort. "You want to be some rowdy, lip-curling, hip-swinging hood with a guitar? That's not how I raised you, son."

To ward off the threat of fireworks, Jenny picked up a stack of plates and signaled Danny with her eyes. "You get the salad bowls and bread plates, okay?"

He looked up and, reading her expression, he pushed back his chair and promptly began collecting the dishes. He followed her into the kitchen and set the soiled china on the counter while she turned on the faucet and filled the sink with hot, soapy water.

"You see why I've got to get away?" he said, hitting his fist against the counter edge.

"Yes, Danny, but please don't let your dad spoil our last day at home."

He nodded and drew in a deep breath. "You're right, Jen. Besides, we'll have the last laugh."

She slipped several saucers into the soapy water. "Save the laughing for later, Danny. Right now grab a towel and help me with these dishes."

"Brilliant," he whispered, swiping the foamy mound with his forefinger and flicking a rainbow of bubbles on her nose. "You thought of the perfect way for us to be alone."

"Are you kidding? I just wanted to save you from another argument with your father." She rubbed away the bubbles with the back of her hand. "Listen, we have to talk, Danny."

"You sound serious."

She nodded. "Tomorrow we're leaving . . . and I'm scared."

He slipped his arm around her waist and drew her against his chest; no matter how worrisome things seemed, she always felt safe and protected in his arms. "Don't be afraid, Jenny, sweetheart. It'll be okay. I promise."

She sniffed noisily. "I didn't know it would be so hard, leaving everybody and going so far away without saying a word. I don't know if I can do it."

"Sure you can. It'll go like clockwork. We'll go to church same as usual. I'll tell my folks I'm spending the day at your house; you tell your folks you're spending the day with me, so no one will even think to look for us until evening."

"How can I lie to them, Danny?"

"It's no lie. You will be spending the day with me. We'll leave church early, drive to our houses and pick up our stuff, then drive to the fairgrounds and meet up with Callan and the band. I'll leave a note in my room telling my dad to pick up my car—his car really—at the fairgrounds. We'll be halfway to Nashville before anyone even gets suspicious."

"I'm leaving a note too. I want to tell Mom where she can reach me if there's an emergency."

Danny's smoky green eyes darkened. "You can't, Jenny. You can leave a note, but don't say a word about where we'll be—until we've already been there and moved on."

"My family will be worried to death if we leave without telling them where we're going."

"We talked about this before, Jen. There's no other way. You're not going to chicken out on me, are you?"

She lowered the china plates into the soapy water. "Of course not, Danny. It's just—what if it isn't what we expect? What if after a couple of weeks, Callan sends us home? What if we hate being on the road? What if our folks are so angry they won't let us come back home again?"

Danny turned her toward him, his fingertips pressing into her upper arms. "Stop it, Jen. You're going off the deep end. Letting your imagination run wild."

"I can't help it, Danny. I'm scared. What if we're making a mistake?"

He moved his palm soothingly over her arm. His eyes were steady, gentle. "We've planned this for a long time, and we're just lucky Cal agreed to let us join the band. If God didn't want us to go, He could have made Callan say no. Right? So we've got to figure this is what we're meant to do."

"If only it didn't have to be a secret. If only we could go with our parents' blessing."

Danny uttered a hard, scoffing chuckle. "That the biggest joke of all, Jen. Your dad and my dad would hog-tie us for sure and never let us out of their sight again."

"Oh, Danny . . . I know you're right."

"We're old enough to take charge of our own lives, and that's just what we're doing. We're following our dreams, the same as our folks did when they were young."

The kitchen door opened suddenly. Annie entered, her expression registering surprise. "I'm sorry, kids. Am I interrupting something?"

"No, nothing at all," Jenny blurted, jumping back.

"We were just talking about—about the future," said Danny, hooking his thumbs on his trouser pockets.

Annie looked around. "Well, I just came in to get Jon Knowl's cake. I'm afraid he can't wait a minute longer. You know how little boys are." She spotted the cake on the counter and picked it up, then gave Jenny a lingering glance. "Jen, honey, I'll be calling you soon about doing some more research for me. You are still interested, aren't you?"

Jenny's mouth went dry. "Uh, sure. I love helping you, Annie. More than anything."

Annie smiled, her gaze going from Jenny to Danny and back again.

"Well, good, I'm glad to hear that, because I love having your help. It makes my research less tedious. And it's great fun spending time together."

Jenny gripped the edge of the counter and stifled the impulse to run into Annie's arms and confess her traitorous plans to run away. She could feel the blood draining from her face and her knuckles growing stiff where she clutched the counter.

Annie's expression clouded. "Are you okay, Jenny?"

"I'm fine. Why do you ask?"

"You look a little peaked. Get lots of rest tonight. You might be coming down with something."

"I will, Annie. Thanks."

"For what?"

"For caring."

Annie's eyes glistened with sudden emotion. "I'll always care, Jenny. You know that." She looked down at the birthday cake and broke into a smile. "Listen, let those dishes soak and come sing and have some cake! This won't be a party without the two of you out there keeping the rest of us on tune."

The next morning, everything went like clockwork, just as Danny had promised. They went with their families to church and left early, Danny driving first to the parsonage for his things and then to Jenny's house, where she collected her suitcase and overnight bag. She left a note in her top dresser drawer that said simply:

DEAR MOM AND DAD:
PLEASE DON'T WORRY ABOUT ME. DANNY AND I HAVE
JOINED A BAND AND WILL WRITE YOU FROM THE ROAD.
THIS IS WHAT WE WANT, SO PLEASE DON'T BE ANGRY.
WE ARE FINE. I LOVE YOU ALL VERY MUCH.
YOUR DAUGHTER, JENNY

As Danny carried her suitcase and overnight bag downstairs, Jenny called after him, "Wait for me by the door. There's one more thing I've got to do."

He looked up at her, a frown creasing his brow. "Don't take too long. Your folks will be home from church soon. If they catch us, it's all over. We'll never get out of here."

"I won't be long," she assured him. "I just have to say good-bye to my grandmother."

"Don't tell her anything," warned Danny.

"It doesn't matter. Nobody listens to what she says anyway." Jenny stole quietly down the hall and knocked lightly on her grandmother's door. These days the family felt fairly secure leaving Grandma Betty alone for the few hours they were at church each week. Now that she no longer boozed it up with her hidden caches of scotch and gin, Grandma Betty was relatively docile and mellow. It had been years now since she had tried to run away or set something on fire.

Jenny opened the door a crack and peeked in. Maybe her grand-mother was sleeping. But no. There she sat in her usual rocking chair by the television set, stretched out in her chenille robe, watching Fulton J. Sheen. Hearing the door hinges creak, she looked up and flashed Jenny a crooked smile, then held out a gnarled hand and said, "Come. Come in, my little sweetheart. Sit a spell and watch television with me."

Jenny pattered over to the rocking chair and kissed her grand-mother's warm, mottled forehead. She sat on the edge of the bed near the rocker and held the frail hand in hers. "I can only stay a minute," Jenny said, her throat tightening. She felt tears gathering behind her eyes, pressing, making her head hurt, but she didn't dare release them. Tears would only confuse and upset her grandmother, and that's the last thing her family needed now.

"You look sad, child. Why aren't you happy?"

"I am happy, Grandma. But I'm a little sad too."

"Happy and sad? All at once? What makes you happy and sad?"

"Danny and I are following our dream, Grams. Remember what you said at the dinner party last night?"

"Dinner party?"

"Grams, we're going to sing with a band, like they do on *American Bandstand*. Your favorite show, remember? Maybe someday you'll turn on the television set and see Danny and me singing on *Bandstand*. Wouldn't that be wonderful?"

Her grandmother nodded. "I'll watch every day. I'll look for you. You tell Mr. Dick Clark he's a handsome man. Like my Tom. You tell him I said so."

"I will, Grandma. I'll tell him you said so."

"Fine. I'll watch every day. Wave to me so I'll see you."

Jenny blinked back the rising tears. "I will, Grams. I'll wave to you and throw you a kiss like Dinah Shore does when she says good night. With both hands." Jenny demonstrated.

Her grandmother smiled unevenly. "I'll watch for you. Wave and throw a kiss like Dinah Shore."

A knock sounded on the door. Jenny jumped up from the bed. Good heavens, surely her parents weren't home already!

"Jenny?" Danny peered into the room, looking harried, impatient. "Come on, Jen, we've got to go. Right now!"

"Okay, I'm coming." She turned back to her grandmother and threw her arms around her thin neck and buried her face against the gray plaited nest of her grandmother's hair. "I love you, Grandma Betty."

With knobby fingers her grandmother pulled Jenny's face down close to hers and kissed her cheek with warm, moist lips. Jenny could smell cold cream and witch hazel on the old woman's soft, crepe-paper skin. "Come back soon and sit with me. Watch television with me, child. Keep me company until Tom comes home."

"I will, Grandma. I promise. I'll come home and sit with you as soon as I can." A tear escaped down Jenny's cheek. "Don't forget me, Grams, okay?"

But her grandmother had already turned her gaze back to the flickering screen. "Watch, Jenny," she rasped. "This man looks like my Tom. Do you suppose that's my Tom?"

Jenny slipped out of the room and shut the door quietly behind her, a huge boulder of emotion pressing on her heart. Danny was already at the foot of the stairs gesturing wildly. "Come on, Jen," he hissed, his hand tight on the doorknob. "If we don't get going now, we might as well forget it!"

Early August, 1960

Danny and Jenny had been on the road with Callan Swan and his band, the Bell Tones, for nearly a week now, traveling from Willowbrook to Nashville and stopping at every one-horse town on the way. Jenny never knew an old bus on the highway could rumble and clatter and bounce up and down so hard it made her teeth hurt, and her bottom, and every other muscle in her body, ache until all she wanted to do was scream.

So far they'd spent most nights sleeping on the bus while the guys took turns driving. There was no way to get comfortable, with the Indian summer heat and the mosquitoes and the hard, narrow seats. The only bathroom Jenny ever saw was inside a grimy gas station or an outhouse in a roadside park or picnic area. She had already stopped worrying about styling her hair or putting on makeup. Most nights she slept in her clothes because there was nowhere to change. She felt like a wandering gypsy or a nomad, with no place to call her own.

Danny kept telling her, "Don't worry, Jen, it'll get better. In the towns where we're performing we'll get our own motel rooms with a private bathroom and hot running water." She couldn't wait. She was going to stand under that hot water and wash her hair until she'd used up all her shampoo. Right now she didn't feel like she would ever get the grit and grime of the road off her skin or out of her scalp.

Already she was tired of the long hours on the road, riding the bus all day and all night, the guys playing poker and passing around a flask of gin or cans of beer. Or smoking their stogies and Lucky Strikes until a blue haze floated like a cloud along the ceiling of the bus and the noxious smell stole the breath from her lungs.

Things she took for granted at home seemed like cherished treasures now. Regular mealtimes. Sitting down at the same time every day for breakfast, lunch, and dinner. Eating at a table with a linen cloth and china plates and polished silverware and maybe a bouquet of fresh flowers on the table.

The guys rarely gave a thought to mealtime; they preferred to snack on whatever they could lay their hands on whenever the mood struck them. Sometimes they ate in a greasy spoon or a drive-in restaurant on some Main Street somewhere, gulping down cheap burgers and fries. But more likely, the guys would stop at a grocery store like A&P or Kroger and load up on canned tuna, Spam, loaves of day-old bread, cheese, peanut butter and jelly, and fresh fruit. A typical meal, whether it was breakfast, lunch, or dinner, was canned tuna bathed in its own oil and slapped between two slices of Wonder bread. It was a favorite of the guys, so they had it at least once a day. After a week of oily tuna on soggy bread, Jenny was ready to revolt. She was sure she had lost five pounds already. She was always what Grandma Betty called "skinny as a rail," but now she was getting downright scrawny.

A week into the trip she told the boys, "If we stopped at a roadside picnic area or somewhere with an outside grill or cook stove, I could fry up some fresh fish or chicken or steak. And some fried potatoes and onions. Or even just a pot of chili."

Cal answered back, "Sorry, Jen, we've got a schedule to keep. Besides, I never promised that traveling with my band would be a satisfying culinary experience."

After that, Jenny tried not to complain. She told herself maybe she was too fussy or spoiled by having it so good at home. She would never admit it to Mama, but she was beginning to realize how fortunate she had been to have all her material needs met all of her life without giving it a second thought.

In her diary at the end of ten days she wrote, "They say anything worth having is worth sacrificing for, so maybe this is my time to sacrifice and put up with tedious days and poor living conditions and a pack of rowdy guys who act like they never had an etiquette lesson in their lives. Not that all the guys are so bad. Danny always treats me kindly and with respect, and he refuses to drink with the others. I think he knows if he started drinking, I'd insist on going right back home.

"And Emmett Sanders, the black man who plays piano and sings like an angel, has been very polite and concerned about me, always inquiring whether I'm comfortable or need anything, like a candy bar or a bottle of soda pop. Like Danny and me, he doesn't drink liquor, so sometimes when we're parked somewhere at night and the guys are drinking, Emmett and Danny and I sit at the back of the bus and sing Negro spirituals and old camp songs. The whole world should hear Emmett. His soul has wings when he sings; you feel it right to your bones so deep you shiver. And when the three of us sing together, it's almost like a spiritual experience, as if God were sitting right there in our midst, listening and enjoying the music.

"I wish Callan would let Danny and Emmett and me sing together in his band sometime as lead singers, not just backup. We sound as good as Cal, and I think the audience would like our sound. But Cal says no; our camp singing is just for fun and the sound isn't professional enough for the Bell Tones. He says Danny and I had better concentrate on creating the sound he wants from his backup singers, or he'll have to start looking for someone else. And, of course, when he makes threats like that, you can see the pleasure he takes in lording it over us. He reminds us that he's the brains and talent behind the Bell Tones, and without him we'd just be a two-bit bunch of ho-hum musicians without a gig to call our own.

"When Callan starts talking like that, Danny gets mad as a hornet, but he doesn't let it show, except to me. His face will turn scarlet and he'll mutter under his breath, 'Any of us in this band are as good as Callan Swan without the swelled head.'

"Anyway, I'm rambling on like a dithering fool. I shouldn't even be writing in my diary about all these troubling things. What if somebody finds it and reads it? I'll really be in trouble then.

"What I should be doing is writing Mama or Annie a letter, but I just can't find the words. I know how upset they must be. Since my first day out I've been sending postcards home, mailing them as we leave each town, with no return address. I've scribbled short messages that give no clue to my whereabouts: 'I'm fine . . . Don't worry about me . . . I love you all very much.' But one of these days I've got to write a real letter home. Maybe tomorrow. Or next week."

By the end of Jenny's second week on the road, homesickness set in like a rain cloud. A regular downpour. More than anything, she wanted to hear Mama's voice, or Annie's, or Grandma Betty's. Even Laura's. But she dared not phone home; she might inadvertently tell them where she was. And she couldn't bear to hear the anger and disappointment in their voices. Maybe it was time to write that letter. But to whom? Mama? Annie? The only one who wouldn't be angry with her was Grandma Betty.

So one night, after Lee Slocum had driven the bus over an endless stretch of two-lane highway and finally stopped at a Kentucky park, Jenny sat in the back of the bus with a flashlight writing her grandmother while the others slept.

Betty Herrick
Honeysuckle Lane
Willowbrook, Indiana

Dear Grandma Betty:
    I'm writing you this letter because I can't write Mama. I know

she's mad at me for running off and won't want to hear anything I have to say. She'll be too bent on giving me a piece of her mind to even try to see things my way. Maybe you won't understand my going away either, but I know you'll hear me out and love me no matter what.

Or maybe after I've written this letter I'll just tear it up and throw it away. Right now I don't know what I feel like doing, except I've got to pour out my thoughts to somebody.

Please don't worry about me, Grams. In spite of everything, I'm happy. I'm singing with a band and doing what I want to do. I have to be the person I am in my heart of hearts, not the person Mama thinks I should be. Please understand, and help Mama and Papa Robert understand. I know they don't always listen to you, but maybe they will when they see this letter. By the way, tell Bethany Rose and the reverend that Danny's doing fine too.

I'm in the bus writing in the dark with a flashlight while the guys are sawing logs loud enough to break the sound barrier. I'll write more later, after our performance this weekend. That's going to be the real test, the thing that will make or break us, and I'm already shaking inside thinking about it. If Danny and I don't please our bandleader, we could both be headed home before this letter even reaches you. Well, I'd better close for now. I'll always love you, Grams. Keep watching for me on *American Bandstand*. I'll be waving at you.

Your Jenny

In her letter Jenny had been careful not to disclose her location, but she wished she could have described the gorgeous scenery and rustic towns they had traveled through. Tonight they were parked somewhere in Kentucky at a place called Pennyrile Forest State Resort Park, on the outskirts of the park so they didn't have to pay. They had crossed over the Ohio River today and driven through homey little bergs with names such as Dixie, Sebree, Slaughters, Fryer, and Farmersville. Tomorrow they would make the short drive east to Hopkinsville, where they would be performing at the fairgrounds. Grandma Betty would have enjoyed hearing about all the picturesque little towns so far from Willowbrook. Someday Jenny would tell her all about them.

Jenny mailed her letter early the next morning just before they left the campgrounds. She slipped it into a camp mailbox without anyone knowing. She knew Danny would have a fit if he even suspected she was writing home. "I don't want our families knowing anything we're doing," he told her repeatedly. "You know my dad. He'd track us down and force us to go home." Jenny had argued that his dad wouldn't dare come drag them home, but privately she knew the reverend might just be mad enough to do it.

The letter was momentarily forgotten as Jenny turned her attention to the band's performance at the Hopkinsville fairgrounds. She knew things were on an upswing when they arrived in town and the fair promoter already had them registered at the Aberdeen Motel, a plain-as-a-mud-fence establishment—two rows of pint-size motel rooms facing each other across a narrow parking strip. But the motel was wonderfully convenient, situated just two blocks from the fairgrounds. Best of all, Jenny had a room all to herself while the boys had to double up, two to a room.

When she stepped inside and shut the door and looked around at the sagging bed, the drab wallpaper and patched curtains, she thought she'd died and gone to heaven. For the first time in nearly three weeks, she had a bed to sleep in and a rusty, claw-foot tub to soak in, and best of all, privacy, glorious privacy!

The band spent all day Friday in a drafty room under the grandstand rehearsing for their Saturday show. It was exhausting and nerve-wracking, practicing the same songs over and over, trying to make them perfect. Cal wouldn't let them rest until they performed the entire program like clockwork, flawless and graceful and synchronized as the inner workings of a watch. When they had finished, they all felt pretty good about themselves, as if they could do no wrong. Even Callan was pleased. He gave Jenny a big hug and told her she was great, and for the first time since starting their travels she felt euphoric and filled with anticipation.

After their long hours of rehearsing, most of the guys headed for a beer hall down the street, but Danny, Emmett, and Jenny wandered over to the booth across from the grandstand. In a large, open-air tent, the First Baptist Church Women's Auxiliary served home-cooked meals—meatloaf, chicken fried steak, goulash, beef stew, and barbecued spareribs.

Mrs. Kimmins, a gray-haired, tallow-hued lady who served the meals, reminded Jenny of Grandmother Anna, smiling and gentle and always hovering, wanting to please. Right away she took Danny, Emmett, and Jenny under her wing and gave them second helpings for free. For Jenny, it was wonderful having home-cooked food again. While they sat at the counter eating, the woman started telling them how much Jesus loved them. Jenny told her, "I know all about that; I was raised on Jesus and His love."

When Danny told her, "My daddy's a minister back in Indiana," her smile grew as bright as the sun. Then she looked at Emmett and said, "How about you, sir? What do you know about Jesus and His love?"

Emmett matched her smile and said in his deep, sonorous voice, "Ma'am, I been raised on the love of Jesus since I was dandled on my daddy's knee. He was a Holy Roller preacher who sang gospel in Memphis and practiced his horn on the corner of Beale Street. He taught me real good about the love of God."

"Then you know He's real?" she prompted, as if they were Sunday school pupils and she the teacher.

"Oh, yes, ma'am. God is as real to me as you standing here. I talk to Him all the time and He talks back to me," said Emmett with his wide, crinkly eyed grin. "I don't fret about them that says there ain't no God, because I already made His acquaintance long time ago. We be real good friends; better than brothers."

Mrs. Kimmins's voice got all breathy and bright and she said, "I knew it. I seen the love of Jesus in your faces. We're all His precious children, aren't we?"

Jenny thought Mrs. Kimmins and Emmett were going to break into song on the spot. Emmett started humming "Swing Low, Sweet Chariot," and Mrs. Kimmins started tapping on the counter, keeping time and nodding her head with Emmett's. Jenny looked at Danny; he looked back at her, and they both busied themselves with their spareribs.

Jenny couldn't help thinking how much Mrs. Kimmins sounded like Annie when she talked about God. Listening to her and Emmett talking, Jenny felt a niggling pang inside, as if she were missing something. She had been raised on all the same teachings as Emmett, but she had never felt the way he felt about God, as if Jesus were his most intimate, caring friend. Jenny doubted that Danny had ever felt that way either. They were always on the outside looking in, wondering what all the fuss was about.

But these days, traveling so far from home and never knowing what to expect, she mused that it would be nice to know God that way. Maybe she wouldn't feel so alone and scared when she woke in the middle of the night in the bus or motel room and couldn't remember where she was or why she was there or where she was going.

In spite of Mrs. Kimmins's penchant for preachiness, Jenny enjoyed their brief time at her booth. And it was obvious Emmett and Danny were enjoying themselves too, eating high on the hog while listening to her regale them with stories of other performers she'd met at the fairgrounds. "We've had lots of Grand Ole Opry stars perform here in Hopkinsville," she told them. "Roy Acuff, Kitty Wells, Mother Maybelle and the Carter Sisters, and Slim Whitman and his band.

And just last year we featured Hank Snow with Faron Young as his opening act."

As Jenny fell asleep that night in her cozy motel room, she thought about tomorrow night when she and the Bell Tones would be performing on the same stage where so many music legends had performed. A knot of anxiety tightened in her chest. "Please, dear God," she whispered into the darkness, "let everything go all right. Give me the courage to walk out on that stage and sing my very best."

The next day both Jenny and Danny were nervous as cats on a high wire as the band unpacked and set up their equipment, did sound checks, and made sure each guitar had its own amp plugged in. The Bell Tones rehearsed one last time, then everyone went back to their motel rooms and got ready for their performance.

Jenny wore her pink chiffon dress and her hair pinned up on top and flowing down her back in long ringlets. The guys wore black suits and pink shirts with maroon ties.

When it came time to walk out on stage and take her place at the microphone, Jenny was glad she was only a backup singer. Every fear she had ever known came goose-bumping under her skin, turning her ankles weak and knotting her throat. She wasn't sure she would even be able to croak out a note when she stared out at the immense black sea of shadowy faces and the blaring lights beaming down on her like enormous blinding moons. But then suddenly Emmett started the intro on the piano, Gil hit the drums, and Callan began to sing. Somehow Jenny and Danny picked up their notes on cue and sang as well as they had ever sung. The rest of the program went just as they had rehearsed it. It seemed they'd been on stage for only a handful of moments when the show was suddenly over and the audience was applauding and making catcalls and stomping their feet, wanting more. Callan led them in three encores and then the curtain closed and they were done.

Afterward, as they slipped out the side entrance, a group of young girls came running up, begging for their autographs. One pretty blonde girl in a ponytail, only ten or twelve, held out her program to Jenny and said breathlessly, "Please sign this for me. You were wonderful!"

Jenny signed her name with trembling fingers and gave the paper back. Impulsively the girl threw her arms around Jenny, thanking her profusely, and cried real tears. "I want to be just like you someday," she said.

Jenny was so shocked she didn't even answer. She just stood watching the girl run off with her friends into the darkness, giddily clutching her autographed program.

In her motel room that night, Jenny described that magical moment in her diary. "It was so amazing. I'm sure I was more delirious with joy than that young girl was. I thought, *This is what performing is all about. This makes it all worthwhile!*

"So, as hard as it was to leave home, and as difficult as it's been traveling and living on the road, I am blissfully content at this moment, anticipating our next performance and our next eager audience. And maybe there'll be another young girl who wants my autograph and dreams of being me someday. Seeing the admiration in her eyes will be enough to buoy me up and help me face the hard, discouraging times I know lie ahead. But for now, I have caught a glimpse of my future and I must pursue it, wherever it takes me."

8

Jenny, wake up! Come on, get up, sleepyhead!"

From a sound sleep Jenny jumped at the sound of the urgent voice outside her door. "Emmett? That you?" she asked groggily.

He knocked with a little rat-a-tat rhythm and called back in a lyrical singsong voice, "Come on, girl. You and me and Danny are going to church!"

Jenny sat up and threw back her covers, sweet filigrees of dreams lingering in her mind. She gazed around the room as cogs of memory slipped into place. That's right. She wasn't at home in her bedroom in Willowbrook; she was in a plain little motel room in the heart of Kentucky. "Emmett," she said sleepily, "I'm dead to the world. Why don't you go on without me?"

"Not on your life, girl. The sun's shining and we're heading for church. We'll give you five minutes to get ready; then we're coming in after you."

She jumped out of bed and reached for her cotton robe. "Oh, no, you don't. You stay right there. I'll be out in ten minutes." She washed, ran a brush through her long thick curls, and pulled on a light cotton dress, sleeveless, a pale peach hue. She dabbed on a hint of makeup and pinched her cheeks for color, then slipped on her leather sandals as she headed out the door.

Danny and Emmett were waiting, leaning against the masonry wall, both looking spiffy in short-sleeved shirts and slacks, Emmett wearing his usual white straw hat with the red and black band. "So what's this all about, gentlemen?" she quizzed, tossing her head back jauntily.

"I'm taking you to my church," said Emmett with a sly smile and a gallant little bow.

"Your church? You've never lived here in Hopkinsville. How could you have a church here?"

"I don't, but my people are here, my brothers and sisters in the Lord, in a church right down the road, a mile maybe. And I'd like the two of you to make their acquaintance."

Jenny held back. "We have a rehearsal today and a performance tonight."

"But we're free till after lunch," said Emmett, gently taking her arm, "and we need to feed our spirits."

Jenny looked at Danny, as if to ask, *Are you going along with this?* Danny shrugged and Emmett answered for him. "Danny's humoring me. I told him a little of my soul music will do wonders for his song writing."

She smiled. "In that case, what are we waiting for?"

"It's a short walk and a beautiful day," said Emmett as the three of them fell into step together, heading away from the motel.

Jenny breathed the fresh air deep into her lungs. The climbing, midmorning sun was a golden orb monopolizing the sky, bright and shimmering, toasting the top of her head, as if someone had placed a friendly, nurturing hand on her hair. The air was scented with sweet, tantalizing fragrances that stirred fragile memories of childhood, faint, fleeting images familiar as her own face and yet just beyond her reach.

After so many weeks of riding in their stuffy, rattletrap bus and days of rehearsing in the cramped room under the grandstand, it felt invigorating to be out walking on the open road in the sunshine, surrounded by miles of lush greenery and overripe fields. But the road was paved with gravel and the pebbles got into Jenny's sandals. "I should have worn better shoes!"

"If it gets too bad, I'll carry you," said Danny, making a swooping gesture, as if to sweep her up in his arms.

"We'll both carry you," said Emmett, on the other side of her. The two, without breaking the rhythm of their stride, latched hands and lifted her up between them and swung her back and forth like a child.

She broke into laughter. "Put me down! I can walk on my own."

"Not a chance," said Danny, tightening his grasp around her waist. "We'll carry you all the way and save those delicate feet."

With an amused bubble of laughter, Emmett burst into song and Danny joined him, harmonizing perfectly, until at last Jenny joined in too, adding her light, clear soprano. "Swing low, sweet chariot, coming for to carry me home . . ."

By the time they reached the whitewashed, clapboard church with its narrow steeple and arched, stained-glass windows, they were breathless with laughing and singing.

"You ain't heard real preaching and singing until you been in a Negro church," Emmett whispered. "You're in for a treat."

"If they sing half as good as you, Emmett," said Danny, "I'll think I've died and gone to heaven."

"And just maybe you have," said Emmett. "Those angels could learn a thing or two from us."

Jenny and Danny grew self-consciously quiet as they followed Emmett up the steps and entered a small, shadowed vestibule that led into a plain, white stucco sanctuary with a cement floor. A silver-gray, barrel-chested man shook their hands and said, "Welcome! Come right in, sister and brothers." Inside, people were already standing and singing energetically, some waving raised hands, others swaying rhythmically and clapping. "Gonna lay down my burden . . . down by the riverside . . . down by the riverside . . ."

In single file—with all eyes on them—Jenny, Emmett, and Danny made their way down the center aisle past rows of straight pine benches and found an empty pew near the front. Jenny stole a glance around at the sea of ebony faces caught up in the rapture of praise, eyes closed, lips parted prayerfully, their rich mahogany skin glistening with summer heat. No one in the congregation used hymn books; they seemed to have known these songs from birth. The words erupted from deep within their souls, vivid, emotion-packed, spontaneous. Jenny joined in singing, tentatively at first, then, feeling a delicious sense of abandon, she gave herself to the music's compelling beat. Surrendering herself to the music, she felt almost as if she were surrendering herself to God.

When the congregation broke into the mournful, "Nobody knows the trouble I've seen; nobody knows but Jesus," tears stung Jenny's eyes as she thought of Mama and Annie and her family back home. And, yes, Danny's family too. They would all be in church this Sunday morning, but they would be grieving the loss of their children, for surely they would see it as a loss; they wouldn't think of Jenny and Danny out facing a great adventure, the chance of a lifetime. No, their families would be heartsick with grief, thinking that their children were missing, in danger, perhaps even dead.

I've got to phone Mama and let her know we're okay, Jenny resolved silently. *Maybe Grandma Betty has my letter by now; maybe Mama's read it too. No, it'll probably arrive tomorrow or the next day. But if I call, maybe Mama will understand and tell me it's okay, I'll have her blessing, and she'll be waiting with open arms when I'm ready to come home.*

But that seemed like too big a miracle even for God. More likely, her mother would rant and rave and insist that Jenny come home immediately if she knew what was good for her. But whatever her mother's response, Jenny had to call, had to let everyone know they were okay. Better than okay. Living their dreams. How many young people got to live their dreams?

Jenny realized suddenly that the singing was over and everyone had sat down, the sound of their rustling still in the air. She had sat down too, reflexively, with everyone else; and now the preacher—the same

smiling, barrel-chested man who had greeted them at the door—
strode to the altar and, ignoring the small pulpit, began to stride back
and forth like a prowling lion, his deep voice booming with authority. "Brothers and sisters, do you love Jesus?"

The congregation chanted in unison, "Yes, brother, we love Jesus!"

The square-jawed minister stopped in mid-stride and pointed a
long, knobby finger, seemingly straight at Jenny. "I said, brothers and
sisters, do you love Jesus?"

The reply came exploding back, "Amen, we love Jesus!"

Jenny mouthed the words but didn't quite say them aloud.

"I said, do you love Jesus?"

"Preach it, brother! We love Jesus!"

"Do you love Him with all your heart?"

"We love Him with all our heart!"

"With all your soul?"

"With all our soul!"

"Do you love Jesus with all your mind?"

"Yes, brother! With all our mind!"

"And with all your strength?"

"Amen, with all our strength!"

"That's the first commandment, my children," boomed the preacher.
"The first and greatest commandment, my brothers and sisters. Love
God! He wants your love! He hungers for your love! It don't matter if
you walk the walk and talk the talk, it's no good if you don't have it
in here!" He thumped his barrel chest. "You gotta feel the love!"

"Feel the love!" someone echoed.

"Feel your love for God, and feel His love coming straight back to
you, pouring out on you like the rains coming down—I said, like the
rains coming down, flowing over you like the mighty floods, like Noah's
flood. Do you hear me?"

"We hear you, brother!"

The preacher cupped his hands together and leaned out over the podium, his voice growing soft as a mother's whisper. "Brothers and sisters, God's holding you in the palm of His hand, like He held Noah's ark, like He holds a wounded little bird. Do you see Him, children? He's got you surrounded by His love. He's got His arms around you, holding tight. Do you feel the love?"

"Amen, we feel the love!"

The preacher's lips curved into an exultant smile. "Ain't nowhere you can run to get away from love like that. Nowhere you can hide. You can run your whole life long and never escape His love. He's right there, brother. He's close as your heartbeat, sister. Do you hear Him? I say, do you hear Him?"

"We hear Him, preacher!"

"Are you listening with your hearts, children? He's saying He loves you! He spilled out His blood on a cross and died for you!"

"Amen!"

"He rose from the dead and broke out of a sealed tomb for you!"

"Preach it, brother!"

"All because He loves you!" The preacher pulled a handkerchief from his vest pocket and mopped his brow. He leaned across the podium and said hoarsely, "What are you gonna do with love like that? Look the other way?"

"No, brother!"

"What are you gonna do with love like that? Run until you can't run no more?"

"No, brother!"

"I say, what are you gonna do with love like that? God's asking, not me. God wants to know what you're gonna do with His love. You gonna trample it in the dirt, or you gonna open your heart and let Him in?"

The preacher rapped his knuckles on the podium. His gaze seemed to settle on Danny and Jenny. "Do you hear Him knocking, children? I say, God's knocking on your heart's door. He's not gonna let you rest until you open the door and let Him in. Praise God, let's pray!"

After the service, as they walked back to the motel, Emmett looked over at Jenny and asked, "So how'd you like being the only white folk in a black church?"

She smiled faintly. "I guess I felt a little . . . outnumbered."

Emmett grinned. "We been feeling that way for two hundred years."

"But I liked the service," she assured him. "It's so different from ours. Isn't it, Danny?"

"Sure is."

"How so?" asked Emmett.

She and Danny exchanged glances. He was going to leave the explaining to her. "Well, at our church," she began, groping for words, "we sing hymns and study the Bible, but it's more regimented. The same routine every Sunday. Sort of like a habit we get into. We can do it without even thinking about it, without feeling anything." She looked quickly at Danny. "It's not that Danny's father isn't a good preacher. He is. It's just different, that's all."

"Different?" said Emmett.

Jenny started feeling flustered. They had stopped on the roadside under the glaring sun, and the rays were hurting her eyes. "It's just— we don't worship God with all the emotion you folks do. Our services are more subdued and . . . predictable. A certain time for the doxology, and the Scripture reading, and the Lord's prayer. Everything in its place."

"That's fine," said Emmett, "as long as you got the love of Jesus in there somewhere."

"It's there," said Danny quietly. "I . . . I just don't remember where."

"Well, then, as long as you got the love of Jesus in your own heart," said Emmett, pressing his forefinger against Danny's collarbone.

Danny backed off from Emmett's touch and said coolly, "My dad's the religious one in the family. I see my future in music . . . and maybe politics someday."

Emmett laughed good-naturedly. "Well, brother, you take the whole world . . . but give me Jesus."

They all chuckled, as if Emmett had made a joke, but Jenny knew Emmett was dead serious. She felt a strange, hollow feeling inside, as if she had nearly grasped something vital, then had let it slip away.

At the motel, after Emmett had gone on to his room, Jenny clasped Danny's arm and said, "We've got to call home and let them know we're okay."

He didn't argue, just nodded and uttered a sigh of resignation. "They could have the police after us, you know. They could make us go home."

"We won't tell them where we are, but they need to know we're safe and well."

They went to the pay phone in the lobby and Jenny dialed. As it rang, she imagined her family sitting around the dinner table eating a pork roast and browned potatoes, her mother's specialty. Her mother had never liked cooking, but she cooked some things quite well.

On the third ring, someone answered. Jenny felt a wave of panic as she heard her mother's voice. "Hello? Is someone there? Hello!"

"Hello, Mama," she whispered.

"Jenny? Is that you?"

"Yes, Mama."

"Oh, my heaven—Jenny, where are you?"

"I'm okay, Mama. Danny's here and we're okay."

Her mother's voice grew shrill. "Where are you? Tell me where you are! Do you hear me, Jenny? Wherever it is, stay where you are and we'll come get you."

"No, Mama. We're not coming home."

"What do you mean, not coming home? You and Danny ran off together and broke our hearts and now you call to tell me you're not coming home?"

"Mama, it's not what you think with Danny and me." *I'm not you, Mama,* she wanted to shout. *I'm not having an affair with Danny like you had with my daddy.*

Anger and a note of hysteria edged her mother's voice. "You listen to me, Jenny. You are coming home, and that's it. Robert will come get you. Now tell me exactly where you are. You hear me, daughter?"

Jenny swallowed hard and hung up the phone. She looked at Danny and sniffed noisily. "I couldn't tell her. I couldn't!"

He pulled her into his arms and held her close, massaging the back of her neck with his right hand. "I know, Jen. It's okay."

"No, it's not okay. Mama sounded so angry. She hates me. She thinks . . . she thinks we ran away together . . . that we're living in sin."

"Honey, let her think what she wants. We know better." Danny kissed her hair, his earnest voice soothing against her ear. "Listen, Jen, we've got to forget about everybody back home. It doesn't matter what they think we're doing. We've got our own lives now, our future. It's just the two of us. I'm your family, and you're mine. We don't need anybody else. We'll be on stage again tonight with a whole new audience watching and cheering. We've got all our dreams just waiting out there for us to reach out and grab them."

She heard everything he was saying, but one phrase stood out from the others. *I'm your family, and you're mine.* It was true. As long as they had each other, they had everything they would ever need.

But then why did she feel this nameless yearning, a void somewhere at her center, in a shadowed corner of her heart? Was it finally dawning that she had truly broken all ties with her family and could never go home again? Or did this peculiar emptiness have something to do with the black preacher and his question, "What are you gonna do with love like that . . . God's love?"

So far in her eighteen years she had avoided answering such a weighty question. She had managed to listen to a thousand sermons and sing a thousand hymns and had never seriously entertained the idea that God's love required a response from her . . . and that the answer she gave could make all the difference.

9

"We're going to Memphis," Callan Swan announced when the Bell Tones had finished performing at the Hopkinsville fairgrounds. The band was having breakfast at Mama Sadie's Café around the corner from their motel, sitting at a back-corner table finishing their grits, eggs, and sausage.

"Memphis?" echoed Gil Russo, the lead guitar player. "You got us a gig there?"

"Better than a gig. I got us set up to cut a demo record with Sun Records."

"With Sam Phillips?" said Danny. "He's the man who first recorded Elvis!"

"That's right. Elvis was looking for the big break we're all looking for," said Gil, swallowing a mouthful of fried grits.

"Well, he found it," said Andy Loomis, his round cheeks apple-red. "Phillips always did like black music and recorded lots of it. But when he looked at Elvis, he saw a white man singing like a black man."

Emmett joined in as he nursed a cup of steaming coffee. "Sam Phillips was smart enough to know he could make a star out of a white man with a black sound, and that's just what he did. Half the music Elvis sings was recorded first by some black man somewhere that nobody paid a mind to."

"Not half his music," said Callan.

"Maybe not, but plenty," said Emmett.

"You aren't bitter about it, are you, Em?" asked Andy.

Emmett turned his coffee cup between his charcoal palms. "No, I know that's just the way things are. A decade or more ago, my daddy sang and played his horn on WDIA. Before he took to preaching full-time."

"WDIA? Oh, yeah. The black station," Lee Slocum acknowledged.

"It was called the Mother Station of the Negroes," said Emmett, a note of nostalgia in his voice, "but we always knew a whole lot of whites tuned in. And they liked my daddy. We knew it was just a matter of time before our music would be played by whites all over the country."

"Anyway," Callan broke in, "Sam's helped a whole lot of singers get their foot in the door. He gave Carl Perkins his chance."

"I know Carl Perkins," said Emmett. "Talented fellow."

"You know everybody," drawled Gil, his crinkly eyes forming smiling quarter moons in his lean face.

"I do know him," said Emmett. "Been twenty years maybe. He was just a boy and so was I. His daddy was a sharecropper and Carl worked the fields right beside us blacks, like he was one of us."

"Emmett, you were a sharecropper?" Jenny had become so engrossed in the conversation her eggs and grits sat congealing on her plate, no longer appetizing.

"I worked the fields every summer until I was grown."

"And you actually worked the fields with Carl Perkins?" said Danny, marveling.

"I did, and we made the acquaintance of another black field hand named John Westbrook. He taught us both how to play the blues." Emmett chuckled, remembering. "You should have seen Carl. He was just a mite of a boy, six maybe, and he made himself a guitar out of a broomstick and a cigar box. Right then, I knew he was going places. It wasn't many years before I ran into him in Jackson, Tennessee, playing in honky-tonks with his brothers."

Cal drained the last of his coffee and set the cup down hard on the table. "Well, like I said, Carl Perkins got his start with Sam Phillips, and I don't see why we can't do the same."

"Perkins did okay for a while," conceded Lee, rubbing his bony chin. "Sold a million of his hit song, 'Blue Suede Shoes.' That song put him near the top of the charts in '55. But where's he been lately?"

"Elvis made that song an even bigger hit," said Gil.

"And Elvis is prettier to look at," said Andy with bemused sarcasm.

Callan reached across the table and placed his hand possessively over Jenny's. "Speaking of prettier to look at, I have some news."

Jenny was about to withdraw her hand, then thought better of it. "What news, Cal?" she asked.

He eased into a generous grin, his dark brows shading his shrewd, olive-brown eyes. Sunlight streaming in the plate-glass window cast a golden glow on his three-inch pompadour. "I think we all agree that Danny and Jenny have proved themselves to be capable and—yes, valuable—members of the Bell Tones."

"Amen," said Emmett.

"Yep, they're talented, all right," Lee agreed.

"Their voices blend well with our sound," said Gil.

Andy grinned, his round, ruddy cheeks blazing. "Looks like we're gonna keep you guys. Is that what you're saying, Cal?"

"More than that. I've made a decision." Cal's hand tightened on Jenny's. "We're making a little change in the band, trying something new."

Everyone looked puzzled. "What are you talking about, Cal?" asked Emmett.

He looked directly at Jenny and winked. "I'm making Jenny my new lead singer."

"Your new lead singer?" blurted Danny, his face paling.

"You heard me. From now on she's singing lead with me."

As Cal's words struck home in Jenny's mind, she caught a glimpse of troubled expressions around the table. She immediately withdrew her hand from Cal's and cried, "I couldn't. I'm not ready to sing lead."

"I think I'm the best judge of that," said Cal, his dark gaze riveting.

"Jenny's a fine singer," said Emmett, "but a change like that just before we make our demo? Could spell trouble."

"Now, that's where we don't agree. I think Jenny will add an attractive new dimension to the Bell Tones. She'll captivate an entirely new segment of the audience."

"The male audience," said Lee with a hint of irony in his small, marble-black eyes.

Cal removed his wallet from his slacks pocket, pulled out several bills, and tossed them on the table, then pushed back his chair. "Look, fellas, Jenny and I will try a few numbers together in Nashville and Jackson, before we get to Memphis. If it doesn't work, nothing lost, okay?" He looked at Jenny. "What about it, doll? Are you game?"

She looked over at Danny and could tell by the set of his jaw that he was grinding his teeth. The two of them were supposed to be a team, not Jenny and Cal. She waited wordlessly for Danny to meet her gaze and respond, and when he did, she could feel the connection between them, like an electric shock. Quickly, edgily, he said, "Go for it, Jenny. This could be your big chance."

She looked back at Cal and said softly, "Okay, I'll try. I'll do my best."

Just outside Mama Sadie's Café, Cal slipped a comradely arm around Jenny and pulled her close against his chest. She could feel the solid curve of his muscles under his silk sport shirt. He bent his head to her face so that his slick pompadour grazed her long, tousled curls. "You won't regret this, Jenny," he said huskily. "We're gonna be good together, you and me. Partners, right? We're gonna play glorious music together, you just wait and see."

She shivered in the suffocating warmth of his embrace. Her voice quavered. "I hope you won't be disappointed in me."

He held her at arm's length and winked. "Why would I be disappointed? You're gonna give me a hundred percent, right?"

Her mouth went dry. "I told you, I don't know if I'm ready, Cal."

He leaned over and brushed a kiss on her cheek, his spicy aftershave filling her nostrils. "Oh, you're ready, sweetheart. You just don't know how ready you are."

Her face turned crimson under his searching gaze. She turned away, looking desperately for Danny. He was waiting for her on the corner, head down, one polished brown loafer toeing the sidewalk.

Cal caught her arm at the elbow. "One more thing, Jenny."

She whirled around and looked up at him, heart pounding. What more was he going to ask of her?

He fingered the scalloped collar of her white cotton blouse. "Listen, honey, I want you to go shopping and buy yourself a nice evening gown, something slinky and shiny to show off your figure."

Her throat tightened. "I have the gown I've worn before."

"That was when you were singing backup. Now you're gonna be on center stage. You gotta look like a star. Glamorous. Sexy." He smoothed her collar in place. "Don't worry, I'll give you the dough. It won't come out of your paycheck."

She stood speechless, numb, the muscles in her arms and legs refusing to move. She was about to tell Cal that the money wasn't her concern; it was the idea of wearing something she wouldn't feel comfortable in. But before she could assemble the words in her mind, Callan Swan had swiveled away from her and was already striding down the street with Emmett, the two of them launching into a spirited conversation.

Jenny joined Danny on the corner and they fell into step side by side, silent, their pace slow, their minds preoccupied. When they reached the motel, he walked her to her room, took the key from her hand, and unlocked the door.

"Do you want to come in?" she asked.

He looked around cautiously. "I'd better not."

"Then when will we talk? We're never alone."

He shrugged, his hands in his slacks pockets, his expression clouded. "What's there to talk about?"

"Everything." Tears gathered behind her lids. "Please don't be mad at me, Danny."

He looked at her, stricken. "I'm not mad, Jen. You think I'm mad?"

"You look mad."

"It's just—" He pushed her door open and coaxed, "Come on. Go in."

She slipped inside. After casting another look around, he followed and quietly shut the door behind him. "Sit down," she invited.

He glanced at the bed and the straight-back chair beside the bed and chose the chair. She sat down on the bed and looked at him. "I'm sorry, Danny."

He eyed her quizzically. "Sorry for what?"

"Sorry that Cal made me a lead singer and not you."

He shrugged, as if it didn't matter, but she could read the hurt in his eyes. "I don't begrudge you your success, Jen. I'm happy for you. It's just—"

She finished the sentence for him. "You figured that you and I would be singing together, not Cal and me."

Danny shifted his weight, tapping his fingers nervously on one knee. "Okay, I admit it. I always saw the two of us on stage singing together. You know how good we sound. A whole lot better than you and Cal."

Jenny smoothed her pleated skirt over her knees. "I know, Danny, and I'll tell him that. I'll tell him I just can't sing with him."

He reached over and seized her hand, looking miserable, clutching her slender fingers so hard she winced. "You can't do that, Jen."

"Sure, I can."

"No, honey, I mean it. This is your big chance. Do you think I'd take that away from you? That I'd be that jealous and mean-spirited?"

"Oh, Danny!" She drew his hand up to the side of her face and pressed his palm against her cheek. She closed her eyes and rocked slightly, savoring the solid warmth of his open palm on her skin; she breathed in the fresh, lemony scent of his aftershave.

She opened her eyes, aware of the rustle of movement around her. Danny had moved over beside her on the bed. Before she could speak, he pulled her into his arms and held her tight against his chest, so hard she could feel his heart pounding under his shirt. "Oh, Jenny," he moaned, his fingers sinking into her tangled hair, "when we ran away, I thought we would be together all the time. But we're never alone. We never have a chance to talk or just sit and hold each other like this. Do you know how much I've missed holding you in my arms?"

"Everyone thinks you're my cousin," she said breathlessly.

He kissed her hair. "I know. I never should have told them that. I was a stupid coward. I was afraid Callan wouldn't let us join the band if he knew the truth."

"But we are cousins, in a way."

"Not the way they think. In name only, not by blood or birth." He searched her eyes. "I want to tell them the truth, Jen."

"The truth?"

"That I love you and you love me, and someday . . ." He clamped her chin in his hand. "You do love me, don't you? That hasn't changed."

Her voice came out hardly more than a whisper. "We've never said the words before, Danny."

He stroked her cheek with a nervous agitation. "But we've always known. Haven't we, Jen? Surely you know. I love you. I'll never love anyone the way I love you."

Tears streamed down her face. "And I love you, Danny."

He broke into a fractured smile. "I think I've waited all my life to hear those words, Jen." He brought his mouth down hard on hers and kissed her until she had to gasp for air. They had kissed before, playfully, teasingly, but never had she felt such hunger and urgency in his kiss, his touch. He pressed her head against the crook of his neck and whispered huskily against her ear, "We'll be together someday, Jen, in every way that matters. I dream of that day."

She wriggled out of his embrace, her breathing labored. "You'd better go, Danny, before . . ."

"I know. I've always tried to be respectful of you, Jen."

"You have been. Always a perfect gentleman."

He chuckled ruefully. "Maybe not a perfect gentleman."

"But I've always known I could trust you with my life."

"And you can. But some things have changed, Jen. We're not at home under our parents' watchful gaze anymore. We're far away in a city of strangers." He nudged her chin wistfully. "Sometimes I wish we could just let ourselves go. Give in to our love. Not worry about what the world thinks."

She reached out and brushed back his hair. His forehead was moist, glistening, his hair damp at the roots. With his clean, chiseled features and velvety green eyes, he was the most handsome man she had ever known. But with his hair mussed and his collar askew, he looked like a lost little boy. She combed her fingers through his thick hair, smoothing it into place. "Danny, we can't—"

His voice took on a hard edge. "Why? Because we're both illegitimate? Why should that make us so different from everyone else?"

She tucked a stubborn wisp of hair behind his ear. "Danny, I came into the world without a father to love me. We both did."

"That's not our fault. I'm sick of people throwing that in my face."

"Oh, Danny, even though we both have fathers now, nothing will ever fill that terrible emptiness for either one of us. It'll always be there, no matter what we do. We can't bring that same pain to . . . to a child of ours."

"We won't, Jen. We'll be married someday."

"We can't think about marriage now. We're trying to establish our music careers. For now we have to keep pretending to be nothing more than cousins."

"Why? You think if Callan knew about us, he'd send me packing? That's what you think, isn't it?"

She stared down at her hands. "I can't help wondering if Callan Swan wants more than a singing partner."

Danny jumped up from the bed and hit his doubled fist against his palm, his voice raw with rage. "If that man ever lays a hand on you—I swear, Jen, if he ever touches you, I—I'll kill him!"

She went to him and embraced him. "He won't, Danny. I won't let anything happen. I promise." They walked together to the door. "Maybe we're wrong, Danny. Maybe Cal is just trying to give me a break. Maybe he really thinks my singing with him will be good for the band."

Danny studied her intently. "You really think so?"

"It's what I have to believe, or how can we even stay?"

He nodded, but he didn't look convinced. "I'd better go, Jen, before someone finds me in your room and gets suspicious." He opened the door and slipped outside, looking back to mouth the words, *I love you.*

She whispered the words back to him, then shut the door and turned the lock. She leaned back against the door, feeling suddenly weak and light-headed. She closed her eyes and felt a tear escape under her lashes. What was she going to do? More than anything in the world she wanted to be with Danny and let the world know of their love.

But now, more than ever, Callan Swan would be calling the shots for both of them. As bandleader and Jenny's singing partner, he would exert even more influence over her, telling her when she must practice and how to interpret and perform their songs. No matter how much she denied the feeling, she knew in her secret heart that Callan Swan would not be satisfied until he had exacted a price from her for his supposed benevolence—a price she would never agree to pay.

10

If Jenny had expected the worst from Callan Swan when she became his singing partner, she was soon pleasantly surprised by his courteous and deferential treatment of her. Before their first performance together, as she quaked with terror in the wings of the old Nashville theater, Cal assured her the audience would find her as enchanting and irresistible as he did. He held her chin gently in his hand and looked deep into her eyes and asked her to trust him.

"I know what I'm doing, Jenny," he told her, his voice hushed, his smoky gaze riveting. "Don't be afraid. Just follow my lead. Ride with me. Fly with me. Sing with me. We'll soar to heaven and back and take the audience with us. After tonight, nothing will ever be the same."

Somehow, she believed him, knew he spoke the truth. His quiet authority and unflappable demeanor gave her the courage to step out on center stage and sing her heart out.

And everything Callan had promised came true. The audience loved her, loved Callan Swan and Jenny Wayne together, loved their sound, their chemistry, their look. She was the tall, willowy girl with the wide-set hazel eyes and flowing auburn tresses, and he was her dark, dashing Prince Charming with the seductive bedroom eyes and shiny black pompadour to rival Elvis's. As they took their closing bows, Callan presented Jenny with a dozen long-stem red roses, and the audience ate it up. Even Jenny was genuinely touched.

Cal and Jenny would become, as Gil Russo predicted only half in jest after their first performance together, "an overnight sensation."

Lee Slocum agreed. "If we play our cards right, you two could become America's rock 'n' roll sweethearts."

"Jenny, girl, that voice of yours could make an angel jealous," Emmett praised, but in a whisper he added, "I still think you and Danny have a better sound."

Jenny thought so too. But what could she say? Cal was calling the shots.

During their first few engagements, Jenny felt deep misgivings about being linked romantically with Callan Swan in the public eye. But as the weeks passed and the audiences responded with increasing enthusiasm, she realized Cal must have known what he was doing all along. Through September, the band received greater acceptance each time they performed, and the buzz of excitement was carrying over to local radio stations.

What had been a ho-hum response was now becoming eager, even electric. Often, these days, when Cal notified disc jockeys that his band was coming to town, they invited him to appear on their station or perform for their local televised bandstand show to promote his local engagements. The exposure was good for the stations and good for the band.

And when Cal took the band to Memphis to cut their demo record featuring Cal and Jenny, the local stations promptly agreed to play the record, including renowned disc jockey Dewey Phillips of WHBQ.

"At this rate, we're sure to have a hit," Cal predicted. The band was having lunch in a small beanery just off Beale Street. "When you've got Dewey Phillips on your side, you're on your way to the Top Forty."

"Without even having to put out a dime to prime the pump," said Gil, dousing his burger with ketchup.

Jenny looked over at Gil. "Prime the pump?"

Lee beamed his toothy grin. "Our star prima donna hasn't been keeping up with the headlines."

"Cut the prima donna talk," said Danny.

"No offense," said Lee, palms raised placatingly. "Just making a joke."

"Danny's right," said Cal. "No put-downs. Jenny's helping put us on the map. We owe her big."

"I agree." Lee gave Jenny's hand a paternal pat. "I wouldn't hurt you for the world, dreamboat. You know that."

Jenny smiled. She knew Lee was sincere. "No offense taken. But about priming the pump . . ."

"Some musicians think they gotta grease the palms of disc jockeys to get their records played," said Cal. "But with the payola scandal making big headlines these days—"

"We've read all about it," said Danny. "It's been in the newspapers on and off all year."

"They even dragged Dick Clark up before their congressional sub-committee," said Andy. "Dick Clark. Can you imagine?"

"He got off okay," said Gil. "Insisted he never took payola, and I guess they believed him. But other guys weren't so lucky."

"Look at Alan Freed," said Lee. "Arrested on charges of commercial bribery. Man, he's the guy who came up with the name 'rock 'n' roll' in the first place."

"Well, we don't need to pay anybody to listen to our stuff," said Cal. "I sent our demo to a couple of dozen radio stations in Tennessee, Kentucky, Ohio, and Pennsylvania. At least half of them have agreed to give us air play. I've got my connections working with Dick Clark, too, and if things fall into place the way I expect, we'll be singing on *American Bandstand* before the world rings in 1961."

"You really think so?" asked Jenny. "That Dick Clark will book us on his show?"

"I think the day will come when he'll be begging us to be on his show. What do you think of that, sweetheart?"

Jenny opened her mouth to reply, but no words came. She could think only of her Grandma Betty back home in Willowbrook sitting in front of her television set, watching *American Bandstand* every afternoon. What an amazing thing if her grandmother tuned in one day and actually saw Jenny performing!

One of the side benefits of the band's growing popularity was the quality of the motel rooms they stayed in on the road. The rooms were becoming cleaner, more roomy, and attractive; they had a television set and sometimes even air-conditioning. Rarely was the band forced to sleep on the bus anymore, since the distance between most of their gigs was rarely more than a day's drive.

In October the band headed north, then west, first cutting up through Kentucky, then swinging into Ohio and Indiana, with two and three-day engagements in Lexington and Louisville; Columbus and Toledo; and Elkhart, South Bend, and Gary. In Gary, they stayed in a small mom-and-pop motel along US-12, where the wafting smells of Lake Michigan mingled with the pungent, metallic fumes of the steel plants.

For the first time in several weeks, Jenny found it impossible to sleep. Each time she began to drift off, she envisioned the worried faces of her family. Willowbrook lay only a couple of hours away, so close and yet so far. It would take so little to say, "I want to go home. I need to go home."

She and Danny had been on the road for nearly two months now, and except for her letter to Grandma Betty, her phone call to her mother, and half a dozen post cards she'd mailed with no return address, she and Danny had made no contact with their families. And as long as no one at home knew the name of their band, they would be hard to trace.

For weeks Jenny had tried to convince herself she felt no guilt, no regrets for running away, that what she and Danny were doing was not wrong, but rather a matter of their own survival. At home their dreams had been squelched repeatedly by parents who were convinced they knew what was best for their children. There was no reasoning with Danny's father or with Jenny's mother. No, she and Danny had done the only thing possible. They had taken charge of their lives and were carving out their own future.

But each day, in spite of her blossoming musical career, Jenny felt less sure that she and Danny had made the right choice. On stage each night she felt euphoric, every fiber in her body hungering for the audience's approval and her entire being thriving on the applause.

But success hadn't delivered the joy and satisfaction she had anticipated. It was like walking a tightrope. Would she perform her best? Would she win the love and admiration of the people? Would she carry it off, thrilling the crowd, mesmerizing them with her talent? Or would she flub a line, or be off-key, or stumble on a cable, or do some other insane thing to humiliate herself and disappoint the fans? When everything went off without a hitch and she sensed the band had the crowd eating out of its hands, she felt ecstatic, part of a miracle.

But it was always over so quickly—the glory and adulation. One minute she was on stage with Callan in the center of a white-hot spotlight, basking in the thunderous ovation, feeling like the most loved person on the planet. And then it was over. The spotlight died and the people went home to their own lives, forgetting the young girl they had just applauded.

And what was there for Jenny to do? She could join the fellows at a local pub or tavern for a few drinks and small talk, but that routine would become old all too quickly. Sometimes she joined Danny and Emmett for a midnight stroll around whatever town or berg they happened to be in, but even that seemingly innocent activity was fraught with danger. Once a pack of wild dogs chased them; another time, a drunk accosted them and cut Danny with a broken wine bottle. And once they were nearly struck by a careening vehicle on a narrow side street.

So usually, when the Bell Tones finished their performance, Danny walked Jenny back to their motel and they went reluctantly to their own rooms, parting with only a chaste good night kiss. She would bathe and dress for bed and lie in her anonymous room staring up into the darkness, the impervious silence louder than the applause of the previous hour.

As thrilling as the applause had been, the loneliness and silence afterward left her feeling desolate and empty. Each night she thought, *Perhaps tomorrow night the applause will be enough to satisfy me; maybe it will be enough to make me happy.* But each night, as the cheers faded, her sense of futility and yearning returned.

On their last night in Gary, as Danny walked Jenny to her room, she refused to release his hand when he turned to go. He stopped and looked at her, his sturdy, chiseled face accented by moonlight and shadows. "What is it, Jen?"

"Don't go, Danny. Please. Not yet. I can't stand to be alone tonight."

He gazed at the half open door, the sallow lamplight spilling out onto the concrete walkway. "I'd better not, Jen. We don't want to start any rumors."

"The guys are all at Gilley's Pub. This is our last night in town. They'll be there half the night."

He shrugged, glanced around, and followed her inside. The room was cold and damp, so she turned up the wall heater and switched on another light. Besides a double bed and dresser, the room had a small table and two chairs. Danny took one chair, she the other. "I have a bottle of Coke, if you want some," she said, "and a bag of chips."

He shook his head. "I'm not hungry."

"You're usually always hungry after a show." She was wearing a white shawl over her long, form-fitting silk gown; she shivered and wrapped the shawl tighter around her arms.

"I'm not that hungry lately."

She studied his golden features in the hazy lamplight and wondered what to say. Should she keep the conversation light and superficial, the way they usually did these days, or should she venture into uncharted territory and speak her heart?

"You haven't said much lately, Danny," she ventured. "Are you okay?"

He looked at her, his eyes narrowing. "Sure, I'm fine."

"Would you tell me if you weren't?"

He shifted in his chair, thrumming his fingers on the table's cheap veneer. "What is this, Jen? Twenty questions? I thought you just wanted some company because you were feeling lonely."

"I am. I do. I just want to talk to someone where it means something."

"What about Callan?" Sarcasm edged his voice.

Her veins went to ice. "What about Callan?"

"You two are so chummy these days, I figure you've got all the company you need."

She traced an invisible circle on the table and said stonily, "You know there's nothing between Cal and me."

His narrowed eyes shot darts at her. "Do I, Jen? To tell you the truth, I don't know anything anymore."

"What's that supposed to mean?"

"Whatever you like. You figure it out."

Her voice came out quivery. "If you think Callan Swan has ever made a pass at me or even made a rude remark in all the time we've been singing together, you're wrong, Danny."

"So he's not the big, bad ogre you thought he was?"

Her voice grew small and defensive. "No. He's been a perfect gentleman. He treats me like a queen."

"So I've noticed."

She hurled the words impulsively. "You're just jealous, Danny."

He slammed the words right back at her. "Jealous? Of what?"

She lowered her gaze, her eyes tracing the fake marble swirls in the tabletop. In all their weeks on the road, the two of them had never come so close to wounding each other. She chewed her lower lip, refusing to answer.

"You think I'm jealous of Cal?" Danny demanded. "You think I'm jealous because he's stealing my girl?"

"He's not stealing your girl."

"Okay, so he can't steal you when he doesn't even know you're mine in the first place, right?"

"That's not what I meant."

"It's what I meant. He treats you like you're his lady love and he's Sir Galahad. Half the world thinks you two are sweethearts."

"That's just a part we're playing on stage, Danny, you know that."

"What about off stage? I see the way he treats you. Like you're a fragile princess he's sworn to protect."

"He's just being nice, Danny." She allowed her shawl to slip off her shoulders. The room was too warm now, a mixture of the overheated furnace and their overheated conversation. She leaned across the table, close enough to touch Danny's hand, but she refrained. "Danny, you're the only one I love, the only one I'll ever love. Cal means nothing to me. He's a friend and my singing partner, nothing more."

Danny crossed his arms. "That's plenty, if you ask me."

She stared at him, a wave of comprehension washing over her. "Oh, I see. This isn't personal, is it? You're not worried about Cal becoming my boyfriend."

Danny eyed her, arching one thick brow. "What are you talking about?"

She blurted out the words. "The real issue. You're angry because Cal made me his singing partner."

A tendon along Danny's neck throbbed momentarily. His lips narrowed and he worked his jaw slowly, as if digesting some bitter truth.

"I hit the nail on the head, didn't I?" she persisted.

He looked at her, his eyes too shadowed for her to read. "I thought when we left home it would be the two of us singing together. I never imagined it being anything but the two of us."

"It still will be, Danny. But right now we have to do whatever it takes to make the Bell Tones successful."

"Even if it means you singing with Callan?"

"Why not? What's wrong with me singing with Cal? Everyone says we sound great together."

"You and I sound better. Even Emmett thinks so."

"But it's Cal's band. He's not going to let us sing together, Danny. I'm sorry. I wish I could change things, but I can't."

"Do you, Jen? Wish you could change things? Every time you and Cal walk out on stage together, my heart twists in my chest. But you always look so happy, so gloriously radiant, like you were made to stand there in Callan Swan's arms and sing with him."

"I'm not in his arms, not most of the time—"

"It doesn't matter. Nothing matters anymore."

She stared at him. "What do you mean by that?"

A deep, smoldering anger darkened his tone. "I mean, I do my job. I try to be the best backup singer I can be, and that's all I have. I hold on to that and try to tell myself it's enough." He reached out and touched her hand, moving his fingertips over her knuckles. "But you know what, Jen? Sometimes I think it's not enough, and I wonder what I'm doing traveling all over creation with a band that isn't even mine, being a stooge, a flunky to some guy I don't even respect. And some-times I think about just packing it up and going home."

"Not without me!" Tears gathered, making her eyes ache. "Oh, Danny, I think the same thing. Sometimes I just want to go home, espe-cially now when we're so close to Willowbrook. Just two hours away. Think of it. My family and your family going about their lives, sleep-ing and dreaming in their beds just two hours from here. What if we went home and just walked into our houses and said, 'Hi, we're home,' and picked up our lives as if nothing had ever happened? We could do it, Danny."

He massaged her hand, rubbing her knuckles too hard. "Are you kidding? We can't just go home. Too much has happened. We've created a nightmare for ourselves, a terrible roller coaster ride, and we can't get off."

A tear slid down her cheek. "For a minute, I hoped . . ."

He reached across the table and caught the glistening tear on his finger. "Why are you so unhappy, Jen? You're Callan's golden girl. You're going to make him a star. You can do no wrong. I would think you'd be overjoyed, thrilled, walking on air."

"I thought so too," she confessed, "but it's not what I expected. When I'm on stage, Danny, I'm caught up in the magic and it's wonderful. But when it's over, the magic is gone, and I feel emptier and more miserable than ever. And I wonder what life's all about if even the most wonderful things are meaningless and can't satisfy you."

His voice took on a slightly mocking tone. "Well, Jen, now you're starting to sound like the wise old men of the ages dissecting life's deepest questions. Why am I here? Where am I going? What is the purpose of living?"

"Don't you wonder about those things too, Danny? Our families never seemed to wrestle with such questions; they never seemed to have any doubt about anything. If the Bible said something, it was true and that was that."

Danny released her hand and sat back in his chair. "We both agreed a long time ago that we needed to find our own answers, Jen, not just accept all the platitudes our folks handed us."

"I have been looking for answers, Danny."

"You have? Where?"

Her voice grew very small. "In the Bible Annie gave me."

His brows shot up. "Really? I'm surprised."

She hugged herself and rocked back and forth in her chair. "Sometimes I'm so lonely, so scared. I think about Annie, and I see the peace in her face, in her eyes. No matter what happens to her, she always has this incredible peace. My own mama has that peace too, Danny. Sure, sometimes she gets upset and frets and stews, but she always returns to that special peace inside."

Jenny paused, rocking absently, searching for the right words. "I've tried praying for peace like that, Danny, and sometimes I think I feel it, but then it's gone, and I'm left with this big empty place in my heart."

"We all feel that way sometimes, Jen. You just have to keep yourself busy and not dwell on things that make you sad."

"No, Danny, I'm not talking about sad feelings," she argued, clenching her hands. "This is so much more. But I can't find words to describe it. Can't you help me?"

"I wish I could, Jen, but I'm fresh out of words myself." Danny stood up and took several loping steps to the door. "I'd better get going, Jen. It's getting late, and we'll be hitting the road tomorrow."

She got up and followed him to the door. "Why won't you talk with me about this?" she pleaded. "I know you must feel the same things I'm feeling. We've always shared everything, Danny. You're struggling too. I can see it in your eyes. You must have some idea what to do."

He drew her gently into his arms and kissed her, but there was a remote, distracted air about him.

"We're losing each other, aren't we?" she whispered, running her fingertips over his lips, his chin.

"It's not that, Jen. It's just . . . I'd like to think our love for each other would be enough to chase away the darkness and the emptiness. But right now, even my love for you makes me feel sad and empty. I'm sorry. I have nothing to offer you."

She swallowed a sob. "I'm sorry too, Danny. I thought our love was strong enough to withstand anything."

He opened the door, stepped outside, and looked back at her, his eyes glinting with regret. "Maybe our love is strong enough, Jen. But right now I honestly don't know."

He fingered a curl that hung over her shoulder. "Lately I have more questions than answers about us, our music, our future. Don't you see, Jen? I'm searching too."

"For what?"

"I don't know. For years all I ever wanted was to make a difference in people's lives. Make them happier, make the world a better place. I wanted my voice to be heard—in my music, in my life, in my work, in my soul. But right now I honestly don't know what I'm supposed to be saying, Jen. I have nothing to give to anyone, not even you."

He touched her face, his expression filled with anguish and desolation, then blew her a kiss, his fingers barely touching his lips. She remained in the doorway, watching as he pivoted sharply and strode off into the darkness without once looking back.

11

"Hey, guys, I just got the word! The Bell Tones are going to Philadelphia!" Cal's voice as he bounded on stage was as buoyant as Jenny had ever heard it. It was the first week of November and she and the group were rehearsing in a drafty downtown theater in South Chicago, a turn-of-the-century edifice with a sky-high baroque ceiling, mountains of gingerbread trim, and carved gargoyle faces accenting rows of fluted columns.

"Philadelphia?" Gil stopped strumming his guitar. "Does this mean we're on *Bandstand*?"

"The one and only Dick Clark original," said Cal, rubbing his hands together as if he were already counting royalty checks.

Andy did a little stiletto chop on the drums, his round cheeks flushing beet red. "When? This century, I hope."

"Next week. Friday. Bobby Darin had a conflict and had to cancel out, so we're in. Just like that. It'll mean some heavy driving time after this gig, but with Lee at the wheel—"

"We could take one of those fancy little planes that'll get us there in two hours," said Gil, running his lean, limber fingers over his guitar strings for effect.

"No planes," said Lee. "After what happened to Buddy Holly, Ritchie Valens, and the Big Bopper, planes give me the willies."

"Come on, man, that was a freak accident," said Andy.

"What do you know about it, man?" Lee shot back. His lips twitched nervously on his long, narrow face. "I played a gig with Buddy two weeks before his plane crashed. He talked about me joining up with him. I could have been on that plane when it went down."

"So, okay, fellas, no planes," said Cal. "Lee, you just make sure that bus is in tip-top condition so we get to Philly on time."

"I'll get us there with hours, even days to spare."

Lee kept his promise. The wheezing, antiquated bus arrived in Philadelphia on Thursday, a brisk, snowy afternoon. Except for sleet and ice in Youngstown and a flat tire in Altoona, the drive was uneventful. But cold! Even bundled in a parka, leggings, wool scarf, and boots, Jenny felt numb, her fingers and toes like icicles.

Lee drove the weary travelers to a nondescript two-story hotel a block from the WFIL-TV studios. With noses red and teeth chattering, they checked in and settled in for the night, thawing out, eagerly consuming a hot meal in the hotel café, and catching up on much needed sleep.

Early the next morning Danny was at Jenny's door, knocking loudly. Still in her nightgown, she opened the door a crack and peered out. "Danny, don't tell me it's already time to go!"

"Sure is," he said with a little bemused wink. But there was a solemn, subdued look in his eyes that overshadowed his light, breezy tone. Jenny felt a tiny stab of guilt. Was Danny remembering their dream of singing on *Bandstand* together? Would he ever forgive her for singing with Callan instead?

"Hurry up, Jen," he said. "Get ready. Put on your prettiest dress. This is the day for fame and fortune to come our way . . . for some of us anyway."

"Fame?" she challenged.

"Sure. The whole country will be watching *Bandstand*."

"Oh, Danny," she whispered, but no other words came. She reached out and clasped his hand; it was cold, but solid and reassuring, as always.

He bent close, his face nearly inside the door, his head pressed against the white, cracked molding. His cheeks were ruddy, his mouth pouting slightly, petulant, endearing, like a little boy's. "Jenny? Oh, Jen!" he sighed. His dusky green eyes met hers with an expression that said a million things, and yet there were no words between them, only a painful silence. Had they reached the place in their relationship where everything they felt was below the surface, hidden, unreachable, unspeakable?

"I wish it could be different," she murmured, hoping he understood what she meant, but not really sure herself.

He shrugged. "I know. Those are the breaks."

Her fingers tightened around his hand. "You must know. This is a wonderful opportunity, Danny. Being on *Bandstand*. Even if we're not singing together."

"Yeah, I know. I just never pictured it this way—you and Callan together."

"We're not together."

"You know what I mean."

"Someday it'll be us, Danny. You and me singing together. On *Bandstand*. Around the world. You still believe that, don't you?"

He moistened his lips. "Sure. Why not?" His eyes weren't on her anymore; he seemed distracted. "Listen, Jen, you better get ready."

She winced at the clipped, surly tone in his voice. There was nothing she could say or do to make this day easier for him, unless she refused to sing with Callan. Would he be cruel enough to ask that of her?

"I could tell Cal I can't perform with him," she ventured, her voice small, wounded. Silently she prayed he would insist she do no such thing.

Danny's brows furrowed. His eyes flashed. "That would be stupid, Jen. You and Cal have already cut the record."

"Are you angry because we're singing your song?"

"Our song, Jen. I wrote 'Born to Love You' for you."

"So in a way, Danny, it's like you'll be up there too. We'll be singing your words."

He scowled. "Yeah, sure. Cal steals my girl and my song in one tidy little package. I should be jumping for joy, right?"

Jenny winced, feeling his pain. "If you didn't want him recording your song, why didn't you tell him?"

"Nobody crosses Callan Swan and stays with the band, you know that, Jen."

She squeezed his hand. "Danny, I won't sing it if you don't want me to."

"That's not it. I just wanted to be singing it with you."

"That's what I wanted too."

"Looks like Callan Swan's the only one getting his way today."

"Maybe I won't sing after all, Danny. What if I'm too scared to sing?"

"It's too late to look for a way out, Jen. Besides, you're just going to be up there lip-synching."

"But what if I can't even do that?"

"Stop it, Jen. The whole thing's set. There's no turning back."

He was right, of course. There was nothing more to say. He wasn't going to make this easier for her, and she had no idea how to make it easier for him. "I'd better get dressed," she murmured. "I'll be out soon."

He nodded. "I'll be waiting in the bus."

When she boarded the bus fifteen minutes later, her gaze met Danny's, and for an instant she read the undisguised rancor, the smoldering resentment. Stricken, she looked away.

"Sit here," said Cal, patting the seat beside him, several rows ahead of Danny.

She sat down, rebuffed by the man she loved. Danny hadn't said a word, but in that fractional glance he had allowed his real feelings to show. He was angrier with her than she ever could have imagined. How would they get past this? How would they ever hold on to the sweet, simple, selfless love they once shared?

"Are you ready for an extraordinary day?" asked Cal. With his stunning three-piece suit and professionally styled hair, he looked like a matinee idol. The girls on *Bandstand* were going to love him. He repeated his question. "Are you ready, Jen?"

She massaged her hands, her fingers already growing stiff and cold in the chill air. "I'm nervous as a cat facing the last of its nine lives," she confessed. "Being on television, Cal, with the whole country watching . . . what if I make a mistake? Everyone will see."

He patted her hand, leaving his warm palm resting on her wrist. "You have nothing to worry about, Jenny. We're lip-synching our record. All you have to do is stand there and look gorgeous and pretend you're singing."

"But what if I'm not in sync? What if people can tell I'm not really singing?"

Cal squeezed her arm reassuringly. "Just go and have fun with it, Jen. Remember, we're going to put on a show America will never forget."

It was nearly noon when Lee drove the group to a nearby deli, where they ordered Dagwood-size sandwiches, potato chips, and bottles of Coke. They sat at round, laminated tables and consumed their food, knowing this would be their only chance to eat until after the show. Jenny hoped her breath wouldn't smell like salami, onions, and pastrami.

From the deli, Lee drove on to the television studios on Forty-sixth and Market streets in West Philadelphia. The television station was flanked on one side by a huge sports emporium called The Arena, and on the other by the elevated railroad running down the center of Market Street to downtown Philadelphia.

Lee parked the bus in the parking lot behind the studio, not far from the Market Street elevated train. It was just one o'clock and already long lines of teenagers had gathered along the brick facade, waiting for the back door to open.

"Looks like we'll have a good crowd," said Cal.

Several girls in bobby socks and penny loafers were spinning hula hoops around their middles, gyrating to keep the hoops in place. They all looked like typical high school kids, mused Jenny, the girls no doubt wearing dresses or pleated skirts and white blouses with Peter Pan collars under their winter coats, the boys wearing suits or sport jackets or sweaters, but always a tie.

"We got some time before we're supposed to show up," said Cal. "Might as well sit back and relax a few minutes. Make sure you haven't got pastrami in your teeth."

While they waited, a shiny black vehicle arrived and parked beside them. Jenny watched out the dirt-smudged bus window as two men climbed out of the car and started walking toward the studio entrance.

"Hey, man, that's Frankie Avalon!" exclaimed Gil.

"He must be the other guest besides us," said Lee, peering out too.

"Great!" said Cal under his breath. "Who's gonna notice the Bell Tones with a teen idol like Avalon around?"

"Is it really him?" cried Jenny, rubbing a spot in the window's cloudy condensation. She recognized him now—a short, wiry young man with a bounce in his step and a healthy head of curly black hair. Wearing a creamy white sports jacket with black trim, black cuffed corduroy pants, and white bucks, the singer looked like little more than a teenager himself.

Suddenly the crowd recognized Frankie too, and the girls swarmed around him with shrieks and screams, begging for autographs. Some girls were actually weeping hysterically. Jenny could hear their high, shrill voices. "Frankie, we love you! . . . Hey, Frankie, you're the greatest! . . . Frankie, you're my life, my whole world! I'd die for you, Frankie!"

Somehow, the dark-suited man beside Avalon pushed through the swooning throng and got the singer inside and slammed the door shut. Jenny looked over at Cal and said, "I don't think we have to worry about a reception like that."

Cal ground his jaw reflectively, watching the crowd. His eyes had a faraway glint. "Someday, Jenny, that'll be me. Someday, I swear it!"

Jenny felt an odd tickle inside, almost a shiver. The idea of being a teen idol like Frankie Avalon seemed so remote, like a fairy tale. But it was obvious Callan Swan wanted that sort of adulation more than anything in the world. But did Jenny? She gazed back at the teenagers, already resuming their lines and turning back to their hula hoops and chatter.

An insight struck her like a lightning flash. *Those kids worship that man!* It was a stunning, sobering realization. It was like Annie always said. "If people don't worship God, they'll find gods of their own to worship; they'll create gods in their own image and worship them." *Even rock 'n' roll singers,* thought Jenny darkly. She shivered again. *Idols. Teen idols! Dear God, I'm part of this system; I'm caught up in this entire process, and I know better. I know the truth.*

"Well, looks like it's time to go in," said Cal, running a hand lightly over his shiny black, lacquered mane. He stood up and gestured to the rest of the band scattered through the bus. "Let's go, guys! And let's knock 'em dead!"

A cheer went up among the musicians and one by one they exited the bus and crossed the parking lot to the studio entrance. As Jenny had expected, there was no stampede from the young crowd, only a ripple of whispers. "Who are they? . . . Should we know them? . . . Are they somebody? . . . Is that the Chordettes? The Monotones?" The teenagers stood watching curiously as the band made their way into the building. A few girls smiled or waved and said hello. Jenny smiled back, her heart already pounding nervously.

A pleasant, dark-haired man in a navy suit and bow tie greeted them at the wide, sliding doors. He introduced himself as the producer, although Jenny didn't catch his name. He escorted them through a large sound stage marked Studio B, out into a hallway, and downstairs to the cellar. "You have a half hour or so before you go on," he said. "Feel free to use the little boy's or girl's room to freshen up. I'll come back in a few minutes and take you back up to the studio."

Danny flashed Jenny a bemused smile and whispered, "Hey, looks like we get the royal treatment, huh?"

Fifteen minutes later the producer led them back upstairs to the sprawling sound stage, where a flurry of activity was underway. A crew in gray janitorial uniforms were pushing pine bleachers out from the wall and setting a podium up on a riser. Already dozens of students were swarming in, pulling off bulky coats and stuffing them with their books and purses under the bleachers.

Jenny gazed around the huge, high-ceilinged room, taking everything in. A score of spotlights hung from the ceiling like round, white moons. The bleachers and a counter-length autograph table stood to the right of the dance floor, and a huge, glittery cutout map of the United States hung on the left. Behind the podium, a field of gold records blazed from ceiling to floor. Past the dance floor, where teenagers were already practicing the latest steps, was the camera area with a maze of cables that looked like writhing snakes. Cameramen were already jockeying for position, pushing around three large cameras hooked to the thick cables.

Amid the whirlwind of activity, the producer showed Jenny and the others around, sidestepping twisting cables and dancing teens, and giving instructions as he spoke. Pausing at the wide oak podium, he said, "This is Dick's spot, with his Top Ten board listing the hits. And right there by the curtain is where you'll be lip-synching your song. You'll notice we don't have any monitors facing the podium because we don't want the kids watching themselves, checking themselves out.

And in case you're wondering, we can get 150 kids on that dance floor. And when you get that many kids out there, this place is hopping."

"It looked like more than 150 kids were waiting outside," said Jenny.

"Probably were." The producer's bland, controlled expression hadn't changed since he'd begun their 'tour.' "Lots of times we have to turn kids away. Especially the girls. We always get more girls than boys. We try to keep it even."

He gestured toward the far wall, droning on as if he'd given this discourse often. "You see those three windows? One's the control room, one's the sponsors' viewing booth, and the other one is where the station executives watch. Don't worry about any of them. Keep your mind on pleasing the twenty million television viewers watching the show."

"That's what we plan to do," said Callan, rubbing his hands together, his chiseled face ruddy, glistening with excitement.

Jenny closed her eyes and pushed from her mind the idea of twenty million people watching them perform. She would concentrate on only one. Grandma Betty.

When she looked around again, she saw that the studio had grown busier and the atmosphere more charged. Broadcast time was approaching. Fifteen minutes at most. The production staff was milling around like bees around a hive.

"As you can see, it takes a lot of people to make the show go like clockwork," said the producer. "Dick's secretary, the stage manager, station manager, director, floor manager, just to name a few. During the broadcast, they make sure the sets are right, the acts arrive in time and know what to do, the kids stay in line, and the sponsors are happy."

Suddenly, from the hallway, a door opened and Dick Clark himself entered carrying a stack of 45 RPM records, followed by a paunchy man in rolled shirt sleeves, checking a chart. Clark, his trim, classic good looks accented by an immaculate navy blue suit and striped tie, looked like a youthful professor or a conservative businessman.

"There's Dick," said the producer. "He's making sure the audio engineer has a copy of his play list. Mr. Swan, have your group take their places over by the curtain. We'll be on the air in a few minutes."

As they crossed the stage to the curtain, Jenny looked at her watch; 2:55. For the next couple of minutes, pandemonium reigned on the sound stage as crew and staff rushed about, attending to last-minute details. Then, as if the entire process had been choreographed, everything fell into place at once. A perfect, calming silence replaced the earlier chaos, and all activity ceased.

At 3:00 sharp, the floor manager yelled out, "Stand by! Five, four, three . . ." Jenny caught her breath as the rapid-fire sound of Les Elgart's "Bandstand Boogie" exploded in the studio. As the music played, the center camera moved in for a close-up of the distinguished host standing behind his solid podium. The theme song faded and Clark flashed the most genuine, disarming smile Jenny had ever seen. With obvious panache, he declared, "Hi, I'm Dick Clark. And this is *American Bandstand*. We're glad to have you with us today. We have some special guests, including one of your all-time favorites, Frankie Avalon, right here from South Philly. He'll be singing 'Venus' and 'De De Dinah.'

"We also have with us an exciting new group called the Bell Tones doing their new song, 'Born to Love You.' Be watching for this song to climb the charts. It's a winner."

The events of the next hour were a heart-pounding blur for Jenny. She half wished the Bell Tones would be first on the program, so the excruciating wait would be over. But no, it looked like they were scheduled for the last hour of the show.

Dick, with his casual, friendly, polished demeanor, chatted with the television audience, announcing new ABC network affiliate stations who had signed on.

Then, with the graceful aplomb of a magician performing his best trick, he slipped a platter on the turntable and announced the first song. It was a fast tune, something by Fats Domino; Jenny didn't catch the title. The teenagers streamed out of the bleachers and began to dance, holding hands, their limber bodies rocking and twisting, bopping and swinging. The girls' full skirts swished against their calves as they gyrated to the heavy, pounding beat.

Jenny watched, fascinated. Many of the couples were regulars who had danced on the show for years. Jenny recognized them and knew her grandmother would be able to rattle off their names.

Another record hit the turntable—a romantic ballad by Pat Boone, prompting a slow dance. After several more records, Clark slipped easily into a commercial for Rice-A-Roni; later he did brief spots for Betty Crocker and Dr Pepper. Halfway through the show he introduced Frankie Avalon, to uproarious applause. Jenny feared a near stampede. But the minute Dick Clark insisted on order, the crowd quieted. Frankie lip-synched his two songs, then sat down at the table and signed autographs. He was quietly whisked out of the studio as the couples hit the dance floor for the next record.

For Jenny, waiting to perform became the longest wait of her life. The minutes dragged; time seemed to stand still; she was certain she would spend the rest of her life in this agonizing limbo. Then suddenly she found herself moving, seemingly in slow motion, as she and the other band members took their places. The all-seeing camera zeroed in on them like a giant, relentless, imperturbable eye.

As their record burst out over the sound system, Jenny was aware of her lips moving. She smiled brightly and allowed herself to sway with the music. She was in the middle of performing for twenty million people, and it had all the hazy, surreal quality of a dream. She heard her voice and Callan's ring out in clear, perfect harmony, reinforced by Emmett's dazzling piano, Gil's mellow guitar, and Andy's robust drums. It was Danny's song, the love song he had written just for her.

I was born to love you,
Born to be the one
To cherish and adore you
From dawn till setting sun.
Born to be true,
Born to love you.
Darling, please don't run away,
Listen to what I have to say.
I was born to love you, only you.

And then, as quickly as it had started, the song was over, and the young people in the bleachers were applauding wildly. Wouldn't Grandma Betty love this! Jenny gazed straight into the camera and blew a kiss. *This is for you, Grams!*

Jenny heard Dick Clark say, "Great job! That's Callan Swan and the Bell Tones! I predict the teens of America will send that song to the top of the charts. Kids, let's welcome the Bell Tones to the autograph table. We're going to hear a lot more from this talented group!"

After the show, as Jenny followed Callan and the others out of the WFIL-TV studios back to their drafty, dilapidated bus, her head still rang with the rousing applause, and her mind was filled with images of eager, smiling teenagers asking for her autograph, treating her like a star. It was heady, mind-boggling stuff.

Callan's voice broke into her thoughts. "Man, we did good today! Right, guys?"

Everyone cheered, except Danny. The guys loosened their ties and shrugged off their sports jackets. Emmett popped open a bottle of cola and was chug-a-lugging on the spot.

Gil reached for a bag of Fritos and tore it open. "Man, if we could get our hands on a kinescope of today's program, we could show it to television stations all over the country."

Cal nodded. "I'll check on that. Let's go somewhere and celebrate."

Lee Slocum started the bus. "Where to? Not the deli."

"No. I saw a place half a block down Market Street. Let's try it."

The Brown Jug, an old Irish saloon and restaurant with drab green walls, oilcloth on the tables, and plain china plates and unadorned silverware, turned out to be a perfect place to eat. The food was good, but more important to Callan Swan, the place appeared to be a favorite haunt of producers and executives in the television and record industries.

"Looks like we picked the right place," he told Jenny as they finished their Irish stews. "We're hobnobbing with stuffed shirt VIPs. See those suits at the table over there? They're talking contracts, record deals. If we were staying in town, I'd make this our regular hangout."

"Sorry, boss," said Lee, stirring his coffee. "We can't get cozy here in Philly. We gotta be in South Carolina tomorrow night. We're booked up all week. Then we head west."

Andy chuckled. "We're a bunch of wandering troubadours."

"But it's going to pay off one of these days," said Cal. "When we've got a few hit records under our belt, we can sit home by our swimming pools and wait for the big guys to come to us."

Danny, sitting across the table, gave Jenny a sweeping glance, then dragged his gaze reproachfully over Cal, who had his arm loosely around Jenny's chair. "If you ask me, we'd better not be in a big, fat hurry to trade our bus in for one of those fancy mansions."

"Oh, yeah? What are you saying, Danny?"

Danny's expression darkened. "Nothing. It's just—we've got a long, hard road before we can nail down the kind of success a guy like Frankie Avalon has. If we start counting our gold records, we'll fall flat on our faces."

Cal let his hand drop to Jenny's shoulder; he drummed his fingers lightly along her bare arm. Jenny could feel Danny's eyes boring into her, his anger seething. Didn't he know she wanted him to be the one holding her in his arms? But how could she protest Cal's gestures of affection without raising questions neither she nor Danny were willing to answer?

"Danny," said Cal with a note of rebuke, "we've just had the biggest triumph in the history of the Bell Tones. This isn't the time for gloomy moods or bleak predictions. This is our night to be on top of the world. Thanks to your song, which we all deeply appreciate, and your cousin's extraordinary singing voice, we have charmed America's teenagers. Right, fellas?"

They all cheered on cue, Emmett raising his glass and Gil tossing chips in the air.

"And this is only the beginning," said Cal expansively.

Everyone was still cheering, applauding themselves, their good fortune.

Impetuously, Callan Swan leaned over and planted a warm kiss on Jenny's lips. Cupping her chin in his sturdy hands, he gazed into her eyes and said disarmingly, "Dear girl, this is the beginning of more than you ever dreamed possible. Hold on to your hat. It's going to be the ride of a lifetime!"

12

Their first day in South Carolina Callan insisted that Jenny needed a new dress, something shiny and sequined that would dazzle the folks of Greenville, or at least the people who came to the Old Cahoots Supper Club, a popular night spot in a renovated basement on the south side of town. Jenny and the band were at the club now, rehearsing, with no one around to bother them, except the owner, Duane Fusco, and he was a quiet, stubby, bald man who kept to himself. The doors didn't open until six that evening, so they had all afternoon to work out the kinks in their program.

But Callan wouldn't let up about the new dress. "Listen, Jenny. Duane, the club owner, says there are some terrific dress shops downtown, so why don't you sneak away for a couple of hours and get yourself something nice? My treat. Maybe a floor-length gold lamé gown. You look like a million dollars in gold."

"How will I get downtown?" she wanted to know. "I'm not about to drive our old bus."

"Take the city bus. It picks you up a block or two from here and takes you right to town."

Jenny couldn't think of any more excuses, and she figured it might be nice to get out in the sunshine. This basement club, which no doubt rocked with heat and energy at night, had the musty, dark, clammy feel of a cave in the pale, empty daylight. So she shrugged and said okay. "I'll be back in time for our final rehearsal."

When Danny saw her slip on her coat, he came striding over, wanting to know where she was going. She told him and he shot back, "Not by yourself, you're not. I heard Greenville's got one of the worst crime rates of any city in America."

"Then come with me," she said, buttoning her coat.

"Can't. I've got to finish the arrangements on a couple of my songs. If I get the bugs out, Cal will use them in the act."

Emmett shuffled over. "Listen, Danny, I'll go with her . . . and I may pick up a new straw hat for myself." His smile spread across his shiny mocha face like a bright half moon. "After all, I got an image to maintain, now that we're all television stars."

"You can come if you want, Em, but don't feel like you have to," said Jenny. "I'm a big girl. I can take care of myself."

"Not in Greenville," said Callan. "Danny's right about the crime rate. But I'm not so sure Emmett should go with you. Remember, you're not in Chicago, Em. Or even South Philly."

"Like the girl says, we can take care of ourselves," Emmett said with a wink.

"Maybe so, Em, but you're in the Deep South now. You know they do things different here. Look what happened when we tried to check you into the hotel last night."

An awkward silence rested heavy on the air. No one wanted to talk about what happened last night, least of all Emmett.

He shrugged, as if it didn't matter at all. "So they won't let coloreds stay in the hotel. That's nothing new."

"We should have gone somewhere else," said Jenny, feeling Emmett's pain, no matter how much he tried to hide it.

"Where else were we going to find rooms for a bunch of musicians at the last minute?" said Cal defensively. "Besides, the hotel's convenient. Just two doors down from this supper club. If you want to go scouting around for a hotel that takes both blacks and whites, Jenny, you go ahead, but we've got a show to do tonight, and that's my first priority."

"Hey, man, it ain't no problem," said Emmett. "I don't mind sleeping on the bus. We done it enough times, all of us."

"Yeah, I know," said Cal solemnly. "So okay, you two go to town. But, Em, watch your back, okay?"

He laughed ironically. "Hard to watch my back when I'm facing forward."

Danny squeezed Emmett's shoulder reassuringly. "Don't let anybody give you—or Jenny—a hard time, okay? Watch my girl . . . I mean, my cousin," he corrected, casting a furtive glance at Jenny.

"We'll be okay, Danny," she assured him. "We'll just take the bus to town, buy a dress for me and a hat for Emmett, and come right back. We'll be back in plenty of time for the final afternoon runthrough."

"Don't say I didn't warn you about trouble," said Cal.

Emmett tipped his straw hat. "Don't worry. Before Chicago, I was raised in Memphis. I know the South and its ways."

"Another thing," said Cal when they were halfway out the door, "don't look too chummy. Folks around here don't take to a white girl and black man being friendly."

"Don't worry," said Jenny, laughing. "We'll act like strangers, if that'll make you feel better."

Cal shook his head. "It's not me I'm worried about."

All the way to the bus stop, nearly two blocks from the supper club and the flea bag hotel that was home for a few days, Emmett chatted about music and his father's jazz playing. "Did you know, girl, my daddy played with Dizzy Gillespie in New York City 'round about '49?"

"I thought he only played on the streets of Memphis." Jenny breathed the cold, brisk air deep into her lungs, chasing out the must and cigarette fumes of the supper club. It was a clear, bright day for

November, the sunshine muted but warm on her head, even though the earth was brown and the trees bare, their spidery black limbs silhouetted against a metallic-gold sky.

"No, my daddy traveled all over during his wandering days," said Emmett, "before my mama made him come home and he settled down to preach. He played with Charlie Parker, the best jazz saxophonist you ever heard tell of. And Thelonius Monk. Now I bet you never heard of him. He was one fine black piano player."

"I wish I could have heard your dad play," said Jenny. She loved hearing Emmett talk about his father and his music; his enormous energy and excitement were contagious. "Em, I bet the two of you together could raise the rafters."

"You kidding, girl? We could raise the dead!"

As they approached the bus stop, Emmett began humming a familiar tune—"Farther Along"—in a voice that flowed smooth as warm honey.

"You've got to teach me that song," Jenny told him. "It just melts my heart. It's like a sweet memory out of the past."

He nodded. "I'll teach you, and we'll sing it together. And we'll raise a few rafters ourselves."

She gave him an appreciative smile. "I can't wait, Em."

They both stepped back as the city bus whooshed to a stop beside the curb, belching a cloud of black soot. The door creaked open and Jenny mounted the steps with Emmett just behind her, still humming his tune. She slid into the first available seat and Emmett paused an uncertain moment before settling down beside her.

Jenny could feel more than she could hear the shock and horror of passengers around her. The bus driver, a beefy white man with full jowls and flaring nostrils, turned in his seat and barked, "Back of the bus, boy!"

Emmett held his place, unmoving, except for several twitching fingers.

The driver stood up, his face flushing. "You dense or just deaf, boy?"

"Me?"

"Yes, you, boy. You see anybody else I'm talking to?"

"This seat was empty, mister," said Emmett, his tone low and polite. "And I'm just sitting here with my friend."

"Where you been all your life, boy?" boomed the driver, his eyes red-rimmed and the veins in his thick neck bulging. The entire bus was abuzz with whispers now. "That seat's reserved for white folk. Coloreds sit in the back."

"Not where we come from," said Jenny, her voice breathy, uneven. "Folks sit where they please."

"You don't say!" The driver stared her down, his face puffy, expanding. Wheezing now, he looked like a red-faced toad about to zap his prey. "Then, miss, maybe you should go back where you come from, if you love colored boys so much."

As Jenny's face turned a scorching crimson, Emmett slipped out of his seat and unraveled to his full rangy height.

Jenny looked up at him. "Where you going, Em?"

His chin hugged his chest. "Back of the bus. No sense stirring up trouble. It's not worth it."

Jenny stood too, her ankles weak. "Okay, then I'm going with you." She followed him down the narrow aisle past rows of stony-faced passengers, their gaze riveted on the tall black man and the willowy white woman. Jenny heard one woman mutter, "Can you imagine the nerve? White trash like her flaunting her association with a Negro! What's the world coming to?"

Emmett sat down in the last row and Jenny sat down beside him. She was trembling now. But if she thought they had appeased the angry driver, she promptly saw she was sorely mistaken.

The driver was still standing, watching, waiting, his vein-riddled face bloated, his countenance darkening like a thundercloud. "Okay, lady, maybe you think you're being cute, but no one's laughing," he growled menacingly. "You're making us late to the next stop, and if you all keep up these shenanigans, I'm reporting the two of you to the police."

"What have we done wrong now?" cried Jenny, appalled.

The driver gestured with his pudgy thumb and forefinger. "Like I said. Coloreds in the back, whites in the front. You can't sit back there."

After a long, excruciating moment, Emmett said quietly, "You go sit in the front, Jen. I'll stay here."

"But—but—" she sputtered, then realized she was bucking a system one lone black man and one frail woman couldn't possibly prevail against. Fighting tears of outrage, she returned to the front of the bus—alone. She rode in silence, her back rigid, her tightly folded hands cold and clammy on her lap. All around her came the stir of indignant voices spewing muffled accusations and racial epithets. *Can you imagine . . . what nerve . . . doesn't he know his place? . . . those uppity coloreds . . . and that shameless girl . . . but what can you expect of white trash!*

Jenny closed her eyes and tried to block out the odious voices around her, the scathing words filled with hatred and scorn, but she had no defense. The words pierced like poisonous darts. She had never felt more like an outcast in her life.

Later, when she and Emmett entered the sprawling department store with its rows of merchandise behind sleek glass counters, she hoped they could put the pain and embarrassment of the bus ride behind them. But she could already sense a change in Emmett's demeanor. He wasn't humming a tune and walking tall and proud the way he usually did; and he was keeping a polite distance from her. Was he afraid to have people see them together? She had half a mind to take his arm and pretend they were a couple. But this wasn't a game; she knew Emmett had good reason to be afraid.

Jenny drifted to the women's dress department, her mind still preoccupied with their humiliating bus ride. She no longer felt in the mood to shop for an evening gown for tonight's show. Half-heartedly she browsed through a rack of dresses, but nothing appealed to her. Yet Callan would expect her to return with something, so she selected several dresses and took them to the fitting room to try on. She finally came out in a sinuous forest-green sheath with a sequined bodice. "What do you think?" she asked Emmett, who stood against the wall with arms folded, looking ill at ease.

"Beautiful, girl. It's you. Get it and let's go." He cupped his hand around his mouth and whispered, "That saleslady's been looking daggers at me. I figure she thinks I'm loitering, up to no good."

Jenny sighed. What was wrong with people? She'd never noticed anyone giving black folks so much trouble back in Willowbrook. Of course, in Willowbrook she'd never known any Negroes personally. She'd seen them only from a distance—cleaning ladies coming and going in her neighborhood or old men operating the elevators in the stores downtown. She supposed Willowbrook had as many black people as any other town, but they had their own neighborhoods and schools and churches. It had always seemed so natural, so appropriate, just the way life was. Odd that she'd never questioned the order of things . . . until now.

She and Emmett were halfway out of the store when Jenny said, "Before we get back on that bus, I need to use the ladies' room."

But the signs over the restroom doors only served to underscore Jenny's growing misgivings. Besides MEN and WOMEN, the signs read, FOR WHITES ONLY and FOR COLORED ONLY. Near the restrooms stood two drinking fountains side by side, one marked COLORED and the other WHITE.

Jenny shook her head. "I think I'm going to be sick," she murmured, rushing into the lavatory. Only when she came out and passed a black woman going in did she realize she had used the wrong restroom.

On the way home, Jenny and Emmett knew enough to get on the bus and sit in the appropriate spots at front and rear, but somehow, Jenny felt violated. She could only imagine how Emmett must feel. How could a system she didn't approve of dictate where she sat on the bus? Jenny knew Emmett had faced this before, but the shame and rage she felt were new to her. Her freedom had been stolen from her as surely as if she'd been held up at gunpoint, and all she could do was just sit there.

When they got off the bus and started walking toward their hotel, neither spoke. Jenny wanted to say something to make Emmett feel at ease again, to bring out the laughing, fun-loving, dry-witted man she had come to care about, but Emmett walked with his head down and his strides long, as if he had forgotten she was beside him. She tried to speak, to traverse the growing emotional distance between them, but no words came; she felt as tongue-tied as a schoolgirl.

At last, in desperation, she looked over at him and said, "It doesn't matter, you know, Em. It doesn't change anything. What happened back there. It's not worth getting upset over. We just have to forget it, okay?"

"Maybe *you* can forget," he mumbled, and looked away.

Shortly before they reached the old, weather-worn hotel, Emmett stretched out a cautious hand and touched her arm. She looked up questioningly at him. "Don't look back," he whispered, "but I think we got company."

"Company?"

"A passel of men following behind, not too close, not too far, but looking mighty suspicious to me."

"Who are they?" she asked.

"I don't know, but I think some of them was on the bus with us going to town, and on the bus coming home. I think they been following us this whole time."

"While we were shopping?"

"I got a feeling they was there too."

"What do they want? To heckle us some more?"

"Or maybe worse. You walk on ahead and get inside the hotel and go straight to your room. Don't you even look back, you hear?"

"Shouldn't we go on to the club? There's safety in numbers."

Emmett shook his head. "I don't want them fellas knowing we're with the band. They might show up at the club tonight and make a disturbance, and then we all be out on our ear."

"Then what should we do?"

"Like I say. You go to your hotel room. Come out when they're gone."

"What about you, Em?"

"I'll walk a pace behind and keep an eye on things."

"Come inside the hotel," she urged. "Go to Danny's room. Or Cal's."

"They're at the club. Their doors'll be locked."

"Then come to my room."

"And have them break down your door and have at us both? No, sister. This is my fight."

"Be careful, Em," she warned, her heart hammering. "Go right to the bus and get inside. Don't get hurt."

His eyes were large as eggs in his ebony face. "Listen, girl, last thing I want is trouble." He shooed her inside and she walked quickly through the small lobby, up two flights of creaking stairs and down the narrow hall to her cramped room. She went inside and locked the door, her heart sinking as she thought about Emmett with no room to go to.

She went to her window and looked out. Sure enough, the bus was parked below in its usual spot. She watched for a long moment and spotted Emmett rounding the corner of the hotel, giving a backward glance as he approached the bus. A fraction of a second later, three husky white men in rumpled leather jackets, Levi's, and heavy work boots came striding up and formed a half circle around him.

"Dear God, they're going to kill him," she whispered, covering her mouth with her hand. "Help him, please!"

The three men exchanged words with Emmett for a minute, explosive words by the looks on their faces. One man pulled something from his pocket and Jenny saw the glint of a knife. He thrust the blade toward Emmett just as Emmett sprang backward, his palms raised protectively. The men started closing in; one lumberjack of a fellow swung his boot at Emmett's groin, but again Emmett sidestepped him. Jenny watched, spellbound, helpless, her body seemingly frozen in place. "God, help him," she breathed again.

A second man stepped forward, tripped Emmett, and shoved him to the pavement, his thick boot pressing Emmett's face into the gravel. The three closed in, ready to pounce like vultures when a red Buick sedan pulled into the parking lot and parked a few feet away. Two white men in business suits climbed out.

The three assailants stopped and looked up, then broke away from Emmett and took off running down the street. The two businessmen glanced over at Emmett on the ground, then looked the other way and kept walking toward the hotel.

Jenny watched from her window, shaking, choking back a sob, as Emmett picked himself up, brushed himself off, and lumbered back toward the bus. He reached for the door handle, then stopped, breathing hard. After a moment he stretched out splayed fingers and pressed them flat against the side of the bus. He leaned forward, his head lowered, his square chin drooping on his barrel chest. He stood that way for a long while, as if wrestling against unspeakable demons.

Finally he let his hands fall to his sides and stepped back. In one sudden, explosive gesture, he swung his leg back and kicked the heavy rubber tire with his booted foot. Again and again he struck the solid, immovable tire until his foot must have throbbed. Jenny couldn't stand it any longer. She turned from the window and ran out of her room and down the stairs to the parking lot.

Breathless, she ran to Emmett and seized his arm as he was about to level another furious kick. He stopped in midkick and stared at her in stunned surprise.

"Don't, Em, please!"

His face contorted in an expression of exquisite pain, then his shoulders slumped and he sagged a little as if all the energy and anger had gone out of him at once. His dark eyes were shadowed and rimmed with unshed tears and his face glistened like polished mahogany, except where the blood trickled down his cheek in a jagged gash. "Whatcha doing out here, little girl?"

"You're hurt," she cried. "They hurt you."

He wiped the blood away with the back of his hand, but it seeped out again in a river of tiny red bubbles.

"I'm sorry, Em," she cried, touching his cheek, covering the blood with her own palm. "I'm so sorry."

"What for? You didn't do this."

No, but someone needed to tell him they were sorry. "You can't stay out here tonight, Em," she said, looking around, fearful of seeing the thugs looming in the shadows. "It's not safe, Em. Maybe you can stay in Danny's room tonight."

"The hotel will send us all packing if we try a trick like that."

"They have no right to turn you away. How can they get away with such cruelty? Somebody should do something."

Emmett chuckled ruefully. "Who? You gonna solve all the world's wrongs, missy?"

"Maybe." She drew in a sharp breath and realized how foolish she sounded. Some things in life were so firmly entrenched in the scheme of things no one person could change them. Surely not a naive teenage girl from Indiana.

Emmett pulled out a handkerchief and wiped his beaded forehead and the trickle of blood. "Listen, girl, we'd better get to rehearsal before Callan Swan has our heads." He paused, then said with an edge of defiance and pride, "Don't say nothing to nobody, okay? We're gonna go strutting into that club tonight and give the performance of our lives."

And they did.

The dimly lit, smoke-filled supper club was packed with a rousing, cheering crowd—old and young, black and white, the wealthy upper crust and freewheeling beatnik eccentrics. The band received two standing ovations—once when Jenny and Cal sang their rendition of a favorite Buddy Holly tune, and again when Emmett, at the piano, sang "Measure of a Man," one of the new songs Danny had written. *Love not the man the world sees me to be; love the hidden person your devotion has set free.* Jenny knew Danny had written those lyrics for only one man—Emmett Sanders.

That evening, as Emmett's agile fingers blazed over the ivory keys with a sizzle that electrified the atmosphere, Jenny thought what a paradox she was witnessing: Emmett, the consummate performer, receiving unbridled applause and adulation, in contrast to earlier today, when Emmett, the man, had been taunted, ridiculed, and attacked by folks who looked no different from those in this very room.

After the show, around midnight, the band was served a private buffet dinner in one of the club's small lounges, where a linen-draped table was spread with a delectable array of fresh fruits and salads and a variety of cheeses, cold cuts, and crusty rolls. Band members were never hungry before a performance, but afterward they were always famished.

Jenny welcomed the down time after a performance to unwind. Like the rest of the band, she was always keyed up and needed an hour or two after a gig to relax and adjust to the real world again. A few of the guys unwound by downing enough beers to have them sloshing around in their boots. But Danny, Jenny, and Emmett refused to booze it up with the others. From childhood Jenny had resolved never to fall into alcohol's clutches, knowing what it had done to her beloved Grandma Betty. She knew Danny and Emmett had lost loved ones to liquor too. For Danny, it was a favorite aunt who cared for him when his mother was in the sanitarium with tuberculosis. And for Emmett, it was the grandfather he hardly knew who died falling-down drunk in a Chicago alley.

It was after 2:00 A.M. before the band made their way back to the hotel. It was a short walk and the street was empty. Still, Jenny shivered with anxiety. A full moon cast deep, whispering shadows that seemed both malignant and mysterious. Danny walked Jenny upstairs to her second-floor room, unlocked her door, and gave her a circumspect kiss on the cheek. "You were great tonight, Jen." He smiled. "Okay, I'll say it. We were all great. It's nights like this you know why you're out there singing your heart out."

"The song you wrote for Emmett was wonderful, and I know he enjoyed singing it. Especially tonight."

"Why tonight?"

She hesitated, remembering her promise to Emmett not to mention the attack. "No reason. It's just that everything came together just right."

Danny lingered in the doorway. "I wish it was right for us, Jen. If only we could be together. I need you."

"Someday, Danny." She took his hand and pressed it against her cheek, reluctant to let him go. "Danny," she murmured, but she was afraid to say anything more. The feelings whirling inside her were a dizzying maze of joys and fears, yearnings and desire.

Danny pulled his hand away from her face and said solemnly, "I hate to leave you, but if I don't go now, I might never go. Good night, my sweet Jenny. Sleep well." He brushed a kiss on her lips, then turned to go.

"Wait, Danny."

He looked back at her, a flicker of hope in his eyes. "Yes, Jen?"

"It's not about us," she stammered. "It's Emmett. Would you go out to the bus and talk him into staying in your room tonight?"

Disappointment was etched in Danny's face. "You know he won't break the hotel rules."

She sighed heavily. "I know. Just try, okay?"

"I already did, but I'll try again. You know Emmett. He's determined to stick it out in the bus. It's like his twisted pride won't let him accept help."

"I know. But ask him again."

"I'll ask him, but don't count on him giving in."

Jenny found it hard to sleep that night. The bed was hard, the sheets coarse, and the pillow lumpy, but she was used to such discomfort. This was something more—a growing apprehension in the pit of her stomach, a sense of foreboding that turned her throat sour, the unwavering conviction that something wasn't right. Enough tension was building inside her to make the bed sheets crackle.

Sometime later—minutes, maybe hours—out of the groggy stillness came a sound so unsettling it caused Jenny to sit bolt upright in bed. Her heart pounded. Was it a dream? No, she heard it again—a commotion outside her window. She sprang out of bed and hurried barefoot across the cold floor to the window. She looked down and her eyes went instinctively to the old monstrosity of a bus sitting on the pavement in all its tarnished glory.

Jenny's gaze focused on six moving shadows converging on both the front and back doors. A shaft of cold terror shot through her. *Dear God in heaven, they're back! That pack of thugs is after Emmett! This time they'll murder him!*

Jenny raced out of her room and ran barefoot down the hallway to Danny's room. She beat on the door until Danny, in baggy pajama bottoms, opened the door a crack and peered out. She pushed her way inside, shivering in her light cotton nightgown, and hysterically bawled Emmett's name. Danny pulled her against his bare chest and wrapped his arms around her. "It's okay," he mumbled sleepily, patting her back. "What was it? A bad dream?"

She wriggled out of his arms and shrieked, "Men! After Emmett! The bus!"

Comprehension swept Danny's face and, grabbing his trousers, he tore out of the room. "Call the police!" he shouted back. "And hotel security, if they have such a thing!"

She ran back into the hall and saw him hammering on Callan's door, then Gil's, pulling on one pant leg, then the other. One by one Danny roused the other band members. While she shakily dialed the local sheriff's office from the hall phone, they flew downstairs in various states of undress.

Haltingly, she spilled out the story to the officer. Her friend was being attacked in a hotel parking lot; please send help immediately. Only after he assured her a patrol car had been dispatched did Jenny drop the receiver back into its cradle. Breathlessly, she dashed back to her room, threw on a light robe and slippers, and hurried downstairs, stumbling, nearly falling on the narrow steps. It was insane to think she could ward off a band of rowdy, blood-thirsty hoodlums, but she had to try.

She padded soundlessly around the corner of the hotel to the parking lot just as the full moon broke free of a low-scudding cloud. What she saw would be imprinted in her mind for the rest of her life. Two of the ruffians had Emmett on their shoulders and were stringing him up to a tree. His blood-curdling scream echoed like a banshee's wail.

Danny, Callan, and the others grappled with the other four intruders, jousting, punching, wrestling—a mass of shadows scuffling in the dark. Bitter shouts rose from the melee. One man roared, "Black boy, you leave white girls be!" Another shouted, "The only good colored's a dead one!"

In the moonlight Jenny saw the rope dangling from a tree limb, saw the noose go over Emmett's head. The two men sprang back and let him go and the rope pulled tight around Emmett's neck. Even from where she stood she could see the horror—his eyes swelling like saucers, his face contorted in a soundless scream. He swung like a pendulum, his boots two feet off the ground. Jenny broke into a run toward him, sobbing, raving like a woman possessed.

Andy and Gil and Lee wrestled free from the other thugs and converged on the two henchmen. Danny and Callan also broke free and seized Emmett around the legs and trunk and lifted him up. The rope slackened. They pulled the heavy cord down from the gnarled limb and laid Emmett on the ground. A siren splintered Jenny's scream with its own ghostly moan.

The siren sent Emmett's assailants shrinking back into the murky darkness. They scattered, bolting in every direction, Danny and the others on their heels, shouting, "Dirty, rotten cowards! Lowlife scum!"

Jenny knelt down on the cold pavement beside Emmett, the gravel scraping her bare knees. Emmett's bulky form lay crumpled, twisted, motionless, his craggy face pulpy with blood, the rope tight around his throat. She loosened the sinewy cord and felt a pulse throb along his bruised, bulging neck. She gathered him into her arms as he gagged and sucked for air. Tenderly she cradled his head on her lap, his blood soaking her white cotton robe, as she prayed for God in heaven to help her make sense of this nightmare.

13

Emmett would live. That was the good news. But it would be weeks before he would be well enough to return to the band. For several days after the attack, between performances at the supper club, Jenny spent every free minute at his bedside in the black ward of the hospital, talking to him, singing to him, assuring him he was going to be okay. Emmett even had her reading Scriptures from his mother's thumb-worn Bible, which he carried in his stuff on the bus. In fact, the guys started calling Jenny Miss Florence Nightingale, the way she hovered over Emmett with such motherly concern.

Danny and the other band members dropped in on Emmett too, sneaking in glazed doughnuts, bacon burgers, and chili dogs. They even brought in a turntable and a stack of 45s, so Emmett wouldn't have to do without his "soul food." When he was spinning his platters, some of the nurses complained about the racket, but others dropped by his room just to hear the swinging pop sounds, including the Bell Tones' own hit single, "Born to Love You."

The morning after their last show at the supper club, the band stopped by the hospital to say good-bye to Emmett and took turns visiting his room. Jenny paced the waiting room, struggling to hold back her tears, and finally turned imploringly to Cal. "We can't just leave like this. We've got to stay here in Greenville until Emmett's released. How can we just leave him?"

Callan sat cross-legged on an overstuffed sofa, thumbing through a dog-eared *Saturday Evening Post.* "I'm sorry, kiddo. There's nothing else we can do. We've got a schedule to keep. But don't worry. He'll get good care. I'm covering all his medical bills."

"But he'll be all alone."

"I know, and it's a shame. But the band's gotta move on. We're booked from here to Hawaii for the next six weeks." Cal paused and added cagily, "But if you really want to stay here in Greenville with Emmett until he's better—"

"No, I'll go with the band," she told him, knowing he was right; it was the only way. They had engagements all across the country; they couldn't disappoint their fans. Besides, she was yearning already for Hawaii. Counting on it. Dreaming of it. No sense telling Cal how excited she was to see Pearl Harbor. Her father had died there. Seeing it was the only way she would ever feel close to him, maybe the only way to ever fill the emptiness inside her. But Cal wouldn't understand. He hadn't spent his life grieving for a father he never got to see.

Cal was still talking about Emmett. "Listen, Jenny, you better go in now and say good-bye to him. The rest of the guys have said their good-byes. We're boarding the bus and leaving in an hour."

Jenny nodded and sucked in a deep breath, gathering her courage as she walked down the hall to Emmett's room. Danny was just coming out the door as she approached. He met her gaze, smiled, and squeezed her hand, as if to say, *Don't worry, Jen, it'll be okay. Emmett will be fine.*

She returned the smile and slipped inside the long, narrow room. There were three beds; Emmett had the one by the window, but there was nothing outside to see, only the brick wall of another wing of the hospital. She strolled over to his bed, her brightest smile in place. He looked up from his lunch tray and grinned, his white teeth flashing in his dark, winsome face.

"Well, you're looking good," she said, pulling the straight-back chair over beside his bed. The wounds on his face and neck were healing well, hardly visible, except for the rope burn; he was looking almost like his old self again. "How are you feeling, Em?"

He gingerly rubbed his rib cage. "With these cracked ribs, it hurts to laugh and it hurts to cry, so I just keep mum. But I'm doing okay."

She sat in silence for a moment, trying to gather the right words to say good-bye, but nothing came, except tears glazing her eyes. "I guess you know we're leaving today," she murmured, her gaze downcast.

He stirred cream into his coffee and set the spoon on the saucer. "I know you gotta go."

"I hate leaving you behind, Em."

"Sure, and I hate to see you go, but that's how life is. I thank the good Lord He watches over me."

"He did, Em. That night—it was so awful. You could have died. I'll never forget. Can you forget, Em?"

"No, I won't forget. Not ever." His bristly brows furrowed over his shiny, coal-black eyes. "But I see things a whole lot clearer since that night."

"What things, Em?"

He turned his coffee cup between his palms. "I watch my back now, like Callan said. And I don't trust nobody unless I knows them. Like you. And the fellas in the band. And God. I figure God's been trying to tell me something, and I weren't listening. But God got my attention real good. He saved me from them brutes. He must be trying to tell me something important, and I better listen."

"You really think God's trying to tell you something?"

"I know it, Jenny. He's been knocking on my heart a long time, and I pretend I don't hear. But this time I hear just fine, and whatever He tells me to do, I'm gonna do."

A tear escaped and balanced on Jenny's lashes. "Oh, Em! How can you talk about God after what happened to you? Aren't you angry at God? Don't you hate those dumb, stupid men who did this to you?"

"Oh, I got a whole lot of raw, surly feelings down deep inside for them men, but I keep the lid on tight." Emmett took a swallow of coffee and wiped his mouth with the back of his hand. His hand was trembling slightly. He looked back at Jenny and smiled, his eyes crinkling with a wistful, bemused compassion. "But, missy, God is another matter. Why should I be angry at God for what them men did? They grieved God a whole lot more than they hurt me."

"But God could have prevented their attack—"

"Sure, He could. And then we'd all be little puppets on a string. No, God loves us enough to let us choose our own ways, and sometimes it's the wrong way and folks get hurt."

"Say what you will, Em. I'm angry enough for both of us."

"Well, the way I sees it, I got two roads open to me. I can set my mind on hate and be like them that strung me up. Or I can set my mind on God's love and be like Jesus. Who do you think I wanna be like?"

She smiled in spite of herself. "Well, when you put it like that, I'd take Jesus any day."

"So would I."

She stood up and placed her hand over Emmett's. "I'd better go. I hate saying good-bye."

"Then don't. Just say, 'I'll see you later, Alligator.'"

She laughed. "In a while, Crocodile! But seriously, Em, it won't be long and you'll be back with the band. You know Callan can't get along without you. You're his right-hand man."

"And his left hand too, don't forget."

"So you've got to get well. Be back with us by Christmas. We'll be in Hawaii. They say sunshine has great healing properties."

"Who says that? You, missy?"

"It doesn't matter. Just join us by Christmas, okay?"

His dark eyes glistened. "That's up to the good Lord to decide. Maybe He wants me somewhere else. Never can tell."

As Lee turned on the highway heading out of Greenville, Jenny could tell she wasn't the only one feeling bad about leaving Emmett behind. All the band members were subdued, staring out the window, silent. A light snow had started and flurries were whirling in every direction at once, turning the road ahead a blinding white. Jenny was sitting in the middle of the bus, but as the cold seeped in, she moved up to the front, close to the grinding, overworked heater that periodically belched a blast of hot air. It didn't help much; she was still shivering between blasts, but it was better than feeling like an icicle six rows back.

After a while Danny moved to the front too and sat one seat behind Jenny. He rubbed his hands together and blew into his palms. "It's freezing back there," he complained, loudly enough for Lee to hear.

"You know this heater," replied Lee, his eyes on the swirling white road ahead. "It coughs and sputters like a dying old man."

Danny looked over at Callan, sitting across the aisle from Jenny. "I suppose we'll be driving all night?"

"If we want to make our next gig in time." Cal slid out of his seat and moved over beside Danny. "Listen, man, I've been meaning to talk to you."

"Yeah, sure. What?"

"Now that Emmett's out of the picture for a while, I need you to pick up the slack. You interested?"

"Maybe. What do you have in mind?"

"It's like this . . ."

Cal lowered his voice, but Jenny could still hear him. She stared out the window, pretending not to listen.

"The truth is, Danny, Emmett did most of our arrangements. He just knew how to put a song together so we'd all sound good. I know you write your own music. You wrote 'Born to Love You,' and that's a great song. So maybe you could step in and fill Emmett's shoes until he comes back. What do you think?"

Jenny could hear the excitement in Danny's voice. "I'd like that. I think I could do a good job for the band."

"Good. That means you'll be arranging songs for Jenny and me to sing, stuff that'll showcase our voices and yet deliver that fantastic harmony the fans eat up. Think you can deliver?"

Danny's voice cooled slightly. "Sure. You and Jenny. Whatever you say. Just let me know what you need."

"That's the spirit," said Cal, giving Danny's arm a good-natured swipe. He leaned forward and clasped Jenny's shoulder through her wool coat. "Hey, baby doll, your cousin's not such a bad guy. You hear? He's agreed to fill in for Emmett. Now you know this guy, so tell me. How can I return the favor? Maybe fix him up with some gorgeous dish at our next gig?"

"That's not necessary, Cal," said Danny thickly.

"You sure? I never see you flirting with the ladies. You sure you don't want some help from someone a little more, uh, experienced?"

Danny's tone darkened. "If I want some female company, I'll find my own."

"Well, for starters," said Cal, casting a sidelong glance at Jenny, "stop hanging around with your cousin all the time. Don't act like a monk. Step out and let the girls know you're available."

"Listen, Cal, you tell me what songs to arrange," said Danny, his voice raw, sullen, "but you stay out of my personal life. It's none of your business."

Cal stood up in the aisle and held his hands up placatingly. "Sure, man, whatever you say. I was just trying to help." He moved on down the aisle to the back of the bus and sat down beside Gil.

Jenny waited until the two of them were absorbed in conversation; then she slipped back a seat beside Danny. In the dusky twilight he reached over and took her hand and tucked it inside his coat, against his chest. She longed to put her head on his shoulder and feel the warmth of his head against hers. But she knew better. Cal would be watching.

She looked up at Danny and whispered, "I'm sorry. All those things Cal said—"

"I wanted to hit him," said Danny. "I wanted to blurt out right here that you're my girl, you and only you, and I don't need some painted hussy in some club somewhere."

"Then tell him," urged Jenny. "Go ahead. I've wanted to all along. Tell him! Then maybe he'll stop treating me like I'm his private property."

"Yeah? You think so?" Danny gave her an odd, brooding look that made her flinch inside. "Come on, Jenny. You don't look so unhappy when you're on his arm, when he's strutting you around, showing you off like a princess. You look like you're enjoying every minute of it."

"That's not true, Danny."

"You bet it is. When you two are singing together on stage, you look like you were made for each other. By the time the show's over, the audience is convinced you two are madly in love."

Jenny felt her pulse racing, her defenses rising. "Stop it, Danny. That's what we're supposed to do. It's not real. You, of all people, should know that."

He shrugged. "You convinced me."

She looked up at him until he met her gaze. Her eyes drilling his, she whispered hotly, "It's you I love, Danny. You I'll always love. No one else. Ever."

He rested his head against hers, his cheek nuzzling her hair. "I love you too, Jen. I'm sorry. This frustration has been building in me for so long, I feel like I'm going to explode."

"Then tell Cal. Let him know we're together. That we love each other. What can he do?"

Danny lifted his head off hers and stared for a long minute out the window. She could feel him drifting away from her, distancing himself emotionally, and it wrenched her heart. "Did you hear me, Danny? What can he do?"

He looked back at her, misery and futility twisting his expression. "Plenty, Jen. He could do plenty. Cal just gave me Emmett's job, a chance to make a real contribution to this band. He could take it all away. Just like that."

She stiffened and said coolly, "Okay, Danny, if that's how you want it. We're cousins, nothing more." Removing her hand from its warm alcove inside his coat, she stood up. "See you later, *cousin*!" Then she returned to her own seat, where she stared out the window at the whirling snow and bit her lip to keep from crying. She was aware of Danny behind her, shifting in his seat, his knees bumping the back of her seat. Was he trying to get her attention? She pretended not to notice. He bumped her seat again, harder, but she ignored him, her tearful gaze riveted on the falling snow.

After a minute, she felt Danny hit the back of the seat with his fist; it jolted her slightly, surprised her. He had to be seething to expose his anger like that. She sensed more than saw him get up; she heard his shuffling footfall as he ambled down the aisle to the back of the bus. She heard him greet Andy; the two started talking animatedly, laughing, joking, as if Danny were in the best of moods. She didn't look around, didn't want him to see her searching the lengthening shadows for a glimpse of his profile.

"When are we going to stop somewhere to eat?" she called to Lee, who sat bent forward over the steering wheel, trying to decipher the highway through the dense, eddying snow.

"We're not," he shot back. "If we don't keep driving and beat this snowstorm, we could spend the night frozen in some ditch. We gotta keep going. Check with the guys. See if they still got some of those peanut butter sandwiches from lunch."

"Yeah, thanks," she said with a sigh. Peanut butter was the last thing she wanted. It was dark now and getting colder still, so if she couldn't eat, she might as well sleep. Anything to blot out her discomfort. She bunched her wool scarf into a little pillow and tucked it between her head and the window.

Just as she dozed off, she felt someone hunker down beside her. Danny! She felt his solid warmth against her, smelled the delicious scents of peppermint and Old Spice. His arm went around her, strong and masterful as he drew her against his chest, the nubby texture of his heavy wool coat tickling her cheek. She felt so wonderfully warm and cozy in his arms, so valiantly protected. He was, as always, her refuge in the storm, her comforter, her safe harbor. Dreamily she turned her face up to his, her eyes still closed, her lips parting to say his name. *Danny. My dearest Danny*. But she had no chance to say the words aloud, for his mouth came down suddenly on hers, smothering her startled protests with a smoldering urgency. "Jenny," he whispered. "My darling Jenny!"

Her eyes flew open at the sound of his voice. There, looming mere inches away and silhouetted by ribbons of shadow and slivers of moonlight, was the smiling, uniquely sculpted face of Callan Swan.

14

Jenny shrank back from Callan's touch. "What are you doing, Cal?"

He reached out to smooth her tangled hair. "I'm sorry, doll. You looked so sweet, I couldn't resist."

"But I was asleep. I didn't know . . . you startled me!"

"My mistake." He ran his finger lightly over her lips. "Maybe we can try again sometime when you're awake."

She hugged herself, shivering. "Please, Cal, leave me alone. Just go."

He lingered, his dark eyes searching hers. "Jenny, listen, don't you see what's happening here?"

She looked away, trembling. "What?"

"That kiss wasn't an idle pass, sweetheart. I wasn't trying to take advantage of you."

"You could have fooled me," she said in a small, hard voice.

He turned her chin back to him. "You must know how I feel about you. I've wanted to kiss you like that since the day we met. I hope, one of these days . . ."

"No, Cal, don't say it."

"I've got to, Jenny. I hope one of these days you'll realize you care for me too."

She turned her gaze to the window. The snow was still swirling in a dizzying ballet, blocking out the world. She looked back at Cal. The evening shadows etched deep lines in his solemn face. "I can't, Cal. I'm sorry. We're friends. That's all we can ever be."

"Why? Is there someone else?"

She hesitated a long moment. "I can't answer that."

"Why not? It's a simple question. There is someone else or there isn't. Which is it?"

"There is," she confessed, "but it's very complicated."

Cal raised his voice, shrugging, looking around. "Well, I don't see anybody staking his claim, so I'm staking mine. I want you to be my girl, Jen, not just on stage, not just in our songs, but for real, in the here and now."

"Cal, please don't—"

"It's too late, doll. I've already fallen head over heels. Would you believe? A hardheaded, no-nonsense guy like me? And from now on, you're my lady, and anyone who doubts it will answer to me." He cupped his hand around the back of her neck, pulled her to him, and kissed her again, soundly. "This seals it, babe. You're mine. And don't you forget it."

She tried to protest, but no words came; her mouth was dry as sandpaper. Cal stood up in the aisle and faced the guys in the rear of the bus. "Listen up, fellas. Jenny and I just had a little conversation up here, and it's decided. Jenny Wayne is my lady, and if anybody has a problem with that, you better spit it out right now."

"Hey, man, that's swell," said Andy.

"You two make a great couple," said Gil, raising his bottle of cola.

"What about you, DiCaprio?" said Cal. "You gonna give your cousin and me your blessing?"

Danny got out of his seat and stalked up the aisle toward Cal, gripping each seat back as he came. He stood facing Cal, the two no more than a foot apart. "You want my blessing?" Danny said hotly. Even in the darkness Jenny could see that he was livid.

"Yeah, let's do this up proper. She's your cousin. We should have your blessing. Right, Jen?"

"No . . . yes . . . I mean, he can't give his blessing!"

"He can't? Why not?"

"Tell him, Danny," cried Jenny.

"How about it, Danny?" prodded Cal, clearly enjoying the moment. "Do we have your blessing or not?"

"Since when do you need my blessing?" Danny railed. "You're gonna do what you please, no matter what I say."

Cal shrugged. "Yeah, I suppose you're right about that."

The bus veered suddenly on an icy patch of pavement. Both Danny and Cal stumbled and fell into nearby seats. Cal's challenge to Danny was forgotten as everyone turned their attention to the perils of the road. But Jenny stole a glance back at Danny and saw the anguish and outrage in his face. It mirrored her own inner turmoil and guilt. Why hadn't Danny told Cal the truth? Why hadn't she? How long could they carry on this painful charade before their unwitting deception caught up with them and ruined everything?

Jenny was getting weary with life on the road. The band's cross-country trek in their tumbledown bus seemed destined to last forever. They had forgettable one- and two-nighters in Memphis, Little Rock, Texarkana, and Shreveport, before heading on to Dallas. They always stopped by local radio stations to make sure their record was being played, and sometimes they made appearances on local televised bandstand shows. They never knew where they would be performing next—in high school auditoriums and gyms, old theaters and ballrooms, honky-tonk clubs, rundown stadiums, seedy dance halls, noisy roller rinks, or dilapidated bandstands.

At each gig they had to unload their equipment and instruments, carry everything inside, unpack the drums, set up and check the sound system, and roll out the amplifiers. By the time the stage was ready, they were sweating and disheveled, with little time to shower, change, and make themselves look presentable. Occasionally Jenny was fortunate enough to have a genuine dressing room or at least a nearby motel room to bathe and dress in (usually one with a bare bulb in the ceiling and a scummy, roach-infested shower). At other times she had to make due with a public restroom or even the bus itself, with its hard, crowded seats and utter lack of privacy.

It seemed to Jenny that life on the bus was rapidly deteriorating. Without Emmett around to ride herd on the guys, they allowed the bus to become a pigsty, strewing their dirty clothing over the seats and allowing garbage and trash to pile up on the floors until the place smelled ripe. Even the aisle was becoming littered with candy wrappers, pop bottles, and beer cans.

Except for Danny, the guys were drinking more too, and sometimes after a show they partied half the night and stumbled back to the bus or motel at dawn, too drunk to stand. Jenny hated that part of touring. Why did the guys have to spoil everything by getting drunk? Usually, when the drinking started, she and Danny would slip off by themselves and talk or drink Cokes and play the pinball machines. But since that night on the bus when Cal kissed Jenny and announced that she was his girl, Danny had kept his distance. She knew he was angry with her and with himself, but there seemed to be little for either of them to say, so they said nothing. Without Danny's funny, endearing company to alleviate the tedium, the endless bus rides were becoming intolerable.

To make matters worse, the guys were insufferably reluctant to make necessary pit stops at passing service stations. Whenever Jenny whispered urgently to Lee that she needed to use a restroom, he was just as likely to stop in the desert beside a cactus or in some woods beside a tree. The men seemed to have no qualms about using the great outdoors for such purposes, but for Jenny, the embarrassment was excruciating.

The band celebrated Thanksgiving Day in a weather-beaten, ranch-style café in Longview, Texas, consuming steak instead of turkey, and chili instead of stuffing. It was the worst Thanksgiving of Jenny's life. She had never felt so homesick. They spent the night at a local motel. Jenny worked up her courage to call home from the pay phone in the lobby. But no one answered. They were probably having a big family dinner with Knowl and Annie, but Jenny couldn't bring herself to dial Annie's number. Confronting everyone would stir up too much pain.

Danny, too, phoned home. Jenny knew immediately by his expression that it had been a mistake. "My dad answered," he told her as he dropped the receiver back in its cradle. "He started yelling at me and telling me how much we've hurt our families, and how I've violated your purity—can you believe that one? Being accused of something I haven't even done?—and we'd better get home if we know what's good for us."

"What did you say?"

"You heard me. I told him I'd call again at Christmas. Maybe. Then I hung up."

"Does he have any idea where we are?"

"He made a couple of guesses, but he was wrong, and I'm not about to tell him. He just knows we're still traveling. We could be anywhere. That's the beauty of it."

Jenny didn't reply. For her, the beauty of traveling had lost its luster.

But if there was one bright spot, it was Dallas, their next stop. Callan had scheduled the Bell Tones for a weekend performance at a large municipal auditorium, for which they were being paid handsomely, so he had booked them at a luxury hotel just off Highway 80. Luxury, meaning the rooms were neat and clean and had working phones and television sets, and the bathrooms boasted real porcelain tubs, without the roaches! The hotel also had an outdoor, heart-shaped swimming pool surrounded by exotic trees and shrubs. Jenny was in her glory.

After a rousingly successful Friday night performance, while the rest of the band celebrated in a nearby tavern, Jenny and Danny went back to their rooms, put on their swimsuits and enjoyed a midnight swim in the heated pool. It was really too cold for swimming, the late November air brisk and biting. But they swam anyway, and Jenny felt more alive and invigorated than she had in weeks.

When they were tired of swimming, they sat on the edge of the pool, dangling their legs in the water, plush towels around their shoulders, and talked. It was like old times. All the tension and animosity they had felt in recent days evaporated.

At first they talked about neutral topics, like how much they both liked Dallas. "I picked up some literature in the hotel lobby on the local attractions and universities," Danny told her. "Never know when I can use this stuff."

But after a while he broached the subject of Callan, his tone turning icy, truculent. "So what's it like dating Cal?"

She answered with an edge of defiance. "I'm not dating him."

"He considers you his girl."

"We're friends, that's all. We talk. We laugh. We have fun together."

"He hasn't made any moves on you?"

"Since the bus incident, he's been quite polite. He respects me."

"Sure. He thinks you have a future together!"

"Whose fault is that, Danny? That night when he asked for your blessing, you said nothing."

"And I've been paying for it ever since. Every time I see him touch you, I cringe."

"Then tell him. It's not too late."

"I will. Soon. Maybe next week."

"We'll be flying to Hawaii, Danny. I want to enjoy the beauty of the islands with you, not Callan. I want you beside me when I stand at Pearl Harbor and see the place where my father died."

"I'll be there with you, Jen. I promise." Danny slipped his arm around her and drew her close. They were both cold and shivering, their hair wet and tangled, their skin turning to goose flesh.

She laid her head on his shoulder and sighed. "Oh, Danny, there's so much I've wanted to talk to you about lately, but we never have time alone, especially now that Cal thinks I'm his girl."

"I know, Jen. I feel the same way. I'm constantly thinking of things I'm dying to tell you, but you're always off with him."

"I'm not with him now. Tell me, Danny. I'm listening. Whatever you want to say."

He chuckled, sounding almost bashful. "When you put me on the spot, my mind goes blank. Later, when I'm alone, it'll come to me. All the raunchy stuff I'm feeling."

"What stuff, Danny?"

He seized her hand and pressed it to his cheek. "I don't know, Jen. I feel all this turmoil inside. It's like I want so bad for my voice to be heard. I'm dying to be the lead singer in our band; I want my record to hit the top of the charts; I want so much. And yet, as hard as I'm trying, I don't know what I'm supposed to be saying. It's stupid, isn't it? I want my voice to be heard, but I don't know what I'm supposed to say. I have no answers; all I have are questions."

"That's how most of us are, Danny. Tons of questions; few answers."

"There's something else bothering me, Jen. It's real strange."

"Tell me."

"You won't laugh?"

"I promise."

He cleared his throat. "Okay, here it is. No matter what I do, I can't seem to get my father out of my head."

"Your father?"

"Yeah. I thought when I left home, that would be the end of it; I'd be on my own, my own man; I'd feel this total separation from my father's life. But he's always with me, Jen. I hear his voice in my thoughts; whatever I do, I feel his approval or disapproval."

"Mainly his disapproval, I bet."

"But isn't it crazy? It's like he's with me wherever I go, walking with me in my shoes, seeing the world through my eyes, experiencing everything I experience, and constantly giving me his opinion about everything. It's driving me nuts, Jen. How do I cut him out of me? How can I ever be a grown man if I'm constantly answering to him in my mind?"

She nuzzled her cheek against his chest. "I don't know, Danny. I've spent my life wishing my father was in my head, in my heart, instead of this empty feeling, this silent, gaping hole inside me. I'd love to hear the sound of my father's voice. I wouldn't care what he said, if I could hear him, just once."

"So maybe I shouldn't complain about my dad, huh?"

"I can't answer that for you, Danny. All I can tell you is how I feel. I'd give anything to make the emptiness go away."

Danny tilted her face up to his. Wet tendrils of hair clung to his forehead; his lashes were wet, his eyes glistening. His dark, brooding gaze held her spellbound. "I can't give you your father, Jen, but I can give you all the love in my heart." He held the back of her head and brought his mouth down on hers, kissing her with a deep, hungry passion. She found herself kissing him back with a delicious urgency she hadn't imagined.

A familiar voice shattered the stillness; it exploded with outrage and astonishment. "Jenny, what in the name of heaven are you doing?"

Danny released her. Jenny whirled around and looked up, her heart racing. Callan Swan stood at the edge of the pool staring down at her, his mouth twisted, his dark eyes flaming. He was still wearing the shiny mohair suit he had performed in and was clutching a bottle of beer in his right hand. There was a thickness in his voice, almost a slur. "Well, I've heard of kissing cousins, but this is absurd!"

Jenny and Danny scrambled to their feet. Jenny wrapped her towel around her. "Cal, I didn't expect you—"

"That's obvious." He stepped forward, his eyes cold as steel. "Is someone going to tell me what's going on here?"

Danny stepped forward and stared Cal down. "I'll tell you. I should have told you from the beginning. Jenny and I are in love."

Cal made a bitter, scoffing sound low in his throat. "You're in love with your cousin? Isn't that a bit, uh—?"

"We're cousins in name only," said Danny, raking his dripping hair back from his forehead. "Jenny and I aren't related by blood. She's no more my cousin than you are."

Cal took a swig of his bottle, swallowing the last of his beer. He pitched the empty bottle into a nearby trash receptacle. "So you two have lied to me from the beginning!"

"Not lied," said Jenny.

"Misrepresented yourselves, then. You must have thought you were very clever. Fooling all of us with your cousin routine. And you, Jenny, making me think we had something going between us."

"I never did anything to lead you on. You pursued me."

"And you didn't bother to set me straight, did you?"

"I wanted to, but—"

"But what, doll baby? You don't have an excuse, do you? And you didn't want to rock the boat either, did you, Danny? Well, now it's too late. That boat of yours has sunk."

"What are talking about, Cal?"

"I'm saying you're out of the band. I won't work with musicians I can't trust."

"You can't do that. You're already working at a disadvantage without Emmett. You need me."

"I don't need anyone, Mr. DiCaprio."

"What about my songs? Half the stuff you're using now is mine."

"And you'll be duly compensated. My attorney will make sure everything is equitable. Meanwhile, go get your stuff off the bus and get out of here. You're finished."

Jenny rushed forward and clutched Cal's lapels. "No, Cal, please! You can't let him go. Don't do this!"

Cal seized Jenny's wrists and held them firm. "Go get dressed, Jenny. You need your beauty rest. We have a show to do tomorrow night."

He released her and she stepped back and looked at Danny, as if to ask, *What do you want me to do?*

Danny nodded, his expression grim. "Do as he says, Jen. Go to your room. Get some sleep. Don't worry about me."

She approached him and touched his mussed hair, fingering the damp tendrils. "I'll come with you, Danny."

He shook her off. "No. You stay with the band. There's no reason for you to leave. You'll be in Hawaii next week. You've got to see Pearl Harbor."

She gave him an impulsive embrace, tears starting in her eyes. "Cal will change his mind. I know he will. I'll talk to him. Don't worry, Danny. You'll be back with us before you know it."

"Sure. Sure, I will." Danny gently pushed her away and started toward the hotel, sidestepping Cal. Looking back, he swung his towel over his head and said with a hint of rancor, "Keep in touch, Jen. And don't give up until you've found your dream."

15

December 7, 1960

After spending half a week in Hawaii, Jenny had to admit it was everything she had anticipated—a paradoxical blend of glistening, marble-white hotels and modern high-rise buildings rising up out of a primeval land lush with exotic vegetation. She loved the great, bold splashes of blood-red bougainvillea, the delicate white orchids etched with crimson and purple, and the lush, blossoming hibiscus.

In fact, everywhere Jenny looked from her sixth-floor hotel balcony, she saw breathtaking beauty—emerald-green plants and flora exploding with a myriad of brilliant colors, towering, graceful palm trees with bushy crowns silhouetted against a salmon-pink dawn, and endless ribbons of luxuriant beaches, smooth and pristine as buttermilk. But until this morning Jenny hadn't had nearly enough time to appreciate this tropical paradise.

The band had arrived in Honolulu on Friday morning, rehearsed that afternoon, then played a full weekend engagement at a local serviceman's club, followed by a two-nighter at one of Honolulu's luxury beachfront hotels. With more rehearsals sandwiched between performances, there had been only one afternoon to enjoy the sun and surf.

After an hour of swimming, they were invited to a luau on Waikiki Beach, where they sampled succulent pork from a whole, red-bronzed pig roasted in a pit of hot rocks. They tried several native dishes, including *poi,* which Jenny didn't care for, and *laulau,* made of chopped taro leaf and chicken wrapped in ti leaves and steamed over a fire. As they ate, native hula dancers entertained them and showered them with fragrant, colorful leis. Topping off the feast was papaya stuffed with shrimp salad, and fresh pineapple with shredded coconut and passion fruit. It was an afternoon Jenny would always remember, and it would have been perfect if only Danny had been with her.

Today, at last, the band's schedule was open again for some relaxation and sightseeing before their evening flight back to the mainland. So now, at dawn, Jenny was standing on her balcony in her floral-print muu-muu, sipping a chilled fruit punch of papaya and guava nectar, and savoring the most beautiful spot on earth.

But the truth was, without Danny at her side, Hawaii might as well have been the Sahara Desert. And now that she had time to reflect, she realized how deeply conflicted she felt.

She had left Danny in Dallas, convinced Callan would realize his error in judgment and send for him in a day or so. But it had been over a week now and Callan showed no sign of regretting his decision to banish Danny from the band.

Jenny was the only one feeling regrets. Maybe she should have stayed with Danny, even though he urged her to go on. If she had threatened to leave the band, too, perhaps Callan would have capitulated and she and Danny would still be together.

With Danny out of the picture, Cal seemed even more entrenched in his belief that Jenny was his steady girl. While he hadn't forced himself on her in a physical sense, he was becoming more familiar and intimate with her in little ways. Like the way he touched her hair, her arm, or her face when they were rehearsing or hashing out the arrangement of a song. And the way he made a point of sitting with her every chance he had—on their flight from Los Angeles to Honolulu, at meals, even at the luau.

He had followed her into the ocean and played water tag, as if they were children, but she sensed that his real motive was physical closeness. Lately he was always there beside her, complimenting her, attending to her needs like a devoted suitor, making small talk or jokes, so solicitous at times she felt she could hardly breathe.

And yet, why was it she did nothing to stop him, said nothing to discourage him, never protested his attentions? Was it because the band was her only way to get to Hawaii? But now that she was safely on the island, to her own bafflement she passively accepted Cal's solicitude. Was she simply growing resigned to the circumstances fate had dealt her?

Even now, as she sipped her fruit punch and watched the pink dawn dissolve into a pale, powder blue sky, she realized she was becoming more withdrawn, remote, reclusive. A private war raged in her soul. She loved Danny but she was here in Hawaii with Callan. Always with Callan.

Without Danny or Emmett to turn to, she had no one but Callan, and maybe he was the one she was meant to be with. He seemed convinced they belonged together. Perhaps he was right; perhaps it would just be a matter of time before she felt about Cal the way she had felt about Danny. But even as the thought entered her mind, she knew it would never be true. Danny DiCaprio was the only man she would ever love. But he wasn't here when she needed him. And Callan was.

Jenny removed a wedge of fresh pineapple from the rim of her glass and nibbled it absently. It was tart and sweet all at once and made her pucker. Callan was that way, a confusing knot of contradictions, sweet at times, yet caustic; kind, yet cunning and cynical. It wasn't as if she didn't care about him; she did. If she admitted it, at times she even felt a physical attraction for him. To her own astonishment, when they were frolicking in the ocean, he had grabbed her around the waist and for a moment she had hoped he would pull her into his arms and kiss her. But the moment passed and she pulled away before either of them could act on their instincts. No matter what, she couldn't betray Danny.

But a worrisome idea struck her. Maybe she was foolishly holding on to her past with Danny when Cal was her future. Maybe Cal was the one who could fill the empty space inside her that nothing seemed to fill.

Even this morning, of all mornings, she was carrying on the argument in her head, trying to convince herself. Everyone said she and Callan made a perfect couple. People said their voices blended like the voices of angels. Since they had started singing together, the band's popularity had soared. Their record was being played on radio stations all across America.

What did it all mean? Was she foolish to fight providence? The questions kept bombarding her, even as her heart ached for Danny. No wonder she had welcomed the band's busy schedule; her inner turmoil ceased only when she was on stage performing.

But today there was another reason for her mounting sense of unrest. She would be visiting Pearl Harbor, her father's watery grave. All of her life she had wanted to see firsthand that terrible spot where her father had lost his life; she had played it over in her mind a hundred times, convinced it was the only way she would ever find peace of mind and a sense of closure.

But now that the day was actually here, she dreaded facing her father's ghost. What if confronting his death only made matters worse? Or what if it made no difference at all? What if that lonely vacuum in her soul remained and nothing could ever fill it?

It would be different if she had Danny at her side. He would know what to say and do to make her feel at ease; he would give her the courage to face her father's death. He would hold her in his arms and convince her everything would be all right, no matter how painful the moment was.

But Danny wasn't here; he might never be in her life again. So she might as well get used to facing the future alone, even the next few hours of this most significant day, December 7, nineteen years exactly since the bombs fell.

Jenny dressed quickly in a pleated skirt and angora sweater. She flagged a taxi outside her hotel, instructing the driver to take her to Pearl Harbor. She had no choice but to go alone. The rest of the band would be sleeping in after a night of partying. Regardless, she didn't want them knowing about her lonely pilgrimage. This was something she had to do by herself; it would be the most painful moment of her life, and perhaps the most meaningful.

Whatever happened, it was the closest she would ever be to the father she had never known. It meant everything just knowing his body was there beneath the water in the twisted wreckage of his ship. Surely, being so close to his physical remains, she would sense his spirit as well. It was a crazy idea, but maybe he had been waiting all these years for her, his only child, to come to him and say good-bye, so he could at last be free.

The taxi driver, a native Hawaiian, kept up a steady stream of conversation while driving the five-plus miles west of Honolulu to the southern coast of Oahu. "Do you not know? Pearl Harbor is *Wai Momi* in Hawaiian," he said. "Means 'pearl waters,' for all the pearl oysters once there."

"I didn't know," said Jenny.

"You never come here before?"

"No, never."

"When you see Pearl Harbor, it is something you never forget."

"I'm sure I won't," she murmured.

"Pearl Harbor is still naval base of United States. Is headquarters for Pacific Fleet. You hear of Pacific Fleet?"

"Yes," she said distractedly. They were crossing Hickam Field now and approaching the harbor. To her surprise, crowds of people were milling about. Somehow, she had expected to be alone, so she could express her feelings to her father privately. "Why are all the people here?" she asked in dismay.

The swarthy, sun-wrinkled driver looked around and gave her a bemused look that said surely she must know the answer to such an obvious question. "This anniversary of Japanese bombing. Nineteen years ago today. Many people come to pay respects."

Of course! She sank back in the seat and sighed heavily. "That's why I chose today too. But I didn't stop to think about it being so crowded."

The driver pulled up beside the curb, checked the meter, and announced the fare. She handed him several bills. He pocketed the money, stepped out, and opened her door. "If you hurry, miss, you get ticket for cruise boat to Ford Island."

"Ford Island?"

"Where you see battleship *Arizona* under water. See? Boat already at dock. Called the *Adventure*. It fill up fast today. Hold maybe 150 passengers. It go at 9:30. Not again till 1:30. Better hurry."

"Thanks!" she called back, breaking into a run. After standing in line for over ten minutes, she managed to get one of the last tickets. Breathlessly she joined the throng filing onto the narrow gangplank of the small, jaunty craft bobbing in the clover-shaped harbor. Once on board, she wended her way through the solemn-faced crowd, passing a sandwich and soft drink bar, and made her way to the starboard side of the boat to stand at the rail. Here she could breathe the fresh, briny air of the Pacific and catch a bird's eye view of the swelling sea.

As the engine coughed and began its high-pitched hum, Jenny felt the craft lurch slightly; she could feel its steady, droning vibration as it began moving slowly over the rolling water. Her clammy palms closed around the metal rail. *Hold on tight,* she told herself. *This could be the ride of your life.*

Static broke over the loud speaker, followed by a deep masculine voice. "Ladies and gentlemen, welcome aboard the *Adventure* on this most momentous of days. Nineteen years ago this morning, at about 7:50 A.M., the first wave of 183 Japanese bombers, torpedo planes, and fighter planes made their sneak attack on Pearl Harbor. Their goal? To destroy the ships on Battleship Row and the planes at the Naval Air Station and Hickam Field and Wheeler Field."

Jenny stole a glance at the face of the man beside her, an Oriental face.

The narrator went on. "An hour later a second wave of 168 Japanese planes attacked. When the smoke cleared, several battleships had been destroyed and many others damaged. Three-hundred forty-seven aircraft were decimated."

The boat was approaching a flagpole looming above the water just off the tip of Ford Island. "Over 2,300 military personnel were killed," the man said, "including 1,177 still entombed in the shadowy depths of the *Arizona* right here below us."

And my father's one of them, Jenny thought darkly. *I never got to hear his voice or feel his arms around me, because his life ended here before I was born.*

Suddenly the motor stalled and the craft wafted in place, tossed rhythmically by gentle, splashing waves. As a color guard raised the American flag to the top of the mast, the sonorous voice broke again from the loud speaker. "Ladies and gentlemen, we are over the grave site of the battleship *Arizona*. Even as she was being attacked, she hoisted her flag and continued to fly it in the face of her enemies. To this day, in her honor, her flag is raised and lowered every morning and evening."

Jenny's eyes welled with tears as she scanned the bronze plaque at the foot of the flagpole. The words branded themselves on her heart, searing her emotions, prompting more tears.

DEDICATED TO THE ETERNAL MEMORY
OF OUR GALLANT SHIPMATES IN THE USS ARIZONA
WHO GAVE THEIR LIVES IN ACTION
7 DECEMBER 1941 . . .
MAY GOD MAKE HIS FACE TO SHINE UPON THEM
AND GRANT THEM PEACE

Jenny blocked out the man's voice and the jostling, crowded humanity around her, blocked out the entire world, in fact, focusing her gaze only on the ghostly hulk beneath the clear, blue-green waters. Her father's ship. Her father's grave. He was there, so close, so far. Chilton "Chip" Reed.

God, it isn't fair! Why did You rob me of my father? Why did he have to die?

Jenny closed her eyes and allowed the flitting, black-and-white images of old newsreels of that fateful morning to resurrect themselves on the screen of her mind. She could see great, billowing black smoke rising like cumulus clouds on the horizon, turning day to night, as if the devil himself had opened the pits of hell and unleashed its sulphurous brimstone. She envisioned the huge, twisted carcasses of ships listing in the flaming waters like blackened skeletons of prehistoric behemoths sinking slowly in the oil-soaked, blood-washed waters.

Her father was somewhere below in that monstrous, rusting, phantom vessel. He would never be closer to Jenny than he was at this moment. Maybe somehow he knew she was here, seeking him out, searching for a way to meld past and present, to connect emotionally with the father who gave her life.

Another wellspring of tears blurred Jenny's vision. "I love you, Daddy," she whispered, her lips barely moving. "I've always loved you. And missed you. There's an enormous space in my heart just for you.

Nothing will ever fill it." She hugged herself, a damp breeze seeping through her angora sweater.

"Daddy, I was born on your birthday," she went on softly, the words hardly passing her lips. "May 13. Did you know that? I bet I'm just like you. Two peas in a pod. I must be like you. I'm not like Mama. We've never gotten along. Am I like you, Daddy? How will I ever know? How can I know who I am if I never know who you were?"

A sob tore at her throat. She choked it back and sniffed noisily, then glanced around, ashamed that someone might have seen her weeping. But no one was looking her way. As crowded as they were on this little boat, everyone was caught up in his own private thoughts and memories.

Jenny stared again at the dark, elusive shadow rippling below the water's surface. She had hoped to come here and feel some sort of satisfaction in seeing where her father had died; a feeling that life had come full circle, so that she could put the gnawing questions behind her and move on. But, if anything, her pain was greater. The loss was deeper, and the emptiness seemed even more pervasive than before.

"Oh, Daddy, I need you!" she cried aloud, tears streaming down her cheeks. "I need you so much! Why did you have to die!"

"*I'm* here, Jenny. Will I do?" A man's deep, resonant voice, warmly familiar, comforting, stirred buried memories and emotions.

Jenny whirled around and stared up into the rugged, tearful face of her stepfather. "Papa Robert!"

"Hello, Jenny." He towered over her, broad-shouldered, barrel-chested, in a navy crew-neck sweater and slacks, his dark, curly hair ruffled by the breeze, his clear blue eyes luminous with love.

She reached back and gripped the railing, steadying herself, her knees weak. "What are you doing here, Papa?"

He reached out tentatively and touched her shoulder, her wind-blown hair. "I came to find you."

"How? No one knew—"

"We've been trying to track you and Danny down for months. We were always one step behind. But a few weeks ago your Grandma Betty saw you on that dance show, *American Bandstand*."

"She saw us? Oh, I'm glad. I had hoped she was watching."

"We didn't believe her at first, but then we heard reports from others who saw you. From the show we learned the name of your band, and our detectives traced you here to Hawaii."

"When did you get here, Papa?"

"I flew in this morning. The desk clerk at your hotel confirmed that you were here at Pearl. I figured you would be. It's where I wanted to be today too."

"But I never saw you get on the boat. Did you see me?"

"I saw you buy your ticket. I boarded shortly after you did, but I stayed back out of the way. I didn't want to intrude on your thoughts. I knew you needed this time alone."

Her voice quavered. "I did, but it didn't help."

Robert nodded. The lines in his face had deepened since she'd last seen him. He looked older, weary. "The pain of losing someone is too big a burden to release all at once, Jenny. I know. We thought we had lost you."

"I'm sorry, Papa Robert." Her chin puckered and her lower lip trembled. "Danny and I never meant to worry you."

He opened his arms and she sank against his chest, her raw emotions erupting in convulsive sobs. He held her close and patted her back, the way he had consoled her as a child. "We'll talk about it later, Jenny. We have a lot to iron out. But right now . . . Pearl Harbor has our hearts."

They both leaned against the rail and gazed out at the sea, his arm loosely around her shoulder. "I keep trying to imagine what it must have been like that morning for my father," she said quietly. "What was he doing when the Japanese attacked? Was he afraid? How exactly did he die? Was he thinking about Mama and his upcoming wedding? Did he have the slightest idea about me? Would he have wanted me?"

Robert leaned over and brushed a kiss on her forehead. "Oh, I'm sure he would have wanted you, Jenny. He would have loved you very much."

"Maybe, but I'll never know for sure. You see, Papa? I have all these questions and no answers. And the worst thing is, I'll never have answers, because my father is dead."

He gently massaged her shoulder. "I can't give you answers about your father, Jenny. But I can tell you what it was like for me the morning the Japs attacked. If you want to know."

She looked up at him and studied the solemn furrows in his forehead. "You've never talked about it before. I knew you were stationed here during the bombing, but that's all I knew."

A grim smile flickered on his lips. "Do you want to hear my story?"

She returned the smile, her lower lip quivering again. "More than anything, Papa."

He cleared his throat as if about to give a speech. "I was stationed aboard the *USS Nevada*, just east of Ford Island. We were moored astern of the *Arizona*."

"You could have known my dad. Could have seen him."

"Might have. At the serviceman's club. The commissary. In town. On the beach. Could be."

"What were you doing that morning?"

His voice took on a nostalgic tone. "I got up early. It was a beautiful day. A little overcast, but nice. Lots of guys slept in, but not me."

"What were you doing when the bombs hit? Something brave—?"

He chuckled ruefully and scratched his head. "To tell you the truth, I was sitting at my desk addressing Christmas cards. I heard a rumbling sound. Airplanes in a dive. I looked out my window and saw two planes. Figured they were our planes taking practice dives. Until I saw the red circles on their wings. The Rising Sun. Torpedo planes heading for Battleship Row."

"You actually saw them?"

He nodded grimly. "They hit the *West Virginia* first, then the *Oklahoma* and *California*. There was outright pandemonium. Air raid sirens blowing, ship horns sounding. I felt the explosion and ran topside. Guys were running every which way, shouting, screaming, bullets whizzing by our heads like angry bees. The thing I remember—our ship's band was playing our national anthem, and they kept right on playing through it all."

"What about my father's ship?" she asked, her voice hushed.

Robert waited a long minute before answering. Jenny could hear the announcer's voice coming again over the loud speaker, but his words seemed distant, remote. The only words she heard were Robert's. "I saw the *Arizona* attacked first by torpedoes, then bombers. Hundreds of men were thrown overboard. We scrambled around like crazy trying to fish them out of that flaming sea. We rescued some, but . . ."

"But not my father."

"No, Jenny. I'm sorry. I would give anything to have rescued your father."

She swallowed another sob. "I know you would."

"The *Arizona* sank like lead with most of its men still aboard. We realized we were the only ship still in commission, so we headed out to sea. But the Japs spotted us and bombed us. We ran our ship aground so we wouldn't block the harbor."

"Is that when you hurt your leg?"

"Yes. Shrapnel got me. I nearly lost my leg, and that's how I got my limp."

"It's so much a part of you I never notice it."

Robert chuckled. "I only notice it when the weather turns damp. I feel the coldness all the way to the bone."

She looked up at him and searched his eyes, her voice filled with alarm. "You could have been killed like my father."

His lips tightened. "I could have. For a long time I felt guilty for surviving when so many of my buddies died. I nearly let alcohol finish the job the war started. That's when I stumbled drunk into a Salvation Army Rescue Mission in California and got my life straightened out with God."

"Isn't that where you met Annie?"

"Right. And eventually she introduced me to your mother." His tone grew wistful. "My darling, unpredictable Catherine."

"And you and Mother fell in love."

He smiled. "The rest is history, as they say."

Jenny gazed out at the cerulean waters. The engine had started again and the boat was beginning to turn back toward shore. She looked up at Robert. "What now?"

He gently squeezed her shoulder. "We go home."

She pulled back. "I can't."

"Why not?"

"I'm with the band. We have a schedule. Callan is counting on me. We're flying back to Los Angeles tonight. I'm committed, Papa. We have gigs all over Southern California."

Robert's expression clouded. "I promised your mother I'd bring you home."

Jenny averted her gaze. "I can't face Mama. She'll never forgive me. She must be terribly angry with me."

"Outwardly maybe. Inside, she's worried sick. She loves you very much, Jen. And she misses you. We all do."

Jenny bit her lower lip. "I'm sorry, but I have a hard time believing Mama's all broken up."

"She is, Jen. Take my word for it." Robert stepped closer, his tone confidential. "There's something else, sweetheart. I didn't want to get into it here, but I guess there's no choice."

"No choice? What do you mean?"

"I don't want to upset you . . ."

She looked sharply at him. "Upset me? What's wrong? Is Mama okay?"

Robert's breath caught slightly. "It's your grandmother."

"Which one?"

"Grandma Betty."

Jenny's heart hammered. "What about Grandma Betty?"

Robert circled her shoulder and drew her close. "There's no easy way to tell you this, honey. I know you and your grandmother have always been close. There's no one else she wants to see, no one else she'll listen to. That's why—don't you see?—I've got to take you home. Now. Tonight. There's not much time."

Tears brimmed in Jenny's eyes. She didn't want to hear this. But somehow she knew, she already knew. "Oh, Papa Robert, no!"

He held her, his hand stroking her hair. "I'm sorry, Jenny. It's her heart. The doctors say there's nothing more they can do. Your grandmother is dying."

16

Willowbrook in December was snowy and cold, with drifts piled mountain-high on the curbs and icicles as long as harpoons hanging from frosty windows. On the train with Papa Robert, all the way from Chicago, Jenny had stared out the window watching the blinding flurries, the white, barren fields, the little towns groaning under their heavy blankets of snow. She had almost forgotten what winter was like. Lord, get me back to Hawaii!

The minute they stepped off the train at the Willowbrook depot, she felt the wind whip straight through her coat and clothes and wrap icy fingers around her bones. She shivered and hugged herself, but the chill seeped under her skin just the same. *Please, Lord, give me the warm, sun-spangled island I left behind!*

Now Jenny was heading home in Papa Robert's roomy Packard. A cold, pale sun was setting in a gunmetal sky. Overhead, violet-black shadows were stealing in like interlopers in gauzy shrouds. It would be pitch dark soon, except for a profusion of stars glinting like ice chips.

It seemed strange to be home again. Jenny felt oddly disoriented, as if, in a matter of moments, she had been uprooted from her normal life and set down in another time and place. Everything was familiar—the old red brick station, the faces of her family, the cobbled streets of her hometown. And yet nothing seemed quite real. She felt as if she were floating in a dream. Was she really living this moment or was her mind playing tricks, summoning old memories and convincing her they were new?

The past twenty-four hours were already compressed into a passel of jumbled images: The bitter confrontation with Callan as they separated. The long, sleepless flight from Honolulu to Chicago with Papa Robert. The grinding train ride to Willowbrook. Stepping off the train and seeing Mama and Laura and Knowl and Annie waiting, welcoming her home as if she had just been off to school or on vacation somewhere; everyone laughing and crying with joy and relief to have her back again.

But as Papa Robert headed home, steering gingerly over the icy streets, Jenny's own emotions were riding a roller coaster. She hadn't realized how much she missed everyone until she saw them again, even Mama. Especially Mama. The enormity of what she had done—running away without letting her family know where she was—struck her with a swift, aching reality. For four months she had all but put her family out of her mind, convinced herself they would go on and be fine without her. Now, seeing them again, seeing the love and concern in their faces, she sensed how deeply she had hurt them, and the shame of it burned inside her.

To Jenny's amazement, even her annoying younger sister seemed thrilled to have her back. In the backseat, Laura held Jenny's hand and talked nonstop, her voice coming in quick, breathless bursts. "I can't wait to show you my room, Jenny. Grandmother Anna made me a new comforter and curtains. Lavender. My favorite color."

Laura was wearing a heavy wool coat with a fur collar that made it look like she had no neck. Even in the streaks of light and dark passing through the car window, Jenny could see Laura's eyes flash with excitement; her face looked thinner, more angular than Jenny remembered. She was losing that baby-fat look, growing up already.

"And Grandma Betty and I saw you on television," Laura rushed on eagerly in her breathy, singsong voice. "But nobody believed us. Until the neighbors called and said they saw you too." She snuggled closer to Jenny. "You and Danny and your band were great. And that Callan Swan is so cute. Do you like him, Jenny?" Laura's hazel eyes danced. "I bet he likes you a whole lot. When you two were singing, you looked like you were in love. Are you in love with him, Jenny? Why don't you marry him? Then I can meet him and get his autograph."

Jenny finally got a word in. "Goodness, Laura, I can get you his autograph without marrying him."

"Swell! The girls at school think it's so neat you're singing with a rock 'n' roll band. We heard your song on the radio too—the one Danny wrote. 'Born to Love You.' I just love that song, Jenny. Will you sing it for me sometime? Oh, Jenny, I'm so glad you came home."

The mention of Danny's name carved a new ache in Jenny's heart. She hadn't heard from him since the band left him in Dallas. Well over a week ago. She wasn't even sure how to reach him. Surely he'd want to know she had left the band and come home.

"Mama," she ventured, knowing it was a touchy subject, "has anybody heard anything from Danny?"

Her mother looked around from the front seat and said coolly, "Now that's a fine question. We all thought he was with you until Robert got to Hawaii and found out he wasn't with the band anymore."

"Then nobody's heard from him?" Jenny persisted.

"It's no wonder. He's probably too ashamed to face us after making you run off with him and live a life of . . . of—"

"We were wrong to run away, Mama, but Danny and I didn't do anything wrong like you mean."

"I hope not. I pray not."

"Catherine," said Robert, "Jenny asked you whether we've heard from Danny."

"Well, the fact is, Bethany Rose got a letter from him today. She came over to watch Grandma Betty while we came to pick you up."

"Danny wrote her a letter?"

"Hardly a letter. Just a few lines. But she was beside herself with relief."

"What did he say?"

"Just that he was staying in Dallas and enrolling in a university there for the winter classes. Not a word about you. Thank God, we'd already tracked you down. But it looks like he came to his senses about going to college instead of playing in that horrid rock 'n' roll band."

Jenny felt her cheeks grow crimson. "It's not horrid, Mama. And Danny would never give up the band. He's going back with the Bell Tones. Just as I am."

"Well, I promised Robert we wouldn't talk tonight about the band and your running away. But we're going to have a long talk about it one of these days, daughter. A real long talk."

"I know, Mama. I'm sorry. I was wrong to run away like that and not tell you."

"I'm glad you came to your senses. But it's not something we can just forget about. You've brought a lot of grief to this family."

"I'm sorry, Mama. I don't know what else to say."

"Catherine," said Robert, "we agreed not to get into this tonight."

"I know. I can't help it. All these feelings just—"

"Right now we've got to concentrate on your mother."

"Mama, how is Grandma Betty? Papa Robert says she's real sick."

"She is, honey. The doctors don't hold out much hope. But she knows you're coming. I told her."

"Papa Robert said it's her heart. What happened?"

"Oh, it's her heart, all right. All that boozing she did all those years took its toll."

"Don't say that, Mama. We have to forgive her for that." Jenny's throat tightened. She could feel tears gathering. "Does she know she's . . . dying?"

Mama's voice sounded as pained as Jenny's. "She refuses to talk about it. You know your grandma. Stubborn and close-mouthed as they come. Especially around me."

"You and Grandma never got along," said Jenny.

"It's not like I haven't tried. Your grandma and I—we're like oil and water. Nothing I do pleases her. It's been that way all my life. You're the only one she'll talk to. I'm counting on you getting through to her, Jenny."

"Getting through? How?"

Her mother didn't answer right away. When she did, she sounded hesitant, groping for the right words. "You know, Jenny. About heaven. God. Where she's going when she dies. Your grandma's never gone to church, never talked about what she believes. Maybe she'll talk to you."

Jenny turned from Laura's curious eyes and gazed out the side window. They were driving along Honeysuckle Lane now, passing Knowl and Annie's stately house. It was strung with colored lights and looked like an old-fashioned Christmas card. Jenny always felt a nostalgic tug in her heart when she saw that house. She could never forget that it had been her home once, for the brief time she was Annie's little girl.

"Did you hear me, Jenny? I asked you a question."

"I didn't hear a question, Mama."

"I asked if you'd talk to your grandmother. You're the only one she'll listen to."

They were turning on Maypole Drive now. Through the night shadows, Jenny could see her house coming into view. It had no lights, except the stark porch light. It was a nice house, neat, nicely kept, familiar, and yet a poor imitation of Annie's house; Jenny had never felt the same emotional connection with it. And yet she did feel something, a response, seeing it now in the shadows. She had missed it; it was home, the only home besides Annie's she had ever known. Robert pulled into the driveway and turned off the engine and Jenny sat still, waiting, feeling a mixture of expectancy and dread.

"Jenny? Are you deliberately avoiding my question?" The streetlight caught her mother's scowl as she looked back at Jenny. "I'd appreciate an answer, young lady."

Jenny shifted uncomfortably. All she wanted to do was go inside and see her grandmother, and then run to her room and collapse in her own bed and sleep until noon tomorrow. "I don't know, Mama," she said solemnly. "I wouldn't know what to say to Grandma. You and Robert are the religious ones."

Her mother refused to back down. "Well, you think about it, Jenny. Your grandmother's eternal destiny is at stake. But she rejects anything I say. Always has, always will." Jenny heard the hurt and envy in her mother's voice as she said, "You're the only one who can help her. She dotes on you, you know that. The sun rises and sets on you. The least you can do is talk to her."

"Please, Mama, I told you. I'm no good at that."

"Well, then, sing 'Jesus Loves Me.' Read from the Bible. Do something. Do anything you can to reach her, Jen. She'll listen to you. In her eyes you can do no wrong. Please, honey. It's not like I'm asking for the moon."

You're doing it already, Mama, Jenny wanted to cry. *Pressuring me to do things your way and be something you think I should be. This is why I ran away in the first place. Please, don't make me regret coming home!*

"Stop it, Catherine," said Robert, opening the car door. "We're all tired. We can talk about it tomorrow. Let's just get inside before we all freeze to death."

"I was only . . ."

"I know, Cath. Come on. It's been a long day for all of us."

They got out of the car and crunched through the rutted, hard-packed snow in the driveway over to the sidewalk where the drifts had been cleared, except for a fine, powdery dusting of new snow. They climbed the steps to the sprawling porch and Robert unlocked the door. The minute Jenny stepped inside she breathed in the warm, familiar smells of home—bacon and onions, lemon oil, cedar wood, and a dozen other faint, indefinable smells that stirred her emotions more than she could have imagined.

"Do you want something to eat, Jenny? Some hot chocolate?" asked her mother.

"No, I want to see Grandma," she said, stomping snow from her shoes and shrugging out of her coat.

"It's late. She's probably asleep. Maybe you should wait till morning."

Jenny headed for the stairs. "I can't wait, Mama. I'll just look in on her."

"Jenny," cautioned Robert, "she's not the same. She's been very ill."

Jenny hurried up the stairs and strode down the hall to her grandmother's room. Her heart pounded. What would she find? The door was ajar and lamplight cast a sallow streamer into the hallway. Holding her breath, Jenny nudged the door open and padded inside. The room smelled stale, medicinal, overheated. Grandma Betty was lying in her bed still and pale as a corpse, her eyes closed, her cheeks gaunt, her hands lying motionless on the comforter. Her frail body hardly made a ripple in the covers.

Bethany Rose, her long ebony hair hanging in waves over her shoulders, sat in the rocker near the bed, crocheting something. Seeing Jenny, she put her needlework aside, stood up, and hastened over, her arms open. "Jenny, welcome home."

As they embraced, Jenny groped for words. "Grandma Betty—is she . . . she's not—"

"No, don't worry. She's just sleeping."

Jenny emitted a sigh of relief. "Thank God, I'm not too late!"

"Your grandmother's been holding on just to see you."

"I never dreamed she was so sick."

"It started after you left. I think she gave up, let her damaged heart get the best of her."

"I never meant to grieve her." Jenny met Bethany's solemn gaze. "Danny and I never meant to hurt you either. I'm sorry we worried you. Try to understand. We had to go. It was the only way. Will you forgive us?"

"Honey, I have forgiven you. And my son."

"And you don't think evil of us? You don't think we . . ."

"I believed in you," she said simply. "I understand the two of you better than you think. It hasn't been so long since I was your age. I know what that wanderlust is like. I had it myself."

"Danny thought you'd understand. But the reverend—"

"Yes, his father is another story. For a long while he was very upset about Danny joining the band." Bethany smiled, her dark eyes glistening. "But now we're both very hopeful."

"Hopeful?"

"Yes. Didn't your mother tell you?"

"She mentioned a letter . . ."

"Yes, a wonderful letter. From Danny. It came today. He's going to college. Enrolled last week for the winter quarter. He says he plans to stay in Dallas for now."

"Until Callan takes him back with the band," said Jenny. "That could be anytime."

Bethany shook her head. "I got the impression Danny is serious about college. He didn't say a word about going back with the band. In fact, he said he's taking extra classes so he can graduate early."

Jenny stiffened. She didn't want to hear about Danny going to college somewhere far away. But there was no sense in arguing with her family or his. Humor them. Let them believe what they wished. But she had no doubt Danny would drop his classes as soon as Callan invited him back with the band.

Jenny heard a sound from the bed, not words, not a groan, but definitely more than a sigh. She hurried over to the bed and leaned close to her grandmother; she stroked her mussed hair and kissed her lined forehead, catching the over-sweet fragrance of her lilac perfume. "Grandma Betty, it's me, Jenny. Can you hear me?"

The fragile figure stirred, the wrinkled face turning toward Jenny, her glazed eyes opening partway. Her pale lips struggled to form the words. "Jenny . . . is that you?"

"Yes, Grams. I'm home. I came to see you."

Her grandmother's mottled hand lifted off the comforter and moved toward Jenny, then fell short onto the bedding. "Stay with me, child," she rasped.

With hot tears coursing down her face, Jenny clasped her grandmother's arthritic hand in hers and pressed the bony fingers against her wet cheek. "I will, Grams. I'll stay. I won't leave you. Not ever again."

"Promise?"

"Promise."

After a few days back in Willowbrook, Jenny felt as if
her four months on the road had been an incredible
dream, a bizarre, bittersweet illusion, a cruel trick of
her imagination. Surely none of it was real—the terrible malaise of
endless hours on the bus counterbalanced by the thunderous applause
of the crowds and the heady excitement of performing. It seemed now
that she had never left home, that her life was a seamless progression
of the mundane, predictable routine it had always been.

But life wasn't the same; under the surface, everything was radi-
cally different. Jenny had breached her family's trust; even though
little had been said, Jenny saw the questions, the doubts, the disappointment in their faces, felt it in the cautious ways they treated her
now. As if they weren't certain what sort of mercurial creature she
was or whether she might take flight again without notice.

Only her mother was vocal about Jenny's transgression. In little
ways she wheedled Jenny about it day and night, saying, "You know
you broke your grandmother's heart going off like that. No wonder
she's failed so much . . . You broke all our hearts; not that you care;
if you'd cared you would have told us where you were going."

Jenny tried to keep silent, to accept her mother's rebuffs and
harangues as her due punishment, but inside she simmered, wanting
to lash out at the mother she had missed so much and yet could barely

tolerate now. Why couldn't Mama be the mother in her imagination who welcomed her home with forgiveness and unconditional love?

On Jenny's fourth morning home, it all came to a head. Grandma Betty had had a spell with her heart and Dr. Pearson had come to examine her. Robert was at work and Laura at school, so it was just Jenny and her mother waiting in the parlor for the physician's report. Her mother paced the floor, nursing a cup of black coffee. "This could be it," she said, more to herself than to Jenny. "Mama's held on this long, but her heart can't keep on forever. She's just gone downhill since . . ."

"Since I ran away?" countered Jenny, curled on the sofa.

Her mother looked sharply at her. "All right, yes. Since you ran away. This whole house hasn't been the same since then. Not that it seems to matter to you."

"I told you I'm sorry, Mama. What more can I say?"

"Sorry's an easy word to toss around. But you don't act sorry. You act like you were just off at a Sunday school picnic, and everyone should just forget the terrible hole you cut in our lives for four months."

Angry tears scalded Jenny's eyes. "I am sorry I hurt you, but I'm not sorry I went with the band. I know I should have told you, and that's what I'm sorry about. Why can't you forgive me?"

Her mother sat down in the overstuffed chair opposite Jenny and set her cup and saucer on the coffee table. "Because you still don't realize what you did, the grief you caused. I'd like to see some real remorse. Maybe then your grandma wouldn't be dying."

Jenny's anger flared white-hot. "Don't blame Grandma's dying on me, Mama. It's not my fault."

"I didn't say it was."

"That's what I keep hearing. You act like I'm the only one who ever sinned. Well, I'm not."

Her mother's face flushed scarlet as her auburn hair, and her green eyes flashed. "Don't get smart-mouthed with me, young lady!"

"I'm just telling the truth," Jenny cried over a rising sob. "The only reason I'm here on this earth is because of what you did, Mama. Maybe if you hadn't sinned with my father, he wouldn't have died!"

Her mother's face drained of color. She sat forward, her spine stiffening. "Are you saying your father's death was God's way of punishing me?"

"Maybe it was. That's what you're saying about Grandma and me."

"How dare you—!"

Jenny hardly saw the slap coming, but she felt the sting of it against her cheek, and she stared in stunned silence at her mother, who looked back in gaping shock. "Oh, Jenny, I'm sorry! I never meant to—"

Jenny sank back against the sofa cushion and rubbed her cheek. She tried to hold back the flood of tears. Her lower lip quivered; she couldn't speak. It wasn't her reddened cheek that hurt; it was the searing ache inside that no one could see.

Her mother, dissolving in tears, moved swiftly over beside her and offered an awkward embrace. Jenny resisted for a moment, then gave in and welcomed her mother's arms. "I'm sorry, Mama," she wailed. "I didn't mean it about you and my father."

Her mother's voice broke with a sob. "Oh, honey, don't you think I've asked myself that question a million times? Don't you think I've blamed myself for your father dying, for your growing up without your daddy?"

She sat back and looked Jenny square in the face. "I would have gone crazy with guilt if God hadn't forgiven me, Jen. He made me see He wasn't punishing me by taking your daddy. It's just the way things happen. Sometimes I forget and slip back into the old ways. But they aren't God's ways. God's first choice is always to love and forgive us and bring us into fellowship with Him."

"I only said those things because I felt hurt, Mama. I don't believe them."

"Well, I wouldn't blame you if you did. Sometimes I forget about God's forgiveness and start dredging up old wounds. Then I have to scoot back under the umbrella of His grace." She ran her fingertip along Jenny's wet cheek, catching her tears. "I was wrong to accuse you of causing Grandma's ailments. I guess it was my way of striking back at you for leaving us."

More tears came. "I truly am sorry, Mama, for leaving you and hurting you. Please forgive me."

They hugged again. "If you'll forgive me."

"I do." They broke apart and both laughed self-consciously.

"We must look a mess. I'll get us some tissues." Her mother went to the bathroom and returned with a box of Kleenex. She sat down beside Jenny, the box between them. They helped themselves, drying their eyes, blowing their noses. Her mother swept back her burnished hair. "Aren't we a pair? A couple of weeping ninnies."

Jenny wrung her tissue into a white, knotted snake. "We're jittery over Grandma. Worry keeps our emotions on edge."

"And fear. I'm so afraid . . ."

"Of what, Mama?"

"Oh, my goodness, don't get me started." Her mother sat back and brushed at her eyes, smearing what little makeup she wore. She was a beautiful woman, with classic features and a graceful figure, but Jenny saw feathery lines in her face that she hadn't noticed before.

"Tell me, Mama."

She lowered her head in her hands. "I don't know if I can."

"Try, Mama."

The words came at last from somewhere deep, raw, unexplored. "Jenny, baby, I'm scared my mama will die without our ever once being close. And when she's gone it will be like she was never here at all, because I never broke through the wall to her and she never broke through to me. And I'll bury her and it'll be over. Too late to know her. Too late to feel some connection. Too late to know if she really loved me, or if I loved her."

"You do love her, Mama, and she loves you. The two of you just don't know how to show it."

"Like the two of us." Her mother reached over and clasped Jenny's hand. Her skin was cold, her fingers taut. "It's the same with us, isn't it, Jenny, baby? The connection has never been there between us either."

"No, Mama."

"You always blamed me for taking you away from Annie."

Jenny looked away. She couldn't bring herself to reply.

"I know it's true, Jenny. You always wanted Annie to be your mother, not me."

Jenny's voice came out small, hardly more than a whisper. "I love you both, Mama."

"Oh, I know you do. In different ways. I've always envied what you felt for Annie. In your eyes she's the real mother."

"Don't say that, Mama."

"But it's the truth, Jenny." Her mother's voice was gentle, earnest. "I've always known you preferred her. Maybe that's why in some ways I've kept you at a distance. I was afraid if we got too close you'd see what a poor mother I really was, and I'd lose you for good."

Jenny clasped her mother's hand. "Oh, Mama, don't you know that my loving Annie doesn't make me love you any less? I've always longed for your love, your attention."

"And I was always so afraid to give it."

Jenny choked out the words, "Don't be, Mama. I need your love so much." Suddenly they were clinging to each other again, rocking together, weeping, their tears streaming freely.

"I love you, my precious Jenny," her mother whispered. "With all my heart." They were silent for a long while, savoring a new closeness. Finally her mother released her and they exchanged wistful smiles. "Oh, Jenny, I wish I could make the same connection with my mama that you and I are making today."

"You will, Mama. Grandma Betty loves you."

"In her own way she does. But I see the connection between you and her. It's strong, unbreakable. She loves you the way I always dreamed she'd love me."

Jenny laid her head on her mother's shoulder. "Oh, Mama, I'm sorry."

"No, don't be. I'm glad she has you. I'm glad at last in her life she opened up to someone. With you, she's a different person than she ever was with me." Her mother paused a moment. When she spoke again, her voice had a deliberate tone. "That's why I keep hoping you'll talk to her, honey."

Jenny sat forward and twisted her ragged tissue. "Mama, I told you before. I'm not like you and Papa Robert and the rest of the family. You're all very religious, and that's fine for you, but sometimes I feel . . ."

"What, Jenny? What do you feel? Tell me."

"I don't know, Mama." Jenny didn't want to get into this now, not when she and her mother were just starting to get along. "I guess I feel stifled. Smothered. Like I can't be myself. Like you expect me to be this proper young lady, this perfect Christian all the time."

"No one expects that, Jenny."

"Don't they, Mama?" A wave of emotions caught her. "For crying out loud, our whole family's in some kind of ministry. Papa and Knowl run the publishing house, Uncle Todd's the preacher, Aunt Alice Marie and Uncle Helm are missionaries. I feel like you all expect me to live for God too."

"Jenny, no one's ever said—"

"Don't you understand, Mama?" Jenny's voice grew ragged. "I want to decide for myself what to do with my life. That's why I ran away.

That's why Danny ran away. He couldn't take the pressure from his dad either."

Her mother was silent for a long moment. When she spoke her voice was soft as cotton and she kept her eyes lowered, as if she weren't quite talking to Jenny. "Being a parent isn't easy, honey. We've tried to raise our children in the church. We've prayed they would come to know God."

"You've done a good job, Mama. I'm not complaining."

"But at some point it stops being what we want and what we believe. It has to come from you. You can't rest on your parents' faith, sweetheart; it's not about us anymore. It's just between you and Jesus, no one else."

"I know, Mama."

"He's there for you, Jenny. Jesus fills the void; He's the only one who can love you with unconditional love—the kind you want from me and the kind I want from Grandma. But no one else can make that connection with Him except you."

"It's not like I don't believe, Mama. I do. Everything."

Her mother met her gaze and gave her a bittersweet smile. "I know, honey. It's all there in your head, all the right teachings. But He wants your heart."

Jenny looked away, thinking of Danny so far away and Grandma Betty dying. "All I have is a broken heart."

"That's His specialty, baby. Mending broken hearts."

Jenny heard the heavy sound of footsteps on the stairs and stood up. "The doctor, Mama. He's coming!"

They hurried into the living room and met Dr. Pearson at the foot of the stairs. He was a portly man with small spectacles over a bulbous nose; his brown tweed suit matched his sparse fringe of lanolin-slick hair, and his fleshy neck bulged over his tight, starched collar. He cleared his throat solemnly, as if anticipating the report he would be giving.

"How's Grandma?" asked Jenny.

"She's holding her own. I gave her some medication and she's resting now. You can check on her in an hour or so."

"Is she worse? Should I call Knowl?"

The physician's gray eyes crinkled. "Now, Catherine, only the good Lord knows what's in store for your mother." He ambled over to the coat rack and retrieved his wool overcoat and scarf. "Her spirits are up, and that's a good sign. But it would take a miracle for that old ticker of hers to last longer than a few more days."

"There—there's nothing more you can do?"

"Nothing short of giving her a brand new heart. And, of course, that's humanly impossible." He pulled on his coat and wound his scarf around his neck. "There's no need to call Knowl yet. But he should say his good-byes to his mother in the next day or so. Just in case."

"I'll be sure to call him. Thank you for coming."

The doctor tugged on his galoshes and trundled to the door. "That's what I'm here for. Just keep her comfortable. I'll stop by again tomorrow."

That night Jenny tossed and turned; she pummeled her pillow until feathers escaped and thrashed around on her mattress so much that soon she was wrapped in her bedsheets like a mummy. She couldn't sleep; she was caught up in an emotional tug-of-war she couldn't win. She kept hearing her mother's words ringing in her head. *It's between you and God, no one else. You have to decide what you want, Jenny. Only God can give you unconditional love. He's waiting, Jenny. Make the connection. Give Him your heart.*

Just before dawn, Jenny climbed out of bed, slipped on her fuzzy robe, and padded over to the window. She rubbed her hand over the frosty pane, clearing a spot so she could see out. Gnarled, bare-limbed trees cast eerie silhouettes against the crystal-blue snow. Flurries danced in a silent ballet. The whole earth was hushed, quiet as a cathedral.

Jenny curled herself into a wicker rocker by the window and gazed out at the ebony sky studded with stars. "Dear God," she said aloud, and the sound of her own voice in the empty room startled her. "Dear God," she said again, more softly, breathing the words in a prayer, "I've known You most of my life, and yet I haven't really known You at all. Maybe You're out of patience with me too, like the rest of my family has been. I hope not, because I need Your help. Please help my Grandma Betty to get well. The doctor says it would take a miracle for her heart to keep working. I've never asked You for a miracle before, but I'm asking now. Make her a little better every day. If You make her well, I'll give my life to You. I'll do anything You ask of me. Just don't take my grandmother away from me."

First thing the next morning, Jenny hurried to her grandmother's room and slipped quietly over to the bed. Grandma Betty stirred and opened her eyes. Seeing Jenny, she broke into a crooked smile. "How's . . . my girl?" she rasped.

Jenny sat on the edge of the bed and clasped her grandmother's frail hand. "I'm fine. And you're going to be too, Grams. God is going to make you well."

The weary, wrinkled face brightened. "Is that a fact?"

"Yes. I talked to God about you."

"You did?" Her grandmother pulled at a raveling on her bedspread. "Well, I don't want to hear what He said about me."

Jenny paused, searching for the right words. "Do you ever think about God, Grams?"

The elderly woman jutted out her pale lower lip. "No more than He thinks about me."

"I haven't given Him much thought either. But last night, when I was talking to Him, it felt so right. I felt clean and whole. And I could feel His love shining right down on me. I didn't know it could be like that, Grams. It was like Jesus was sitting right there in the room with me, keeping me company. I didn't feel lonely or afraid. I knew He would take care of me."

Her grandmother pulled her hand away from Jenny's and folded her thin arms protectively. "That's fine and dandy for you, Jenny. What's it got to do with me?"

Jenny's voice trembled slightly. "I'm not good at saying these things, Grams. But I've got to know, just in case. Do you have Jesus in your heart?"

"Don't know if I do, don't know if I don't."

"I've got to know I'll see you in heaven someday."

"I hope for heaven, same as anyone else."

"If you ask Jesus to be your Savior, He'll make sure you get to heaven."

Her grandmother raised one bristly eyebrow and scrutinized Jenny with dark, flinty eyes. "Did your mama put you up to this? Did she tell you to come save my soul?"

Jenny squirmed, smoothing out a ripple in the chenille spread. "She, uh, she said I should talk to you."

"She thinks I'm dying!"

Jenny's words wrenched out in a sob. "Are you, Grams?"

"No, child. I'm too stubborn to die. The Good Lord's gonna tiptoe by my door and go on to someone else. And I don't need any fancy sermon to tell me different."

Jenny seized her grandmother's vein-riddled hand again, and she pressed it to her cheek. "I don't know any sermons, Grams. All I know is Jesus loves you, and He wants you to love Him back. Will you?"

Grandma Betty sniffed noisily and fetched a hanky from the lacy sleeve of her nightgown. "I don't cotton to religious things, Jenny. If you ask me, the church is full of hypocrites. They smile at you on Sundays and tear you to bits the rest of the week."

"I'm not talking about people, Grams. I'm talking about God's Son. Folks did a whole lot worse to Him."

Her grandmother sighed. "All right, I'll think about your Jesus. Between my television shows. When I have a mind to. If He makes you happy, He must be okay."

18

Two weeks before Christmas, Callan Swan phoned Jenny from Los Angeles. "Honey, when are you coming back with the band?" he wanted to know, his voice sugar-sweet. "You've been gone over a week, sweetheart, and we can't cover for you much longer."

Jenny steeled herself, knowing this wasn't the answer he wanted to hear. "Cal, I can't come back yet."

"Why not? Your grandmother didn't die?"

"No. Actually, she's doing better. The doctor says it's a miracle. She could live for weeks or months yet, maybe even years."

"Then she doesn't need you anymore. Listen, I'll make reservations for you on the next—"

"No, Cal. Listen, you'd better get yourself a new girl singer."

"I don't want anyone but you, Jenny."

"I know, but I'm not—I can't go back with the band. Not now. I just can't."

"You're deserting us?" His tone turned venomous. "What's got into you, Jenny? How can you just quit like this? The band needs you. I need you. This is your whole life. This is where you belong. You know it as well as I do."

Jenny sat in the straight-back chair beside the small mahogany phone table. She felt weak inside, her mouth dry, her feelings confused. Was she making the mistake of her life to turn Callan down? Would she regret it for the rest of her years?

"Cal, I'm sorry. Right now I have to stay here in Willowbrook. I promised my grandmother I wouldn't leave her again. If I leave, she might die."

"That's irrational, sentimental hogwash, Jenny."

"It's how I feel, Cal. I gave Grams my word."

She didn't tell him her other reason for staying, that she had promised to give her life to God if He healed her grandmother. It looked like God was keeping His part of the bargain; now it was up to her to keep her promise. Not that she had the slightest idea what that meant. How did a person give her life to God? Whatever God might ask of her, she knew one thing. He didn't want her going back with the band. But she couldn't very well tell Cal that God had told her to stay home.

"Jenny, did you hear me?" Cal sounded agitated, annoyed. "I said, I just hired two guys to replace Emmett and Danny, but I'm not getting another girl. If I can't have you, I'll do a solo act for a while. But I'm not letting you off the hook, do you hear? I'll call again in a few days. Maybe your head will have cleared and you'll be ready to come back."

"No, Cal, it's over," she said shakily. "Please don't call again. I've made my decision."

Cal's tone grew solemn, determined. "It's not over, baby. It'll never be over. I told you once you're my girl, and I meant it. When you least expect me, I'll be there to claim you for myself, and for the band. We belong together; we're great together, on stage and off; everyone says so. You can't fight fate, baby."

"Cal, don't talk that way," she pleaded.

"I mean it, Jenny. You'll be mine someday; it's just a matter of time."

"Stop it. You scare me."

"I say what I mean, and I mean what I say. So long for now, sweetheart, but you can bet your life this isn't the end of it."

Jenny slammed the receiver back in its cradle. She was trembling. What if Cal was right? What if she was destined to be with him? He had a way of making her feel powerless, impassive, as if his will alone were law. On the road with him, she hadn't seen how cunningly, how effortlessly he had controlled her, making her believe his wishes were her wishes. But now that she was no longer under his influence, she saw how much he had manipulated her. God help her, she dared not let that happen again.

She shivered involuntarily. *I've got to talk to Danny. He'll know what to do. When he finds out I'm home, he'll come home too, and we can be together again. Danny's the only one for me.*

Jenny phoned Bethany Rose and got the phone numbers for Southern Methodist University and the boarding house where Danny was staying. She dialed the number with trembling fingers. It seemed like months since she and Danny had been together; surely he would be as eager to hear her voice as she was to hear his.

A woman's voice came on the line. "Mrs. Krashinski's boarding house."

Her throat tightening, Jenny asked for Danny and heard the woman shout, "Danny DiCaprio. Phone call! Take it here in the hall!" To Jenny she said, "He'll be with you in a minute, miss. Just hold on."

Jenny murmured a polite thank you and waited for what seemed ages before Danny's voice came on the line. "Danny?" she asked. "Is that you?"

"Jenny?" He sounded surprised, taken aback. "What's wrong?"

Tears sprang to her eyes. "Nothing, Danny. I just—I had to hear your voice. It seems like forever . . ."

"I know, Jen. I've missed you too."

"I'm home now, Danny. Papa Robert came and got me in Hawaii. Grandma Betty almost died."

"I know. Bethany wrote me. I'm sorry."

"She's better since I came home. I never prayed so hard for anything in my life. The doctor says it's a miracle she's still alive."

"That's great. We could all use a miracle these days."

"Danny, I just got a call from Callan. He wants me to go back with the band."

"What did you tell him?"

"I said I couldn't, but he sounded awfully angry."

"Listen, Jen, the last person I want to talk about is Callan Swan."

"But you think I did the right thing, don't you, Danny? Telling him no?"

"The world would be a better place if people had started telling Callan Swan no a long time ago."

"I knew you'd see it that way. I feel better already."

"Is that the only reason you called, Jen? To ask me if you should go back with the band?"

"No, Danny, of course not. I want to know about you. When are you coming home? I can't wait to see you."

There was a heavy pause. "I'm not, Jen. I'm staying here. Didn't my folks tell you I enrolled in college here?"

Her voice quavered. "Why did you do that, Danny? All you ever wanted to do was sing with the band."

His voice took on a cynical note. "And we both know how that turned out."

"It doesn't have to be that way, Danny. We could have our own band. We could look Emmett up. He must be out of the hospital by now. We could have the kind of band we've always wanted."

"Jenny, don't. It's too late for that. I'm in college now, and I love it. I'm studying political science. Who knows? Maybe I'll be president someday."

"Don't tease me, Danny. You were meant to sing."

His voice turned somber. "I don't know what I was meant to do,

Jen. That's why I'm staying in Dallas. I like my classes, I like my life here. It feels safe and right."

"Safe? Right?" She couldn't keep back the tears. "What about us, Danny? You always said we belonged together."

"Oh, Jen, don't do this to me." His voice broke with a palpable agony. "Don't you understand? You're one of the reasons I've got to stay here."

"Me?" She sank down in the chair, her head spinning.

"When I'm with you, you're all I can think of, all I want."

"What's wrong with that?" she challenged tearfully. "I feel that way about you too."

"We're too young, Jen. You're eighteen, I'm almost nineteen. What do we know about life or the world or the future? It's too soon for us to be together the way we want. I realized that after I left the band. It's a good thing Cal caught us kissing and made me leave. Otherwise . . ." His voice trailed off."

"What?" she demanded. "Otherwise, what!"

His voice took on a warning tone. "You know what. The same thing could have happened to us that happened to my parents and yours. We're no stronger than they were."

"You mean we might have had to get married?" She choked back a sob, angry now, scarcely remembering her bargain with God. "Would that be so bad?"

"Jen, you don't know what you're saying. We don't want our love tainted that way. Look at the hard time we've had because of our parents' choices." His tone grew tender. "Jen, if our love is real, it'll still be there when we've grown up and become the people we're supposed to be."

Tears were coursing freely down her cheeks now. "Then you won't come home?"

"No, Jen. I'm taking extra classes so I can graduate early."

"What about Christmas?"

"I'll be staying here in Dallas. There are some nice folks living here at the boarding house. Students like myself. None of us can afford a trip home. So we'll have Christmas here."

"What about next summer?" she sobbed.

"Summer school. Like I said. Extra classes."

Jenny's voice grew shrill. She doubled her clammy hands into fists. She wanted to strike back at Danny, hurt him for hurting her. "You're trying to punish me, aren't you, Danny? Me and your parents. That's what this is all about."

"Good grief, Jen! Why on earth would I do that?"

"Because you're still angry with your dad for trying to run your life, and maybe you're angry with me for becoming a lead singer with Callan. You were jealous of Cal and me, weren't you? You couldn't stand seeing us together, singing together, and everybody applauding."

"Sure, I was jealous," he conceded. "I hated seeing you with that conceited, power-hungry jerk. But that's not why I'm doing this, Jen. I'm trying to save us both. Right now we can be better people apart than we can together. Someday, when the circumstances are right, maybe we can . . ."

"What if they're never right?" she countered brokenly.

"That's the chance we have to take, Jen. I love you. Please don't hate me."

"I could never hate you," she whispered. There didn't seem to be anything else to say after that. They exchanged a few words of small talk, admonished one another to keep in touch, and then they were saying good-bye, and she was left with nothing but a click and a dial tone. She sat holding the receiver in her hand for a long while.

How ironic, she brooded, *that she had just severed any future contact with Callan Swan, and now Danny was doing the same to her, dismantling their relationship with a few shattering words.* Life wasn't fair. She had bargained with God for her grandmother's recovery; was this God's way of making her pay? He had taken away her singing career, and now Danny. What more would He demand before her debt was paid?

"Oh, God, how could You? I thought You loved me!" Jenny wept until her sobs turned to hiccups and there were no more tears to cry. Finally she replaced the receiver and dried her eyes, her resolve hardening. She wasn't about to slouch around with a broken heart. She would put Danny out of her mind and heart forever. She would forget him and concentrate on her family, on carving out a life for herself in Willowbrook. Yes, of course! She would enroll at Willowbrook University and throw herself into her studies, just as Danny was doing. Maybe then the hurt would go away.

By Christmas Jenny was feeling better, more on top of things, more hopeful about her future. She had enrolled at Willowbrook University for second semester, joined the choir at church, and taken a part-time job doing light secretarial work in her father's office at Herrick House Publishers. She deliberately kept schedule crammed from morning to night, seven days a week. When she wasn't at work or at church, she spent her time helping Annie with research or keeping Grandma Betty company, reading to her, crooning hymns and popular old standards, and watching their favorite television shows. Every show except *American Bandstand*, which always brought a lump to Jenny's throat.

On Christmas morning, Grandma Betty was well enough to come downstairs and join the family in the parlor around the huge, brightly decorated blue spruce. She sat wrapped in her flannel robe, her brown hair twisted back in a loose bun at the nape of her neck. Her gaunt face was as lined as a road map, her cheeks pale as oatmeal, but her black eyes shone as bright as licorice drops. "Oh, I like the tree," she raved, clapping her knobby fingers together. She stared down at the mountain of foil-wrapped packages and chirped, "Do I get presents?"

Jenny stooped down and removed a large gold box with red velvet ribbon from under the tree. She handed it to her grandmother. "This is for you, Grams, and lots more."

Her grandmother fumbled eagerly with the ribbon. Jenny sat beside her on the sofa and helped lift the lid. They both pushed back the crinkly tissue paper. "Do you like it?" Jenny asked as her grandmother held up a silk, wine-colored dress.

"Goodness, it's too nice to wear in my room, child."

"It's for church, Grams. So you can come hear me sing in the Christmas cantata tonight."

"Oh, I'm not able."

Jenny's mother sat down on the tufted arm of the sofa and stroked her mother's hair. "Yes, you are, Mama. Doc Pearson said so. If you feel up to it. We'd really like you to go with us."

"No, Catherine. The crowds . . . I couldn't."

"We'll be right there with you every moment," said Papa Robert. "And if you get tired I'll drive you home."

Betty looked at Jenny, her wiry brows arching in a question mark. "I'll hear you sing? Just you? Lots of songs?"

Jenny smiled. "Yes, Grams. I have lots of solos. And I'll sing them just for you."

"Well, then, maybe so. Is it snowing? I'll wear my beaver coat and my rubber boots, if I can find them. And I'll take my fur muff."

"Don't worry. We'll make sure you have everything you need, Grams. You'll look beautiful in your new dress. And with you there at church hearing me sing, it'll be my best Christmas ever."

To everyone's relief, Grandma Betty managed to sit through the entire cantata without growing restless or uttering a word of complaint. Jenny watched her from the stage and sang every song for her, praying that the words would touch her heart and draw her to the Child of Bethlehem. After the service, Jenny and the other choir members handed out candy canes to the children, and Grandma Betty made sure she got one too. Several, in fact.

Later that evening, when Jenny stopped by her grandmother's room to say good night, she found her grandmother sitting up in bed sucking the sweet peppermint stick, her lips and fingers red from the sticky candy.

Jenny sat on the side of the bed and smiled. "Don't tell anyone, Grams, but there are lots more candy canes on the Christmas tree. I'll get you one anytime you like."

"It's very good, but hard, and my teeth are old." Grandma Betty licked her lips, making a clucking sound. "I liked your songs, child. You should sing them on television. Mr. Dick Clark should have you back on *American Bandstand*, so everyone can hear you."

"I'm afraid my television days are over, Grams. I'm staying right here in Willowbrook. Remember? I promised you."

"I remember. What about Danny?"

"He's in Texas. He won't be coming home for a long time."

"That makes you sad. I don't want you to be sad."

"I'm fine, Grams. It's better this way. That's what Danny says anyway."

Her grandmother put her finger to her lips as if she had a secret to share. She leaned toward Jenny, cupped her hand around her mouth, and whispered, "I did what you asked."

"What's that, Grams?"

"I said your prayer."

"My prayer?"

"Yes, your prayer. I asked Jesus into my heart. Like you sang to me. Remember? 'Jesus loves me . . this I know . . . for the Bible tells me so.' Now I'll go to heaven, just like you. Jesus promised."

With a triumphant whoop, Jenny encircled her grandmother in her arms, sticky candy cane and all. Through her tears, Jenny blurted, "Oh, Grams, now I know this is the best Christmas of all!"

19

After a memorable Christmas (thanks in large part to Grandma Betty), the new year, 1961, arrived with a sense of excitement and fresh beginnings for both Jenny and the country, with the inauguration of the thirty-fifth president of the United States on January 20. Already Jenny felt an emotional connection with John Fitzgerald Kennedy; he was a trailblazer—the youngest man, the wealthiest, and the first Catholic ever elected president.

Jenny's entire family gathered around the television set to hear his inaugural address. She sat mesmerized as the handsome president declared, "Let the word go forth from this time and place, to friend and foe alike, that the torch has been passed to a new generation of Americans—born in this century, tempered by war, disciplined by a hard and bitter peace, proud of our ancient heritage . . ."

But Jenny was most stirred by Kennedy's challenge to the nation, "Ask not what your country can do for you; ask what you can do for your country." She took the challenge personally and felt a profound emotional reaction. This was the sort of all-consuming zeal she wanted to experience, a commitment to something beyond herself that inspired sacrifice and service.

But where and on whom should such unswerving devotion be placed? On God? She had promised Him her life in exchange for healing Grams, but she was still sorting out what His claim on her life meant, and she still had more questions than answers. In her brief existence she had already made too many assumptions about her destiny. Just last summer she had sworn wholehearted commitment to Danny and her singing career, but now she had neither the career nor the man she loved. She was determined not to make such a painful mistake again.

As Jenny watched the inauguration, she knew Danny would be watching, too, in his Texas boarding house, surrounded by new friends Jenny would never meet. Afterward Danny would probably celebrate with his friends and cheer on the new president he so admired. If Danny had his way, he would become just like Kennedy. Maybe even be president himself someday.

Jenny was glad Kennedy had won, even though most of her family had supported Eisenhower. In high school she had read Kennedy's Pulitzer prize-winning biography, *Profiles in Courage*, and knew his story well. A navy man like her father, Kennedy had been wounded in the war, nearly killed, when the PT boat he was commanding was rammed by a Japanese destroyer. In spite of his wounds, Kennedy rescued his crew. Jenny's father would have been a hero like that too, she imagined, if he'd ever had a chance.

But now it was time for Jenny to stop thinking about what might have been and never could be . . . for Chilton Reed as well as for Jenny and Danny. As she started classes at Willowbrook University that month, Jenny refused to allow herself to grieve any longer over her father or to brood about Danny. She threw herself into her studies and took on enough extracurricular activities to fill every waking hour. She was determined to be a model student, a model daughter, a model Christian.

From time to time she received letters from Danny—short, factual reports about his classes and activities. He was doing well, getting good grades, leading a choral group on campus, attending a nice church, and tutoring a fellow student who lived in his rooming house, a girl named Donna Garvey, who was failing chemistry. Rarely did he mention his feelings for Jenny or discuss their relationship. As impersonal as they were, the letters might as well have come from some stuffy great-uncle. Still, she hungrily devoured every word, reading between the lines for any hint that Danny still loved her.

Jenny heard occasionally from Callan Swan, too, and dreaded his letters as much as she looked forward to Danny's. With Callan's scrawled notes came press releases and newspaper clippings about the band and little souvenirs from their travels—matchbooks, menus, cocktail napkins, and photographs of Callan with a variety of pretty girls, all devoted fans. He had hired a new girl singer, but he grudgingly admitted that no one would ever take Jenny's place. "Say the word, sweetheart," he wrote in a letter that June, "and you're back in the band. Any time, any place. I still adore you."

She considered the possibility of rejoining the band . . . for all of two minutes. The semester was ending and a long, listless summer stretched ahead. Wouldn't it be fun to travel with the band again? To feel the exhilaration of performing on stage? To hear the applause once more?

But as quickly as the idea flitted through her mind, she dismissed it. Joining up again with Callan would be a mistake; everything that attracted her to him would eventually send her careening off in the wrong direction. He had a hypnotic, intoxicating way of stirring up the appetites of the body with his tantalizing kisses, and of the mind with his seductive offers of power, money, fame, and success.

Instead of joining Callan and the band, Jenny spent the summer of 1961 taking classes, working at the publishing house, doing more research for Annie, and singing at several local churches. She dated occasionally, but the men didn't interest her; they were merely passing acquaintances, casual friends, cordial escorts to academic functions, nothing more.

The letters from Danny and Callan tapered off during the summer months. Danny hadn't even remembered her nineteenth birthday in May. Still, Jenny prayed that Danny would come home to her, just for a brief visit. At last he wrote and told her he was too busy this summer, but promised to come home next summer for sure.

As fall came with another full load of classes, Jenny began to wonder if she and Danny had ever really been in love. Perhaps it had been nothing more than a teenage crush; they had been thrown together for most of their lives, so maybe they had mistaken friendship for love. Determined to put him out of her heart and mind once and for all, Jenny threw herself again into her classes, her work, and her singing. She stopped to catch her breath only during those special times with her family on weekends and holidays.

Grandma Betty remained in surprisingly good health, considering the tenuous condition of her heart. In his regular examinations, Dr. Pearson simply scratched his head and said, "I'm convinced that woman stays alive by sheer will power alone." But Jenny knew it was more than that. It was the miracle God had promised her, and Jenny was doing her best to keep her end of the bargain, whatever it might be.

The months ticked away, the holidays coming and going. As Christmas of 1961 approached, there was talk in the family that Danny might fly home for a visit, but a week into December he called home and told his parents the trip would have to wait; he was cramming for finals and needed to stay in Dallas over the holidays and hit the books. His grades, his very future, depended on it. "But don't worry about me," he told Bethany, "I won't be lonely. I'll be spending Christmas Day in Georgia with a girl from school—Donna Garvey and her family."

Jenny had mixed feelings about Danny's canceled trip. Seeds of jealousy sprang up at the thought of him spending Christmas with another girl, even if she was just a friend from school. But as much as Jenny yearned to see Danny, she feared what being with him again would do to her heart. She had spent over a year making herself believe she could have a life without him. What if she saw him again and realized she couldn't live without him? She couldn't risk that possibility.

Another year came slipping in with such ease and stealth, Jenny wondered if this was how the rest of her life would be—the years rolling by so swiftly she would hardly have time to catch her breath.

Grandmother Anna often said each year went by faster than the one before. "Wait till you get my age, Jenny," she admonished as the family gathered in church to welcome in 1962. "Time is winging away. The years go by so fast I'm tempted to leave the Christmas decorations up year round. Mercy me, we just get them down and it's time to put them up again!"

Jenny knew the feeling. When she was a child, time passed at a snail's pace. It seemed to take forever for Christmas morning to arrive with all the glorious presents under the tree. But these days the season was upon her and gone before she could finish all her shopping, wrapping, baking, and visiting.

During 1962 Danny's letters grew still more infrequent, and when he did write, it was only to tell her what he was doing, rarely to ask about her. "I've joined a grassroots political organization," he wrote in a letter late in February, "and I'm thinking more and more about running for office someday. By the way, Jen, did you see the White House on television last week? Jackie Kennedy gave Charles Collingwood the grand tour. It was something. Makes a guy think being president wouldn't be so bad."

In a card for Jenny's twentieth birthday that May, Danny wrote, "Donna Garvey and I went to see a campus production of *The Sound of Music* last Saturday night. It's a great play. You should see it someday. By the way, happy birthday. And for the record, Donna's the girl in my rooming house I tutored last year. A swell girl. We're just friends."

But if they were just friends, why did he mention her, and why did Jenny feel an ache inside thinking of them together? Maybe they were only friends, but she was with him and Jenny wasn't. And the way time was going, Jenny might never be with him again.

That June Jenny received a surprising phone call; a voice from the past, but she recognized it immediately. "Hey, girl, what you been doing since I last seen you?"

"Emmett!" she cried. "How are you?"

"I'm all right. I'm back in Chicago helping my daddy with his church. We got us a choral group going like nothing you ever heard. We been singing for half the churches in Chicago, and a few beyond. You gotta come hear us one of these days."

"Oh, Emmett, I'd love to. I was so worried about you when we left you in that hospital in Greenville."

Emmett's deep voice grew wistful. "What an awful time that was— that night, them boys—straight out of the devil's pit. But God had hold of me. I stayed in the hospital three weeks. Callan paid the bill, every penny. And when I was on the mend, I took a bus home to Chicago. He paid for that too."

"I didn't know," said Jenny. "I kept thinking you'd come back to the band when you got well, but we never heard a thing from you."

"Well, I had me plenty of time while I was on my back to think about things. And, glory be, I got the call from God to tend to His work. The Lord told me I was done making a name for myself with the band. He wanted me to start making a name for Him."

"I guess you know I quit the band shortly after you did. Right after Hawaii. My grandmother was ill and needed me."

"Callan told me when I called to get your number."

"How is Callan? I haven't heard from him in a long time."

"Then you ain't heard about Andy Loomis?"

"Andy? Cal's drummer? What about him?"

Emmett's tone sobered. "He died a few months ago."

Jenny's breath caught. "Oh, no! What happened? An accident?"

"Worse," said Emmett. "Him and the guys was at a bar one night tying one on. They wanted to see who could chug-a-lug the most beers. Andy won . . . and lost. He collapsed and went into a coma. Never came out."

Jenny uttered a sound that was almost a sob. "I can't believe it! He was such a sweet, boyish, funny guy. Always treated me nice. He had those round, apple-red cheeks and big teeth and mischievous eyes. His feelings were always written all over his face."

"And he was one fine musician," said Emmett.

"How's Cal taking it?"

"Not so good. He blames himself for letting the guys get stewed every night. He made the whole band swear off liquor."

"Then at least some good came from it."

"I been talking to Cal about getting right with God," said Emmett. "Since Andy died, he listens to me. Keeps saying one of these days he'll get things squared away. You be praying for him, Jenny."

"I will, Emmett. Every day. I promise."

"That man still misses you. He keeps hoping you'll go back with him one of these days."

"No, Emmett." Jenny's voice softened. "I can't go back on my promise to God."

"What you been promising God now, child?"

"I promised Him my life if He healed my grandmother."

"That's dangerous ground, girl."

"No, Emmett. Grams got better. And now I'm trying to figure out how to keep my part of the bargain."

Emmett chuckled. "I didn't know God was in the habit of bargaining."

"I tried it anyway. I had to, Emmett. Call it what you will. An answer to prayer. A miracle. I owe Him. And I'm still not sure how to keep my commitment to Him."

"Maybe I can help you out," said Emmett with a sudden lilt in his voice. "I got something going that's a dream come true."

Jenny laughed. "Tell me. What is it? The gig of a lifetime?"

"You guessed it, girl. You hear of Billy Graham?"

"The evangelist? Of course. Who hasn't? He puts on crusades all over the world."

"Um-hmm, and this summer he's coming to Chicago," said Emmett, his voice swelling with excitement. "And you know the big choir they got? We're gonna be singing—me and my church!"

"Really? That's wonderful, Emmett."

"And there's more. When his team invited me to sing, I told 'em I'd be having some others singing with me. I'm talking about you, Jenny, and Danny."

"But Danny's not here. He's in Texas."

"Ever hear of buses? Or trains? I tell you, the three of us is gonna be singing together in the Windy City for Billy Graham."

Jenny's pulse quickened. "Oh, Emmett, stop kidding me!"

"I'm serious, girl. It's all set. McCormick Place is where the crusade is gonna be. Three whole weeks. But they're gonna have the final rally at Soldier Field. There'll be some hundred thousand folks coming, and it's our gig. Just say the word."

"Oh, Emmett, I don't know. Even if I could, what about Danny? He'll be in summer school in Texas. He hasn't been home in a long time. I don't think he'd want to come all the way to Chicago."

"Sure he will. The truth is, I already talked to him. He's coming home between classes. Taking the train. Arriving just in time for the rally at Soldier Field. And heading back to Texas two days later after a visit in Willowbrook."

Jenny nearly dropped the receiver. Her heart was doing a drum roll. "Danny's coming home? You're sure?"

"Sure as day. So tell me, girl. Can I count on you?"

Jenny's head spun. "Yes, Emmett. If Danny's going to be there, so will I. Write me with all the details, okay?"

"Don't worry, girl. I'll be sending a letter mighty fast."

Jenny took the train to Chicago, arriving the day before the rally at Soldier Field. Emmett picked her up at the station and drove her to the home of one of his parishioners, where she spent the night. The next afternoon Emmett drove her to his church for the rehearsal—a modest, rambling, whitewashed structure at the edge of a sooty, noisy commercial district.

And there in the sprawling sanctuary, in scorching one-hundred degree heat, she saw Danny for the first time in nearly two years. They spotted each other across the humid, airless room while the choir rehearsed, singing joyously, exuberantly, heads bobbing, arms waving heavenward in spite of the warmth.

For Jenny, everything halted as she slipped through the narrow pews toward the man she loved. He came striding toward her too, and when they met, it was all she could do to keep from flinging herself into his arms. He looked older than his twenty-one years and even more handsome than she remembered. He had lost his boyish good looks; now he had the solidly sculpted features of a man.

He seemed about to embrace her, then drew back momentarily, and finally swept her into his arms. "Oh, Danny, I've missed you," she whispered.

"I've missed you too." He held her at arms' length and looked at her. "You're more beautiful than ever. Still the same flowing red hair and gorgeous green eyes, but where are the freckles?"

She laughed. "Under the makeup."

He released her and looked over at Emmett. He was instructing the choir, saying something about timing, and counting out measures.

"Looks like we'd better get busy, Jen." Danny gave her a private wink. "Emmett's counting on us."

She nodded. "We've got a lot of work before the rally tonight. We haven't sung for this many people at once since we did *Bandstand*."

"Another lifetime."

She clasped his arm. "Imagine us on the same stage with Billy Graham. Everyone in Willowbrook will be watching."

Danny grinned. "My dad will think he's finally died and gone to heaven . . . seeing me with Billy Graham."

She tightened her fingers on his arm. "This will be a night we'll remember for the rest of our lives. Won't it, Danny?"

Under his breath he murmured, "Whenever we're together, I'll remember it for the rest of my life."

She searched his eyes, but before she could discover what he meant by such a remark, Emmett called them over to rehearse their song. For the rest of the afternoon and evening they had no chance to talk privately. They rode with the church choir on an old relic of a bus to the Chicago stadium—a massive structure that seemed to extend for miles over the landscape. Hundreds of buses lined the parking lots, and thousands of people swarmed in the wide expanse of doors.

Jenny, Danny, Emmett, and his choir joined a much larger choir on the platform in the middle of the horseshoe-shaped stadium. The stadium was jam-packed and, in spite of the sweltering heat, there was a crackling excitement in the air that made Jenny's adrenaline soar.

The rally began and television cameras rolled as Cliff Barrows led the choir in a rousing hymn. Then George Beverly Shea ambled to the podium and in his deep baritone sang "How Great Thou Art."

When it was time for Jenny, Danny, and Emmett to sing, she wondered if she'd be able to hear herself over the hammering of her heart. She found herself standing between Danny and Emmett at the podium, and somehow, in spite of weak knees and perspiration dotting her forehead, she opened her mouth and the words broke from her lips on cue. It was a song she knew well, a moving spiritual Emmett himself had written. The three of them had sung it often together during their long, lonely nights on the bus, traveling from city to city.

Jenny felt a heady euphoria as she sang of Jesus comforting His children and healing their wounds. She had never felt such joy crooning to boozy crowds in smoke-filled dance clubs. She sensed a hungry, eager response from the audience; the song was drawing them closer to God, stirring their hearts, making them tenderly receptive to the message Graham would bring.

Too soon the song was over and Jenny was taking her seat on the platform while the tall, rangy evangelist strode to the podium, Bible in hand. He was even more striking in person than the image she recalled from her television screen, with his tanned, boyish good looks, wavy hair, and classic chiseled features. Jenny had never seen such intense eyes or heard more passion in a preacher's voice.

He began by reading Jeremiah 29:13: "'And ye shall seek me, and find me, when ye shall search for me with all your heart.' Ladies and gentlemen," he intoned, his rich voice reflecting his Southern roots, "you have been searching for something for your entire life, something vital that you never had, something or someone to fill the great void inside you . . ."

He spoke of the chasm separating imperfect man from a Holy God, and of Christ, who paid the price for man's sins on the cross and was knocking on the door of man's heart, eager to enter and fill the void with His Spirit. To Jenny's surprise, Graham cut his sermon short, no doubt because of the suffocating heat. The fierce sun beat down relentlessly, sapping everyone's strength, but the scorching heat didn't quash the crowd's enthusiasm for Graham's message. As the choir sang "Just As I Am," he gave his usual invitation to accept Christ, and hundreds of people streamed onto the field and surrounded the platform.

Jenny had never witnessed anything like it—so many people coming forward, many weeping, others smiling or embracing, all eager to find Jesus. She watched Graham at the podium, his head lowered, hand covering his mouth, his eyes closed in prayer, and wondered what could be more satisfying than ministering to others of God's love.

After the service, Emmett drove Jenny and Danny to the train station and waved them off as they boarded the evening train for Willowbrook. "Praise God, we'll do this again someday!" he called after them. He shouted something more, but his words were lost in the engine's bellowing roar.

As the train began its shuddering roll down the tracks, Jenny and

Danny made their way to the first passenger car and found an empty seat in the smoky, airless coach. They hadn't planned to make this trip together; Emmett, playing matchmaker, had booked them on the same train home.

They settled back, knowing it would be hours before the train rumbled into Willowbrook's familiar red brick station.

Danny offered her half of the hoagie sandwich he'd purchased at a deli near the station. They washed it down with a thermos of black coffee Emmett had given them, taking turns sipping the hot brew from its plastic cup as the teeth-rattling train jounced them through the darkening Indiana countryside.

The whistle blew, its moaning siren song echoing on the sultry air. It was the same sound Jenny had heard as a child when she had lain in bed and dreamed of traveling to distant lands. Now, she'd been to those lands and back again, and they didn't seem so magical anymore.

"Ticket, miss?" It was the conductor, a portly, gray-haired black man, shuffling down the aisle, checking tickets. Danny handed him theirs. After that, the only sound was the muffled hum of conversation and the steady, grinding whir of spinning wheels on steel tracks.

After a while, Jenny looked over at Danny and smiled. "It's been great seeing you again."

He returned the smile, his eyes crinkling in that special way that made her stomach tickle, as if she were taking a dip on a roller coaster ride. "Great seeing you too," he said. "I've thought about you a lot."

"Same here."

He put his head back against the seat and gazed at her. "You're not the same teenage girl I remember, Jen."

She gazed back at him. "I'm twenty now. Not a teenager anymore."

"I know. You've grown up a lot. You seem more focused, more at peace."

"I suppose I am. But today I just feel excited."

"Because of the Crusade?"

"Yes. Being part of it. Seeing Billy Graham in action. Watching all the people come forward. For the first time I can understand what motivates our families to be involved in ministry. There's something about God using you to help others. Changing lives. I think I could get caught up in something like that." She looked over at Danny. "Do you ever feel that way, that God has His hand on you and wants to use your life for some greater good?"

"In a way I do. That's why I'm thinking about politics. It's a powerful way of helping people and making a difference."

"I suppose it is. I hadn't thought about it like that." She sighed wistfully. "I don't know what God wants me to do with my life. I'm just going to have to wait and let Him show me."

Danny turned his gaze briefly to the window. "To tell you the truth, I don't know either. Maybe it's politics, maybe it's not. I have this gnawing feeling inside, like I should know what I'm supposed to do, but I don't. Everything I do is a leap in the dark."

"God will show you, Danny. Just like He'll show me. Trust Him."

"I'm working on that. I still have a hard time distinguishing between God's voice and my father's."

"Maybe you're trying so hard to shut out your father's voice, you can't hear God's."

He gave her an ironic grin. "You know me so well, Jen."

She searched his eyes. "Do I, Danny? Sometimes I wonder if we know each other at all anymore. Everything used to be so simple— our feelings, our plans, our future."

"Yeah, we were great together. It was you and me against the world."

"But the older we get, the more complicated everything seems. Why does it have to be that way?"

He reached over and took her hand. "Maybe it doesn't, Jenny. Maybe we're just making it difficult. I know we can't build a future on the past, and we can't forge a relationship via long distance. But maybe there's something we can do."

"What?"

He stroked the back of her hand. "You could transfer to Southern Methodist University, and we could be together again."

"Is that really what you want, Danny?"

"Don't you? We once had something good between us."

"But we're not the same people anymore. You said so yourself. What if we can't get back what we had?"

He pressed her hand against his lips. "If we don't spend time together, how will we get to know the people we are now?"

Her voice caught. "I can't move there, Danny. I promised Grandma Betty I wouldn't leave her again. I'm the only one she's really close to."

His eyes narrowed. "You're going to put your life on hold for a doddering old lady?"

"She's not doddering."

"Everyone in the family thinks she's touched in the head."

"She's just a little eccentric and forgetful."

Danny released her hand. "Jen, we'll never know what kind of future we could have together if we never see each other."

"Then come back to Willowbrook," she pleaded.

He shook his head. "I'll never live there again. I don't know where I'm supposed to be, but that's not it."

"Not ever?"

"Not ever."

Her voice cracked with disappointment. "That's too bad, Danny. Because after traveling all over the country, I've decided I like Willowbrook just fine."

"Good for you," he said crossly, and closed his eyes, pretending to sleep.

She closed her eyes, too, and allowed the swaying train to lull her into slumber. After a while, she realized her head had lolled over onto Danny's shoulder. He stirred and instinctively pulled her into his arms, her cheek against his chest. She could feel the heat of his skin through his light cotton shirt. She closed her eyes and inhaled the musky scent of his aftershave. When she was with him like this, nothing else in the world mattered.

She looked up at him through the sallow, flickering light, traced his sturdy jaw line, the faint stubble shadowing his chin. All the feelings and memories of their long nights on Callan Swan's tour bus came rushing back, filling her senses, clouding her reason. "Oh, Danny," she whispered, "I love you so much."

He nestled his chin in her tousled curls and said huskily, "Then come to Texas."

"I can't."

"You can."

"Not now, Danny. I'm sorry."

"When?"

"Someday."

His muscles flexed and his voice took on a dark, melancholy edge; she knew his words would resound in her heart for months, maybe years to come. "Don't you get it, Jen? Someday never comes."

20

Jenny never would have imagined that well over a year would pass before she saw Danny again. But maybe that was best. She was beginning to believe that Danny was right. Someday would never come for the two of them.

He had returned to Dallas two days after their performance at the Billy Graham Crusade, promising to write, assuring her of his love. But it was a love neither of them were willing to give first place in their lives. And Jenny wasn't sure it was a love God was willing to bless. Danny's nagging question resurfaced. How could they know if they never spent time getting acquainted with the persons they had become?

Jenny hoped Danny would make it home for Christmas, but his choral group was singing in several Dallas churches over the holidays. All too soon another year rolled around. Jenny prayed he would get home for a few days during the summer of '63, but he wrote and told her he was taking classes all summer so that he could graduate in June of '64. "It works both ways," he wrote. "When are you coming to Dallas?"

Suddenly it was fall again and she had classes of her own. In spite of her prayers, she and Danny seemed to be heading in opposite directions, setting vastly different priorities, planning very different futures for themselves. Whatever Jenny's future held, she wanted to sing, and increasingly she was thinking in terms of a career in gospel music. But Danny was obsessed with politics and determined to carve out a career for himself in the political arena.

Early in November of 1963, Jenny received a phone call from Danny. "Jen, I want you to come to Dallas for the Thanksgiving holidays. You can fly down the week before and I'll pay half your fare," he promised. "I've even got you a place to stay."

"Where?" she wanted to know. "Not some expensive hotel."

"No. Right here in my boarding house."

She hesitated. "You don't mean your room."

"Of course not. Jen, what kind of a guy do you think I am? My friend, Donna Garvey, is going home to Georgia for the holidays. She lives down the hall from me. She says you can stay in her room. No charge."

Jenny bristled at the mention of Donna. "Let me think about it, okay?"

"Try to make it, Jen," he urged. "We've been playing tag with each other for years now. It's time we discovered whether what we feel for each other is more than a teenage infatuation."

Jenny hung up the phone with misgivings. She wasn't sure she wanted to learn the answer to Danny's question. What if it meant she had to give him up for good? She was comfortable with her life just as it was—going to college, spending time with her family, getting to know herself better, dating now and then with friends from church and school, and doing the things she wanted to do without having to answer to any man. Forcing the issue with Danny would mean making a decision about her future she wasn't sure she was ready for. Or was it possible she was afraid of going to Dallas and making the same mistake her mother had made and finding herself trapped in a life she had never bargained for?

Jenny had to pour out her heart to someone. Instinctively, she headed upstairs to her grandmother's room, knocked lightly, then peeked inside. Grandma Betty was sitting in her rocking chair wrapped in a lap blanket and a knit shawl, watching television. Peter, Paul, and Mary were singing "If I Had a Hammer." Her grandmother looked up and beamed. "Come in, child. Sit down and watch this show with me. It's very good."

Jenny sat down on the edge of the bed. "I'd love to, Grams, but I've got a term paper to write. And tests to study for."

"Too busy for me?" Her grandmother made a sad face. "Poor Jenny. You work too hard."

"No, Grams. I just want to get my education." She paused a moment, carefully framing her words. "I got a phone call tonight from someone special."

"My Tom?"

"No, not my grandfather."

"Not that bandleader fellow. That Swan somebody with the big bus? The one who's always wanting you to run off with him?"

"No, Grams, not Callan. Danny."

Her faded eyes brightened. "Danny? Our Danny?"

"Yes, our Danny. He wants me to visit him in Texas."

Her grandmother rubbed her bony, arthritic wrist. "So go."

"Do you really think I should, Grams?"

The wizened, wrinkled face turned from the television to face Jenny. "Do you love him?"

Jenny drew in a sharp breath. "Yes. Yes, I love him, but I don't really know what that means anymore."

"Love is love. It was with Tom and me. You love or you don't love, that's all."

Jenny smiled ruefully. "I wish it were that easy."

Her grandmother pointed one long, knobby finger at her. "Go to Texas. I would have followed my Tom to the ends of the earth."

Jenny stood up and patted her grandmother's shoulder. "You're right, Grams. Maybe I should go."

Jenny flew to Dallas the Thursday before Thanksgiving. Danny picked her up and drove her to the rambling, turn-of-the-century boarding house in a shabby, but venerable, neighborhood near the university. He introduced her to Mrs. Krashinski, the owner, and they chatted for a while; then he showed her to the tiny, homespun room that belonged to Donna Garvey.

Hesitantly she crossed the threshold. The room had a cluttered, pleasantly eclectic air to it. Cozy pine furnishings—a plain bed, desk, dresser, and bookcase—blended with a young woman's personal effects—a record player and popular record collection, paperback novels and glamour magazines, lumpy brown teddy bears dressed in overalls or lace dresses, and an assortment of beauty products, perfumes, and lotions. She sensed Danny behind her as she scanned the walls covered with college mementos—pennants, programs from university plays and sports events, and glossy, black and white snapshots of Donna Garvey and Danny together—everywhere!

Jenny felt a stab of jealousy as she looked at the photographs of Donna and Danny standing arm in arm by some campus building, or sitting with friends at a coffeehouse or restaurant, or horsing around outside the boarding house. And the two of them laughing uproariously over something. The two looked so comfortable together, so natural, as if they had spent many long, leisurely hours together and knew each other well. Perhaps too well.

"I didn't know you and Donna were such good friends," she said, trying to sound nonchalant.

Danny set her suitcase by the bed and looked up quizzically. "What do you mean by that?"

"Nothing," she said quickly. "It's just . . . from these pictures you and Donna look so close. You must spend a lot of time together."

Danny shrugged. "A fair amount, I suppose. We've lived here in the same boarding house since we started college. The guys here at the house remind me of Cal Swan and the band. They spend Saturday nights at the pub boozing it up. Donna's not like that. She's easy to be with." He paused. "Something wrong, Jen?"

"You must like her a lot."

"I do. We're good friends. I don't think I could have lasted here all these years without her."

Jenny's voice wavered. The knife was twisting deeper. "I suppose she feels the same way about you."

Danny grinned unabashedly. "I hope so. She's a terrific girl. I just wish you could have met her. Of course, then her room wouldn't have been available."

Jenny sat down on the bed, picked up a stuffed bear with button eyes and a bow tie, and hugged it to her breast. "Maybe I shouldn't have come to Dallas," she said softly.

Danny sat down beside her and stroked her cascading curls. "Why would you say that, Jen?"

She burrowed her chin into the bear's fuzzy head. "I feel like I'm intruding on your life here. Your friends, your routine, the places you go—it's all settled. I'm not part of your life anymore, Danny."

"Why do you say that? Just because I'm friends with a girl here in Dallas? What about you, Jen? Aren't you still stringing Callan Swan along, even promising to go back with the band someday? You know how he feels about you, and you just keep him there in your hip pocket in case you ever need him someday."

"I do not, Danny! That's cruel! Cal knows exactly how I feel. I've told him I don't plan to go back with the band. We're friends, that's all."

"And what about us, Jen? What are we? Just friends?"

She gazed solemnly at him. "I don't know, Danny. What are we? You tell me."

"Sweetheart, don't you get it? That's what I'm trying to figure out. But how can I when we don't even know each other anymore? And now you're trying to put Donna Garvey between us?" He pulled Jenny against his chest and massaged the back of her neck. "We've got to get to know each other again, Jen. Find out how we've changed, what matters to us, where we're going with our lives. It's our first step back to each other."

"But what if the things we learn just make the distance between us greater?"

He kissed her hair. "Better we find out now. We've let things ride too long." He looked at her and made a face, gently mocking her gloomy expression. "Come on, Jen. Don't look so glum. Wait'll you hear what I've got planned for us this weekend!"

She sighed. "After all those hours on the plane, I'm ready for a good night's sleep."

"That's what I figured. We'll have a leisurely dinner somewhere close—Italian, Chinese, or good old American cuisine—whatever you're hungry for. Then I'll get you back early tonight so you can get your rest. But I warn you, tomorrow's going to be a big day."

"What's tomorrow?"

Danny's eyes gleamed with excitement. "The president's coming to town, and we're going to see him. I've got it all planned."

"President Kennedy? You're serious?"

"You bet. It's going to be a day you'll never forget."

She gave him her warmest smile. "Then I'll be sure to get my beauty sleep."

A misty dawn greeted Jenny on Friday, November 22, with faint ribbons of sunlight seeping through high, narrow, unfamiliar windows. Jenny stretched under the downy, homemade comforter and wondered for a moment where she was. This wasn't Indiana. No, of course not. She was here in Dallas with Danny. In Mrs. Krashinski's boarding house. In Donna Garvey's room, surrounded by Donna Garvey's teddy bears!

But after years apart, she and Danny were together again. His room was just down the hall. And today promised to be a rare and special day. They were going to see the president.

By the time she had washed, dressed, and joined Danny in the dining room for breakfast—a bountiful feast of scrambled eggs, sausage, toast, and grapefruit—a warm sun had replaced the gauzy mist with shimmering gold streamers across the Texas sky.

Everyone at the dining table agreed it was a balmy day for November, even for Dallas, a perfect day for a visit from the president. As she ate, Jenny could feel the excitement in the air, a sense of expectancy, exhilaration.

"When you see the president, you tell him I say a prayer for him every night," said Mrs. Krashinski, crossing herself. She was a squat, well-padded mother hen of a woman, nearly as wide as she was tall, with a propensity for plying her boarders with copious amounts of food and maternal advice. Like Danny, most were students at Southern Methodist University.

"If everything goes as planned," said Danny, draining his coffee cup, "we'll be seeing the president in a couple of hours."

Mrs. Krashinski breathlessly patted her ample bosom. "I'm dying with envy. Imagine, for a few moments you and President Kennedy will be in the same place at the same time."

Jenny nodded. Indeed, it was an invigorating feeling to imagine sharing a sliver of time with a man who held such a prominent place in history. "You could go with us, Mrs. Krashinski," she suggested.

"No, I couldn't. Big crowds make me nervous. But you two go and enjoy yourselves. I'll expect a full report."

Another boarder at the table, a mousy-faced young man with a crewcut, made a slight hissing sound. "You know Kennedy's coming to Dallas with that glamorous wife of his 'cause he needs our electoral votes. He's got his eye on the presidential election next year."

"So what?" said Danny. "I'm thinking ahead to the election too, figuring how I can help Kennedy get reelected. I may even join his staff."

The boarder snorted. "Big political aspirations, eh?"

Jenny looked at Danny. "Really, Danny? I didn't know you planned to get involved in Kennedy's campaign."

"Why not? I'll have my degree in political science next spring. I'll be a college graduate. I can do anything I please."

"I'd like to hear more about your plans," Jenny said softly, blotting her lips with her white linen napkin.

Danny pushed back his chair. "Swell. We'll talk on the way to Love Field. If we don't go now, we'll never beat the crowds."

Minutes later, as they drove along Lemmon Avenue toward Love Field, seven miles northwest of downtown Dallas, Danny divulged some of his hopes and dreams. Except when he had been on stage singing with the Bell Tones, he had never sounded so eager, so animated. "I figure I can join Kennedy's reelection campaign next spring. Get in on the ground floor. Make a difference. I've already made some inquiries, and the possibilities are good."

"You really want to get that involved in politics? Work for Kennedy's election campaign?"

"Why not? It's a start. And who knows where it could lead? Maybe someday I'll run for Congress. Or even the presidency. Who knows, Jen? Maybe you'll even be my first lady. What do you think? Am I crazy or what?"

"I—I think it's admirable you want to serve your country," she said, trying to match his excitement. "But what about your music, Danny? It's always been so much a part of you. You can't just forget your music."

"Music will always be important to me, Jen. You know that."

But, for Jenny, the more pressing, unspoken question was, *Where will I fit into your life if you immerse yourself in politics? First lady is a long way from Willowbrook.* But she held her tongue, not wanting to evoke an answer that had the power to devastate her.

They were approaching Love Field now, and Jenny could see that a crowd of hundreds, perhaps thousands, had already gathered to greet the president and first lady. "I hope we're not too late," he said. "The place is already packed."

After several frustrating minutes of circling the parking area, Danny found a space some distance from the air field. He parked his powder-blue Studebaker, then he and Jenny hurried toward the airstrip, running hand in hand over the hard-packed, uneven ground. At Gate 28 they wended their way through scores of people pressed eagerly against the chain link fence, many waving signs declaring JFK IN '64 and ALL THE WAY WITH JFK, while others waved Texas and American flags or held their youngsters high on their shoulders. Somehow, Danny managed to pull Jenny through the crushing, teeming throng until they were among the first at the fence.

They stood breathless, hearts pounding, as the press plane and the vice president's Air Force Two touched down, one after the other. Then, shortly after 11:30 A.M. Danny cried, "Look! There it is! Air Force One!"

Jenny shielded her eyes against the late morning sun as the silver, blue-trimmed jet glided in like a huge, mythic bird swooping down from a luminous, cloud-scudding sky. The American flag blazed proudly on its tail and the words UNITED STATES OF AMERICA glinted in large black letters along the fuselage.

The gleaming transport struck the tarmac with a jolt and a squeal, then taxied for some distance on the runway and came to a shuddering stop, its massive engines whirring into silence. Jenny waited, transfixed.

After several moments, the cabin door opened and Mrs. Kennedy stepped out, followed by the president, brushing back a shock of umber-brown hair from his forehead. The two stood framed for a moment in the doorway like the perfect smiling couple on a wedding cake. Then, waving, moving with dignity and vigor, they descended the ramp flanked by an entourage of men in dark suits and sunglasses.

"Secret service," Danny whispered, as if reading the question in Jenny's mind.

Jenny lost sight of the chief executive and first lady for a moment as a cluster of dignitaries—the mayor's welcoming committee—surrounded them. As someone handed Mrs. Kennedy a bouquet of red roses, cameras clicked and flashguns popped and a clamor erupted from the crowd, deafening, uproarious. Jenny had an impulse to hold her ears. Instead she clapped and shouted too, her own emotions surging.

"Look, Jen, they're coming this way," Danny exclaimed. "The president's coming over to shake hands."

For an instant Jenny shrank back uncertainly. What could she possibly say to the president?

Danny pushed her forward and stretched his own arm over the fence. "Reach out and shake his hand, Jen. Put your hand out. Make sure he sees you."

Jenny's heart hammered inside her chest. President Kennedy was only a few yards away now, ruggedly handsome, tanned, impeccable in a natty blue-gray suit, gray pinstriped shirt, and blue tie. He was walking the length of the fence, grinning broadly and shaking hands vigorously, as if greeting family and friends. Mrs. Kennedy moved gracefully beside him, just a step ahead, stunning in a nubby, rose-colored suit with navy collar, a pillbox hat perched on her russet, upswept pageboy. In her arms she carried the bouquet of red roses.

Suddenly there they were, bigger than life, extending a hand to Jenny, first Mrs. Kennedy, her white-gloved hand soft and warm, her luminous brown eyes cordial, direct, disarming, as if she had come to Dallas for this moment alone. "Good morning," she said in her lilting, softly accented voice.

"You look lovely," Jenny replied in an awed half whisper.

"Thank you." Mrs. Kennedy impulsively pulled a long-stem rose from her bouquet and handed it to Jenny.

Jenny could hardly breathe as she clutched the rose to her breast. "Thank you, oh, thank you!" she murmured.

Then the president extended his hand, his head cocked slightly, his crinkly, eloquent gray eyes glinting with merriment, his handclasp firm and reassuring. "Hello. Thanks for coming," he said in a deeply resonant voice.

Jenny felt a radiating warmth as his sturdy hand enveloped hers. It was a transcendent moment. Magical. Time stopped. Everyone around her disappeared; the surrounding cheers and shouts dissolved into silence. For a split second she was connected with history, had become part of a legend. She stood spellbound, hardly realizing that Kennedy had released her hand and was moving on down the line, seizing other outstretched hands as he nodded and beamed and welcomed the eager throng.

Minutes later, as secret service men ushered the president and first lady to a waiting limousine, Danny seized Jenny's free hand and said, "Let's go!"

She stared at him, baffled. "Go? Where?"

"To the car. Before the rush. Traffic jams. We'll make a beeline into town and get a good view of the motorcade. I figure the president should be passing through downtown Dallas in less than an hour."

They ran like excited youngsters to Danny's vehicle, jumped in, and were off at breakneck speed, heading for downtown Dallas. "Can you believe it?" Danny shrilled. "We shook hands with the president!"

On the radio the Brothers Four were singing, "Michael, Row the Boat Ashore," but Jenny hardly heard the words. She was cradling the fragile blood-red rose in her arms and replaying the past few moments, pinching herself to be sure it wasn't a dream.

Danny thumped the newspaper lying on the seat between them. "We're lucky. The newspaper published the exact route the cavalcade will take. A maze-like eleven miles through the heart of the city. We'll just drive around and pick the best spot."

But as they drove toward the business district, the towering skyscrapers of the Dallas skyline rising before them, traffic swelled to a standstill. Main Street was jam-packed, an exuberant, volatile crowd spilling off the curbs, nearly clogging the street. Danny inched his Studebaker along bumper to bumper toward Elm Street. "We'll have to take a detour, Jen," he said at last, disappointment thick in his voice. "It looks like a whole lot of people got here before we did."

Jenny stared disheartened at the throngs amassed along each side of the street, surely twelve deep in places. "Where can we go, Danny? We'll never get close."

"Don't worry, I've got a plan. We'll circle around, park a few blocks from Elm, and find a spot beyond the business district where the crowds aren't so heavy."

Danny finally found a parking spot on Commerce and from there they half-walked, half-ran several blocks west, bypassing the crowded downtown area. They crossed a grassy expanse to the corner of Elm and Houston, where the crowd was surprisingly thin, in places only a single line of spectators. It was like a park, the grass a luxuriant emerald green.

"From here we can see the caravan before it heads down the incline into the underpass," Danny told her. "They'll be moving slowly, making a sharp left at our very corner and taking the Stemmons Freeway to the Trade Mart." He chuckled. "The presidential limousine will be so close we could hop a ride."

Jenny's excitement kindled. "Oh, Danny, I wish we had a camera."

"Take a snapshot in your memory, Jen. Someday we'll tell our grandchildren about the day we saw the president."

Our grandchildren? He had said the words unthinkingly. Was she reading more into the remark than he meant?

"It won't be long now," he said, clasping her arm with a nervous urgency.

She glanced at her watch. Twelve-twenty.

Danny was right about one thing—the timing. They had been standing on the corner for less than ten minutes when they spotted the first police motorcycle escorts leading the cavalcade down Houston toward them. The air was suddenly charged, electric, as the cerulean-blue, flag-studded Lincoln convertible bearing the presidential party approached, flanked by police motorcycles.

The presidential limousine inched along and made a sharp left turn onto Elm Street, heading toward the triple underpass.

"Magnificent, isn't it?" said Danny. "It's Kennedy's own 'Bubbletop' from Washington. Flown in. Can you believe it?"

"Where's the president?" whispered Jenny.

Danny pointed. "Governor and Mrs. Connally are in front, the president and first lady in back."

Jenny saw them now. Waving jubilantly to the crowd, their smiles exultant, they looked as fresh and vibrant as they had at Love Field. The triumphant chief executive and his wife were breathtakingly close, eight feet, ten feet, no greater distance than the space of a small room. So incredibly close!

As the enormous limousine passed by, Jenny held up the rose Mrs. Kennedy had given her and called out, "Thank you!"

Mrs. Kennedy, sitting to the left of her husband, looked over and nodded, smiling, her warm gaze fixed on Jenny for one heady, intoxicating moment.

Jenny couldn't tear her eyes away; she was determined to seal these moments permanently in her memory.

A sharp, cracking noise made her jump instinctively. What was it? A firecracker? Motorcycle backfiring? Surely not a gun. In a split second two more shots rang out above the cheers of spectators.

Before Jenny could think or react, she found herself sprawled on the ground and Danny on top of her, shielding her. She felt the warm, solid weight of his body on her back, the lush, pungent grass in her face, and spiky tendrils of grass in her mouth. The hard earth beneath her grazed her bare arms and legs and a needle-like thorn from the rose pricked her palm.

"Stay down! Someone's shooting!" Danny rasped, his head against hers.

In an instant the whole world had somersaulted into mind-numbing pandemonium. Cheers turned to screams. A motorcycle escort veered toward the curb, mere inches away, spewing dust and gravel into Jenny's eyes, then roared off after the presidential limousine.

Another officer darted by on foot, a looming shadow cutting off the sun for a moment, his booted heel crushing the tender rose Jenny still clutched in her palm. She looked up, blinking against the grittiness behind her lids, craning her neck in spite of Danny's heavy hand on her shoulder.

Jenny saw a blur of pink—surely not Mrs. Kennedy!—scramble out of the limousine and crawl over the back seat and across the rear of the automobile. A secret service agent in a black suit and sunglasses sprinted after the Lincoln, jumped on the back bumper, and coaxed the figure in pink back into the car.

Several helmeted policemen and dark-suited secret service men appeared out of nowhere and dashed after the Lincoln, guns drawn. Pistols. Automatic rifles. Dear God, even machine guns! Like truant youngsters who had missed their school bus, agents and officers frantically chased the fleeing limousine as it picked up speed. There was an aura of rank absurdity about the scene. Bedlam, havoc, horror.

The Lincoln was nearly out of sight when the vice president's limousine roared past. Within moments the motorcade's final press cars had sped by and disappeared from view. As quickly as the maelstrom had erupted, it was over, replaced by an eerie, unnatural silence broken only by a random dirge of stunned, mournful laments and sobs from the bystanders.

Danny released Jenny and she sat up, dazed, shaking her head as if waking from a dream. She was still holding the crushed rose, a tiny bubble of blood showing where a thorn had pierced her palm. She looked around at the grassy knolls, a rich verdant green in the warm sunlight, a placid, park-like atmosphere.

"The shot came from over there," Danny said, pointing to a dilapidated warehouse where several policemen scaled a sloping hill. The multistory red brick building had large, drab windows and a white masonry lacework facade with a nondescript sign that read, TEXAS SCHOOL BOOK DEPOSITORY.

With a sharp intake of breath, Jenny scrambled to her feet, then sank back down on the ground, her ankles weak, her head reeling. Danny wrapped his arms around her and held her tight, his taut jaw pressed fiercely against her forehead. "Dear God," he uttered.

Jenny's throat knotted. "Did they hurt him?"

Danny tightened his hold on her. She could feel the tension constricting his muscles. "I don't know." He looked at her and smoothed back her tangled hair, gently removing a twig caught in a stray curl. "Are you okay?" he asked.

For a moment she didn't recognize him. Shock had drained his face of color and jarred his features just enough to distort his expression. His mouth was twisted at one corner, his lips pale, trembling. "I said, are you all right, Jen?"

She ignored his question. "Who—?"

"I don't know. Let's get out of here. It may not be over yet." He pulled her to her feet and led her across the street, past other onlookers who stood frozen to the spot, past an old man on his knees pounding the earth, past a mother hugging her children and weeping. Jenny hesitated, as if to offer help, but Danny yanked her hand, so she kept running. They ran breathlessly down Houston Street, past a curving, white ornamental fence. Danny had parked his car on Houston, several blocks away. Their pace didn't slacken until they reached his Studebaker.

Danny's hands were shaking as he pulled away from the curb. Jenny realized she was trembling too, so hard that her teeth chattered. She hugged herself and closed her eyes, willing the tremors to cease.

Danny fumbled with the radio dial. A familiar tune was playing.

Something by the Christy Minstrels. "It's too soon," he mumbled, "but maybe—"

Static sizzled over the airwaves, cutting off the lyrical ballad. A deep, formal, emotion-filled voice broke in. "Ladies and gentlemen, we bring you this special news bulletin from downtown Dallas. We have received a report that President Kennedy has been shot. He was struck by gunfire as his motorcade left the business district and headed for an underpass leading to the Trade Mart. He is being taken to Park-land Memorial Hospital. His condition is unknown. I repeat, the president . . ."

Danny swerved slightly as he covered his mouth with his hand. He made an odd sound low in his throat.

"It's true," said Jenny under her breath. "We saw it. They shot the president. Oh, God, we were right there." She dug her fingernails into the soft flesh of her arms. A wave of nausea assailed her stomach. "It feels like the . . . the end of the world."

"Maybe he's okay," said Danny. "Maybe he wasn't hurt."

She looked at him. "You don't believe that. Something happened, something bad."

Danny sucked in a ragged breath. "It can't be that bad, Jen. He's not dead!"

Goose bumps prickled her skin. "You don't think . . . no, they couldn't kill him!"

He bit his lower lip. "How could they? Things like that don't happen. It was just a close call. It's going to be okay."

Danny took a circuitous route toward the boarding house, avoiding Main Street and the crowds. Still, the noontime traffic was heavy, moving sluggishly. But, to Jenny's amazement, nothing seemed amiss. The world was still functioning as it had an hour ago. Traffic signals worked, pedestrians crossed the street at a leisurely pace, passing motorists looked detached, nonchalant. Maybe she and Danny had imagined everything. It was a dream. Maybe they had never gone to see the president today. Maybe they only imagined the announcer's dire words.

Danny drove on stoically, his expression hardening, his knuckles white on the steering wheel. Neither spoke for several minutes. Jenny felt numb, her mind a blank, except for the prayer echoing over and over in her head. *Dear God, let everything be okay. Don't let the president be hurt!*

They arrived back at the boarding house shortly after 1:00 P.M. Mrs. Krashinski opened the door before they even reached the sagging, lattice-trimmed porch. "Oh, holy Mother of God," she wailed, her doughy face splotched with tears. "Did you hear? The president's been shot!"

"We were there," Jenny said shakily, following Mrs. Krashinski inside. She still carried the crushed rose.

"You saw it?"

"We saw something," said Danny. "We don't know what."

The television was on in the living room. Mrs. Krashinski shooed them toward it. "Quick. Come listen. There'll be more news."

They sat down on the overstuffed couch just as a droll-faced, stiff-lipped newsman came on and reported what they already knew; then regular programming resumed. Mrs. Krashinski got up and turned down the sound. "You two look like you need something. Hot tea? Soup?"

"Tea," said Jenny, just for something to say. Nothing would help her now.

"Danny? Tea?"

He nodded distractedly, and Mrs. Krashinski bustled off to the kitchen. Danny sat forward and put his head in his hands. Jenny moved over close beside him and rubbed his muscled arm. "It'll be okay, Danny."

He looked at her, his eyes red-rimmed. "Will it?"

Shortly after 1:30 P.M., as Jenny sat sipping a cup of tepid tea she didn't want, Walter Cronkite appeared on the television screen. He was in his shirtsleeves and had a rumpled, disheveled look about him as he put on his dark-rimmed glasses and looked somberly into the camera. In a heavy, barely controlled voice, he announced, "From Dallas, Texas, the news flash is apparently official. President Kennedy died at 1:00 P.M., Central Standard Time, 2:00, Eastern Standard Time, some thirty-eight minutes ago." He removed his glasses and his voice choked up, so that he had to pause before going on. "President Kennedy died of a gunshot wound in the brain."

"Blessed Mother!" cried Mrs. Krashinski, crossing herself. She burst into heaving sobs and ran from the room.

Danny slammed his fist into the tufted arm of the couch and uttered an anguished, "No!"

Jenny sank back against the cushions, her mind reeling. It wasn't true! Couldn't be. She had just seen the president. For one magical moment he had become real to her—a smiling, laughing, vigorous human being. She had felt the warmth of his handshake; they had looked into each other's eyes and connected.

She reached for the damaged rose beside her on the sofa. With a rising sob, she pressed the soft, velvet petals against her cheek and breathed in the sweet fragrance. A knot of pain tightened in her chest, as if she herself had lost something precious and personal. In the span of two brief hours she had experienced the broad sweep of wildly opposing emotions—delirious joy and decimating loss.

Danny stood up and paced the floor, taking long strides over the worn Oriental carpet, pummeling his fist against his palm. "If only we could have warned them," he said in a tight, shrill voice.

She stared up at him, baffled. "Warned them?"

He looked at her, a haunted, hopeless expression shadowing his eyes. "We stood right there at Love Field shaking his hand, Jen, looking him right in the eye. If only I could have known and said, 'Don't go into Dallas. A gunman's waiting for you.'"

"We didn't know!"

Danny's fists tightened. "We were this close to him, Jen; we were connected. We could have changed history if we'd known."

She stood up and seized his hands. "Don't talk that way, Danny. You're not making any sense. How could we have known? We aren't responsible for what happened to him. It didn't have anything to do with us."

He pulled away from her touch. "Then why do I feel like it did? Why do I feel like I let him down somehow, like I should have been able to do something and didn't?"

"It's not our fault, Danny. We didn't know."

"We were this close!"

She went to him again and hugged him, her slender arms circling his waist. He started to resist, but she tightened her hold. He burrowed his chin in her hair. She nuzzled her cheek against his chest, savoring his warmth through his cotton shirt. She needed to be reminded that death hadn't just swallowed the entire world. The two of them were still alive; the promise of tomorrow was still theirs; they could still feel love and warmth and joy.

Slowly Danny's taut muscles relaxed. His chest heaved, but he wouldn't allow himself to cry. A shudder went through him and he held her closer so that she had to draw back her head to breathe. They stood like that for several minutes, holding each other. Time no longer held meaning.

Jenny wanted to speak, wanted desperately to say something to make everything all right again, but this time too much had happened. Maybe they could never go back.

"Why didn't God stop it?" Danny whispered into her hair.

"I don't know."

"He could have stopped it, and He didn't."

"We can't blame God."

"Can't we? I can. This would have been a perfect day, Jen, the best day ever. But now nothing will ever be the same. Not me, not us, nothing!"

"Don't say that, Danny. We'll be okay. Somehow."

She and Danny rocked together with a mournful rhythm, rocked as one, swaying, breathing as one, without words, unmoving. *Hold on for dear life,* she told herself. Hold on to her beloved Danny and never let him go, lest he be ripped from her arms as swiftly as the president had been torn from his wife's loving embrace.

21

Even with Danny beside her, this night was darker than any Jenny remembered. The wind whistled through the eaves like a whisper, a lament. Annie had once told her, "When you hear the wind, it's me whispering to you, Jenny, reminding you of my love." But this was another kind of wind, stirring up deep, primal fears, reminding Jenny of her childhood terrors—ghostly shadows in the night, grotesque monsters under the bed, ghoulish faces at the window.

If a president could be slain before her very eyes, then anything could happen; no one was safe; everyone was vulnerable. Everything she had ever believed and trusted in was suspect; the old rules—the verities of good triumphing over evil—no longer applied.

If a president could die, then she could die; Danny could die. They could have died this very day; a stray bullet could easily have found them. Danny was right. If a president could die like this, so savagely, so randomly . . . where was God?

Jenny was exhausted after spending long, anxious hours before the television screen. Shock blurred her mind to breaking events—newscasters announcing Kennedy's casket being flown to Washington aboard Air Force One while Vice President Lyndon Johnson was sworn in as the thirty-sixth president of the United States; and a slight, nondescript man named Lee Harvey Oswald arrested in Dallas as a suspect in the murder. But only one horrifying fact drumrolled over and over in Jenny's thoughts: *Kennedy was slain . . . Kennedy was slain.*

That night Danny had remained with Jenny in her room; she was afraid of the dark, didn't want to sleep alone in the dark. When she was a child, her mother or grandmother always left a light on or a candle burning to ward off the nocturnal phantoms of her imagination. Tonight neither she nor Danny could imagine being alone. They lay fully clothed in each other's arms on the covers of the small bed. If they clung desperately to each other, maybe they could ward off the feel and taste and smell of death. Candles burned on the dresser and windowsill, their charred wicks scenting the air, their flames flickering like fireflies in the inky blackness. A clock ticked; a train whistle blew; a siren sounded far away.

Once, when Danny half-heartedly mentioned going and letting her get some sleep, Jenny told him no, she couldn't stand to be alone, couldn't possibly sleep alone in the whispering darkness.

Sometime around midnight she almost dozed, but woke when she heard a muffled sob beside her. Danny's body shook and he rolled over, turning his face to the wall. Jenny moved close and wound her arms around him. She pressed her face against his broad back, absorbing his convulsive sobs against her own body. She had never loved Danny more.

After a long while, Danny sat up, stared into the shadows, and said bitterly, "Everything I've done with my life is foolishness, a complete waste of time."

"Don't say that, Danny."

"Why not? All my life I've searched for truth and direction. I wanted to do something, be somebody, serve mankind in some way. But tonight I am as far from knowing truth as I have ever been."

Wordlessly, Jenny held him, his raw pain mingling with her own sense of loss. She could feel him shutting down emotionally, steeling himself, physically shutting her out.

Toward dawn Jenny fell into a fitful sleep. As her slumber deepened, vivid dreams flooded just beneath her consciousness; the action was frantic, slapdash, disjointed, with people shouting and running every which way over emerald-green hills. Jenny was running too, breathing hard, her ribs ready to explode as she chased the president's speeding limousine. But when she reached the convertible and stared inside, she saw her own father, Chilton Reed, lying bleeding and dying among the strewn roses.

Jenny woke with a start, the image heart-poundingly real. She had seen her father! Her brush with death had swept her back to him. What did it mean? She sat up and slipped quietly off the bed and headed for the bathroom, shaking off the dregs of sleep. She stripped off her rumpled clothes and stepped into the shower, turning on the tepid water full blast. For a long while she let the staccato streams strike her face, her body, bringing her to life. Shivering, she got out, toweled herself off, and put on fresh clothes. A knit sweater and an A-line skirt.

She found her Bible in her suitcase and sat down at the small desk and read as the first ribbons of dawn trickled through the green calico curtains. From time to time she gazed across the room at Danny sleeping soundly, his breathing slow and deep. She loved him, but she could not help him or heal his hurts, just as he could not help her.

"I have nowhere to go but to You, dear God," she whispered brokenly. "No one to turn to but You. Help me. Help Danny!" For a long time she sat in silence in the presence of God, listening, waiting, her prayers coming without words from a secret place inside she'd never known.

Later, as the sun streamed golden through the narrow windows, Danny stirred and raised up on one elbow. "Jenny? You up already? What are you doing?"

She closed her Bible, her face flushing slightly. "Just reading. Praying."

He swung his legs over the side of the bed. "It's too late for that."

"It's never too late."

"It's too late for Kennedy."

"We're still here, Danny."

"So what? So God can knock us down too?"

"He's the only One we can turn to, Danny. Without Him, what do we have?"

"What do we have with Him? What kind of God is He anyway? A bully? A sadist?"

"No, Danny. He loves us. He's all we have."

Danny leaned forward and put his head in his hands. "Then I'd rather have nothing."

Jenny touched her Bible, ran her finger lightly over the gold letters on the black leather cover. H-O-L-Y . . .

"Danny," she said softly, "when I was a little girl, I pictured God up in the sky somewhere, in heaven, this vast distance away from me. And once in a while He would look down and nod or frown at me, depending on whether I was being good or bad. He was remote, like a grandfather in the sky, like a distant relative I wrote to once in a while because my mother made me. But He had nothing to do with who I really was. In my mind He didn't have a clue about me."

Danny looked at her, his brows shading his eyes. "So?"

She shrugged. "So . . . I don't know."

"So you were right. God doesn't have a clue."

"But He does. These past few years I've gotten to know Him better."

"Swell."

"I'm serious, Danny. I feel like I'm on this terrible roller coaster ride, hanging on for dear life. Only, Jesus is in the roller coaster too, hanging on to me so I won't fall."

She continued tracing the letters. B-I-B-L-E. "I didn't realize until this morning when I was praying how close He is. I'm not alone. Neither are you."

"Cut it out, Jen. You're starting to sound like my dad. You've been listening to too many of his sermons."

"I'm just trying to tell you how I feel. Even when I'm scared out of my wits or feel like I've lost something precious, like now, Jesus is part of me. When I was praying this morning I heard His voice in my head; I felt His arms around me. He was right there, closer than you are."

Danny's eyes narrowed. "So what are you telling me, Jen?"

"Nothing. Everything. How I feel."

He raked his fingers through his sleep-tousled hair. "Maybe you should be a preacher, Jen. Like my father."

She bristled. "I'm not trying to preach, Danny. I'm just trying to help you find some comfort, like I found this morning."

He stood up and tucked his shirttails into his trousers. "I'm not looking for comfort. I want to see some justice in this crazy world."

"Only God can—"

"Stop it, Jen. Enough talk about God. Like I said, you're sounding too much like my father!"

"Maybe that's not so bad, Danny. Maybe we both should have been listening . . ."

Danny crossed the room and turned on the radio. "Maybe there's some news."

She stood up, gripping the edge of the desk. "Don't shut me out, Danny. This is important. How can we have a future together if we don't feel the same way about things?"

He turned the dial, static breaking over the channels. One announcer described a smiling Kennedy as he greeted Dallas well-wishers yesterday at Love Field. Another newscaster reported on Lyndon Johnson assuming his duties at the White House. Another reviewed the scant information known about the suspected assassin, Lee Harvey Oswald.

Danny leaned one hand on the radio and listened. Jenny listened too, resisting the hypnotic pull of the reporter's voice that would inevitably lure her back into the terrible, unfolding drama. After a moment she turned away, hugging herself. She didn't want to hear any more about the grisly events that had brought the world to a stand-still. Right now she wanted to concentrate on her life and Danny's. Their future.

"Were you listening to me, Danny?" she asked. "We were talking about us."

He gave her a sidelong glance. "How can we talk about us when the whole world's gone crazy?"

"Because that's why I came to Dallas . . . to see if the love we had is real and strong enough to build a life on."

"It is, Jenny."

"You believe God wants us to have a future together?"

Danny snapped off the radio and came over to the desk; he took both her hands in his and drew her to him. "We have a future together, Jen, but it has nothing to do with God."

His words stung. She searched his eyes. "You don't believe that. You've always loved God, even when you were angry with your father."

"Maybe, but that was before."

"Before . . . ?"

"Before we stood watching a bullet take down the president." He stepped back from her and made a fist. "Where's God now, Jen? Now that Kennedy's dead and everything's fallen apart? What's God going to do for an encore?"

She reached for him. Somehow she had to convince him. Their future depended on it. "Please, Danny, don't talk that way. God's the only One who can get us through this."

He seized her wrists. "Stop it, Jenny. We're not going to agree on this. Just drop it!"

She retreated, breaking his hold, feeling as if he had physically wounded her. "I think I'd better go home, Danny."

"Go home? You just got here."

"I shouldn't have come. Once we wanted the same things, but not anymore."

Danny's voice softened. "What is it you want, Jenny?"

She sat down on the bed and smoothed the chenille spread. "I want to sing again."

"All right. What's wrong with that?"

"I don't mean with the band. I want to sing for God. I don't know where, I don't know how, but He's given me this desire, and I don't know what to do with it."

"You mean you want to sing like we did for the Billy Graham Crusade the summer before last?"

She smiled. "Yeah, only maybe not on such a grand scale. It's not every day you can sing for thousands of people. I just want to sing about what God's done for me."

Danny sat down beside her and took her hand again. He stroked it with a nervous agitation. "I don't know what to tell you, Jen. I feel like I've wrestled with God and my father for half my life, and just when I think I know which voice I'm hearing, something happens to throw me for a loop. I've tried to pray, to make peace with God, but after yesterday I'm through trying. So if you're looking for some spiritual giant . . ."

"No, Danny. Just someone who loves God and wants to sing for Him. Or maybe not sing. Maybe serve Him some other way, I don't know. I'm just finding my way myself. I hope the man I marry will help me get to know God better."

Danny released her hand and crossed his arms on his chest. His face clouded and his voice took on a sudden detachment that made her wince. "I'm not that man, Jen."

Tears welled in her eyes. "How can you say that, Danny?"

"Because I don't want anything to do with such a cruel, capricious God. And I'm not just talking about Kennedy now. I'm talking about me. God has taken everything from me—a career in music and probably my future in politics. And you—I wanted you, and now He's taking you from me too. I can't love that kind of God."

"He's not that kind of God."

"He is to me."

"Then I guess there's nothing else to say," she murmured. "I can't give up my faith, not even for you, Danny."

"I'm not asking you to give it up. Just don't ask me to make some sort of spiritual commitment to please you. I can't do it. I've got to be true to myself."

"I wouldn't ask that of you, Danny. You know me too well for that." Her voice quavered. "I just wish you knew how much God loves you."

Under his breath he murmured darkly, "Yeah, I wish I could believe it too."

Jenny got up and went to the dresser for a tissue. She blew her nose and blotted the wetness under her eyes, then turned back to Danny. "It's crazy, isn't it?" she said, forcing her voice to sound light, natural.

"What is?"

"This whole thing. Something so terrible happening. The president killed. It's so unspeakably awful, it makes me want to run straight to God for comfort. It makes me want to tell the whole world that Jesus is the only One who can ever make things right again."

"What's your point, Jen?"

She looked earnestly at him, searching his eyes. "How is it the same event can drive me to God and drive you away? How does that happen?"

He shrugged. "Maybe I'm just being realistic."

"Maybe you're just being . . . wrong."

"Could be. But that's how I feel right now."

Jenny walked over to the window and looked out. The sun had a sallow cast, as if it were forcing its rays through a gauzy veil. "I'm going to phone the airlines and see if I can get a flight home tomorrow," she said with a catch in her voice.

Surprise sharpened Danny's tone. "You're really going home early?"

She nodded. "After all that's happened, it's too painful to stay here, Danny."

"You're not just talking about Kennedy dying, are you?"

"No. I'm talking about us."

"A different kind of death," he said thickly.

She brushed away a tear. "If you ever change your mind, Danny, you know where to find me."

He ground his jaw. "And you know where to find me too."

On Sunday afternoon, Danny drove Jenny to the airport. Like polite but awkward strangers, they said little to each other, even as they said their good-byes and she boarded her plane for Chicago. What could they say? This was an ending, one of many this weekend. Just this morning they had watched in stunned silence as a man—a Dallas nightclub owner named Jack Ruby—darted across the television screen and fired a bullet into Lee Harvey Oswald, killing the president's assassin before their very eyes.

When would the horror end? Jenny wondered. When would the nightmare be over? And when would the pain of losing Danny ever go away?

22

For the nation and for Jenny, Christmas of 1963 was a time of inner contemplation, spiritual self-examination, and heartfelt prayer. Painfully raw were the memories of a month before when the entire world came to a stop because one man died. Repercussions of that day continued like ripples fanning out in a great sea. Folks in Willowbrook still spoke in hushed whispers of the day the world changed. They remembered. Would always remember. On the day a bullet stopped the president, people stopped, schools stopped, the New York Stock Exchange stopped, and the Canadian House of Commons, the United Nations, Congress, the courts, and theaters closed, and sports events were canceled. And when the wheels of time started again, everything was different. Even Christmas.

While the world mourned a president's death and a nation's loss of innocence, Jenny did her own private grieving. Between the pages of her Bible she pressed the crushed rose Jacqueline Kennedy had given her. Every morning when she opened her Bible, she looked at the bruised, withered flower, its lacy petals sheer as butterfly wings, and remembered that fateful day in Dallas and the weekend she and Danny had said good-bye.

She grieved for the fallen president. For his brave widow. For herself. For Danny. For the love they had shared and lost. For the timing that was never right. For the hopes and dreams she was forced to relinquish.

If she had entertained any remnant hopes that her relationship with Danny could be salvaged, they were dashed when she received his Christmas card. "Wish I could get home for the holidays," he wrote in his scrawled hand under the printed verse, "but there's too much to do if I want to graduate in June. I'll be spending Christmas with Donna Garvey and her family in Georgia. They're great people; they treat me like a son. And Donna's been terrific too, nudging me out of my doldrums and helping me get my life back on track. Don't know what I would have done without her. Hope all is well with you, Jenny. Have a swell Christmas. And give everyone my love. Danny."

Jenny's New Year's resolution for 1964 was to throw herself so fervently into her studies, she would have no time to think of Danny. So for the next semester at Willowbrook University she took the largest class load allowed; if she passed every subject she, like Danny, would graduate in June. In addition to her schooling, Jenny led the church choir, helped Annie with her research, and helped care for her Grandmother Betty, who remained chipper and alert in spite of her growing frailty.

Early in March Jenny received a rare letter from Callan Swan, saying, "Jenny, my girl, just wanted to let you know that, after over eight years together, the band has disbanded. That's right, baby. To my great regret, the Bell Tones is kaput. As you know, the music has changed from what we knew and celebrated in the '50s. These days, pimply faced kids are gyrating to dances with animal names like the Chicken, the Monkey, and the Dog.

"I booked the band in a few New York discotheques and even the Whiskey a Go-Go in Los Angeles where bikini-clad girls dance in suspended cages, of all things! I tried the new sound, but I just can't dig it, and frankly, the audience doesn't dig us the way it used to. Maybe we'd have a chance if we changed our name to the Kangaroos or the Chameleons! What do you think? Or the June Bugs, maybe? Bugs seem to be in style these days.

"Speaking of bugs, did you see that new British group on the *Ed Sullivan Show* last month? The Beatles! What kind of name is that? And did you get a look at their outfits and hair styles? Man alive! Any self-respecting male would laugh them out of town. But oh, no. Audiences are wild about them. Who would have thought?

"After breaking up the Bell Tones, I hit rock bottom for a while. I was like a dead man without my music. Even wished I was dead like our good buddy Andy. When Andy died a couple of years ago, that's when everything started falling apart. I blamed myself for letting the guys booze it up, for letting them get carried away and make Andy drink himself to death. But things are better now. I'm finally getting my life straightened around.

"Anyway, Jenny girl, I want you to know I've teamed up again with our old friend, Emmett Sanders. He's formed his own group and travels all over the country, performing old-time gospel music in churches and fairgrounds and civic auditoriums and what have you. I know you won't believe this, but Emmett has seen to it that I 'get religion.' Losing Andy the way we did made me sober up in a lot of ways. So now I'm singing for the Lord, and it's not half bad. Imagine Jesus taking an old renegade like me and cleaning him up. So, you see, sweetheart, I've got something to sing about now.

"And that's my other reason for this letter, Jenny girl. I figure you must be about finished with college and ready for a real career. So how about joining Emmett and me and going on the road again? You and I can still make beautiful music together, only this time we'll be singing for the angels. How about it? I've never stopped loving you. Yours always, Cal."

After reading the letter, Jenny felt stunned, euphoric, and suspicious, all at once. Had Cal really changed? Surely if anyone could reach him, it was Emmett. Em radiated the love of God. Was it possible God wanted her with Callan? Had He kept things from working out with Danny so she would be available for Cal? The idea seemed incomprehensible—

that she was meant to be with Callan Swan! Would God play such an immense practical joke on her, letting her think Danny was the one when it was really Cal all along?

Jenny needed time to digest this new development. Lots of time. She had never seriously considered loving Callan Swan; he was half the man Danny was. And yet if Jesus had gotten hold of his life and changed him, maybe he was a man she could love. The thought boggled her mind. And the idea of joining Emmett's group tantalized her. She would love to perform with him again, and with Callan, too, now that he was singing for God. Maybe this was her destiny, her calling, her future.

But Jenny wasn't about to rush things. She wrote Callan a warm, friendly letter, telling him she was delighted about his new musical venture with Emmett and she would think and pray about his invitation to join them. But she couldn't make any promises until God gave her peace. Even then, she wouldn't be able to join them until after her graduation in June. Cal wrote back immediately and said he would be waiting for her favorable response.

And Jenny—what was she waiting for? For Danny, the one man she had always wanted.

On May 13, Jenny's twenty-second birthday, she received a card from Danny with a scribbled note telling her he would be graduating in June as planned and coming home to Willowbrook at last. "I'll be home the middle of June," he wrote. "Will you meet me at the depot? I have a big surprise. My life has taken an entirely new direction, one I can't begin to share with you in a letter. I'll tell you all about it when we meet face to face."

Puzzled, Jenny tucked the cryptic letter back into its envelope. It said so little and yet so much. What surprise did Danny have? And why couldn't he tell her in his letter?

When she could stand the suspense no longer, Jenny went to the phone and dialed Bethany Rose. If anyone knew what was happening with Danny, it would be his stepmother. But when Bethany answered, Jenny found herself stammering awkwardly. Would Bethany think she was prying into Danny's personal life? And did Jenny really want to know the truth when it had the power to wound her?

After a few moments of hemming and hawing Jenny blurted out, "Have you heard from Danny?"

"Yes, we got a letter today," said Bethany, her tone guarded. "He said he was writing to you too, Jenny."

"Yes, he did. I got a letter."

Bethany sounded relieved. "Well, then you know. I hope you weren't terribly upset, honey."

"Upset?" Jenny echoed.

"You know." A long pause. "He did tell you, didn't he?"

Jenny's voice wavered. "He . . . he just said he's bringing home a surprise. He wouldn't tell me what."

Bethany's voice swelled with sympathy. "Oh, Jenny, I'm sorry. I thought he told you. How could he think he could wait until he gets home? That's a man for you."

"Tell me what, Bethany?" Jenny's throat constricted and her mouth felt like cotton. "Please. What's Danny's surprise?"

Bethany's voice turned guarded again. "Oh, Jenny, I shouldn't be the one telling you. But, well, you'll have to know sooner or later."

"Know what?" pleaded Jenny.

"Honey, Danny's getting married. He and that girl in Texas—that Donna Garvey—are planning a July wedding."

Jenny's head spun. She held the receiver away from her ear for a long moment. "Danny's . . . getting married?"

"I don't know why he didn't tell you. It's not like him to be so cruel."

Jenny choked back a sob. "He had no reason to tell me. We broke up last Thanksgiving."

"But you still care, don't you, Jenny? I can hear it in your voice."

"I'll always care." Jenny steadied her voice. "But love wasn't enough.

We wanted different things from life." Another long pause. "Bethany, did he say anything else in his letter?"

"Probably the same things he wrote you. He said his life has taken an entirely new direction, and he's bringing home a surprise. He said he hopes we'll be happy for him. We will. We must be."

Jenny's fingers tightened on the receiver. Her palm was clammy. "What did Danny say about the wedding?"

"Oh, honey, I hate to tell you. He said he's helping Donna with the wedding plans and he never knew how much there was to do. Her parents are planning a lavish reception with a guest list of hundreds. Danny is flying to Georgia in July for the ceremony. He said he's never seen Donna so happy, and he can't wait to see her coming down the aisle."

Jenny sank down in a nearby chair, weak-kneed. "It's true then. He's not just thinking about marrying her. He's made up his mind. The wedding's already arranged. He must have no doubts she's the one for him."

"He has known her for a long time, Jenny."

"And lately he's spent more time with her than he has with me," Jenny said feebly. "But I never thought . . ."

"I'm sorry, honey. I know what a shock this must be."

Jenny forced a lilt into her voice, but it came out brittle. "I'll be fine, Bethany Rose. It just takes a little getting used to."

"Donna must be the surprise he's bringing home," said Bethany. "He'll want his father and me to get to know her before the wedding."

"But why would he ask me to come to the depot when he's bringing home his fiancée?" Jenny lamented.

"I'm sure he's not trying to be mean-spirited, Jenny. He probably just wants you to get to know Donna. After all, you and Danny have been close all your lives. He wants you to share his happiness. You will go, won't you, Jenny?"

"I . . . I don't know." Jenny wanted to shout into the phone that she never wanted to see Danny again, that he could whisk his darling

Donna off to some distant planet, for all she cared. But she forced her voice to remain civil, detached. "I'll try to make it, Bethany Rose. I suppose it's the last thing Danny will ever ask of me."

During the next few weeks, Jenny went through the motions of studying, taking final exams, and receiving her diploma. At the edge of every action was the brooding thought, *Danny's getting married. He loves someone else, not me!*

In her prayers, Jenny tried bargaining, arguing, and pleading with God. But she always came back to the same realization. God had taken Danny out of her life forever; she couldn't have the one thing she wanted more than anything—the man she loved. Somehow she had to accept her loss and go on.

She recalled a song she had sung in childhood, one of Emmett's favorites. "You take the whole world, but give me Jesus." Such easy words to sing, but could she live them? Could she relinquish Danny without bitterness? Could she truly be satisfied if she had nothing else except Jesus?

The night before Danny was scheduled to arrive in Willowbrook, Jenny knelt on the floor by her bed and gazed up at the moonlit window. The house was silent except for a ticking clock, creaking floorboards, and a persistent branch scratching the window panes. Jenny felt like a child again saying her prayers. *Now I lay me down to sleep* . . . But this wasn't a child's prayer; it was the anguished cry of a woman struggling to surrender everything to her Lord.

Jenny vowed not to get off her knees until she had given God everything she still clutched in her hands . . . and her heart. "Jesus," she whispered into the darkness, "You gave up everything You had for me. Your very life. Help me to give everything I have to You. Even Danny. Especially Danny. Help me to love You so much it won't matter if I lose him."

Sometime after midnight, as Jenny's bare knees ached from the hard floorboards, she sank against her bed and rested her head on the plush comforter, her mussed hair falling over her moist forehead and cheek. She felt as if she had laid her head in Jesus' lap, and He was offering her a father's comfort, the way her own father might have done if he had lived. But this went beyond a human father's touch. She could feel Christ's love spreading through her like sunshine, like a balmy breeze, a gentle, soothing hand.

She stretched her arms over the bedspread and opened her hands, her fingers splayed wide. All the resistance, anger, and disappointment eased from her tired limbs, from her broken, defenseless heart. She had given God all she knew how to give; she was holding nothing back, not even Danny, not her music, nothing. She was starting over, from scratch, her hands and heart empty, except for Christ's Spirit, His tender love. And He was enough. Jesus was enough. For the first time in her life she understood what it meant to have nothing but Christ and to know He was sufficient; He was her all in all. And whatever He chose to give back to her she would accept gratefully.

It was a sweet, startling revelation, a joyous epiphany. With Jesus she had everything, without Him she had nothing. With that knowledge she could face whatever life threw at her. Even Danny. Even Danny and Donna getting married next month.

The next morning Jenny telephoned Bethany Rose and told her she wouldn't be going with them to the depot to meet Danny. "This should be a private time for you and the reverend to meet Donna and welcome Danny home. I wouldn't feel comfortable intruding . . . But give Danny my love and best wishes."

And she meant it. Her heart was free of bitterness. She wanted God's best for Danny, and if Donna was the one, so be it. Meanwhile, she would keep herself busy so she wouldn't think about the train arriving this afternoon, bringing Danny and Donna to Willowbrook. She wouldn't think about how much she wanted to be there and run into Danny's arms. No, all of that was behind her; she had given it to God, given Him all her hopes and dreams and expectations.

For an hour or two that morning Jenny wandered around the house looking for something to occupy her time, her thoughts. She wandered into her mother's art studio at the back of the house and watched her mother spread a rainbow of oil colors on a canvas, creating a lush summer landscape with her quick, deft brush strokes.

After a while Jenny drifted upstairs to Grandma Betty's room and sat by her bed and read her the twenty-third Psalm. At lunchtime Jenny brought up a tray of chicken noodle soup and tuna fish sandwiches, and she and her grandmother had lunch together. Halfway through, her mother joined them, wiping turpentine from her fingers and pulling a bandanna from her auburn curls. She sat down with them and had a sandwich and they all watched *Truth or Consequences* and laughed easily at all the funny parts.

This was one of God's unexpected gifts—she and her mother and grandmother in the same room laughing and having fun together. For the rest of her life she would treasure such ordinary, extraordinary moments—sitting with Mama and Grandma Betty, eating sandwiches, watching television, laughing, the summer sun shining in, making the room golden and warm.

Shortly, Grandma Betty drifted off to sleep and Mama went back to her painting. Jenny headed upstairs to her room. It was nearly 2:00 P.M. Danny's train would be arriving soon. Bethany Rose and the reverend would be greeting him and his bride-to-be and they would be heading to the parsonage for a celebration.

Jenny wouldn't be there. She wouldn't be sharing any of the big events in Danny's future, nor the small, insignificant moments that shaped an entire lifetime. Someone else would be at his side, loving him, encouraging him, sharing his burdens, and bearing his children. Not Jenny. But God would give her the strength to go on without Danny.

Shortly after 3:00 P.M. Jenny heard the doorbell ring. She waited for a moment, hoping her mother would get it. But Mama wouldn't hear the bell from the back of the house, and the ringing was growing more insistent.

With a sigh Jenny headed downstairs. "I'm coming," she called as she crossed the living room to the entry. She swung open the door and stared up open-mouthed at the towering figure before her. "Danny?"

He flashed her his crinkly eyed grin and handed her a long-stem red rose. "For you, Jen." He looked healthy and vigorous in a maroon polo shirt and beige slacks; his face and arms were tanned and the breeze had sent strands of his umber-brown hair curling over his forehead. He had never looked more handsome.

"What are you doing here?" she blurted.

"I came to see you. May I come in?"

She stepped aside and allowed him to enter. He strolled in and headed for the living room. She followed him and watched in perplexity as he made himself comfortable on the overstuffed sofa. He looked up at her, his arms spread over the back of the couch. "Sit down, Jen. It's good to see you."

"Same here," she mumbled and sat down in the armchair opposite him. She set the rose on the glass coffee table between them, then smoothed her pleated skirt over her knees and crossed her arms stiffly, waiting, wondering.

"Why didn't you meet my train, Jen?"

"I thought it was best," she said, "considering."

"Considering?"

"I wanted you to have a special time with your folks."

"But I especially wanted to see you. Things were pretty bad the last time we were together. Kennedy getting shot . . . us breaking up."

"That was the worst weekend of my life, Danny."

"Mine too. But a lot has happened since then. We have a lot to talk about, Jen."

She rubbed her hands nervously; her fingers felt like icicles in spite of the summer heat. "Bethany already told me," she said in a small, controlled voice.

"She told you?"

"Yeah. About Donna. The wedding."

Danny drummed his fingers on the tufted sofa. "Oh, yeah. I did write her about Donna and the wedding."

It hurt just hearing him say her name, but Jenny managed to say, "I hope she'll be very happy."

Danny smiled unabashedly. "Oh, she will be. She's waited for this day for years."

Jenny's heart twisted. How could Danny be so callous, so blasé? "And you're happy, Danny?" she asked thickly. "About the wedding?"

"Me? Sure. Why not? Who doesn't like a wedding?"

"It's next month. Isn't that awfully soon?"

He shrugged. "No, I don't think so. Donna has her degree now. She's ready to be a wife. Of course, she'll be teaching too. She's already lined up a position in Atlanta. Junior high. I don't envy her trying to keep a bunch of little rascals in line."

"Atlanta? That's awfully far away."

"Not really. She wanted something close to her family. You know, so her parents will be able to enjoy their grandchildren."

"Grandchildren?" Jenny echoed in horror.

Danny chuckled. "Not right away, of course. I told her she should just enjoy being married for the first year or two, without the patter of little feet to spoil the romance."

Jenny clasped her hand over her mouth, afraid she would be sick. "If that's all you came to say, Danny," she began.

He sat forward and rested his hands on his knees. He gave her a baffled, disquieting look. "What do you mean, Jen? We haven't begun to talk . . . about us."

Us! A shiver crept up her spine. "What else is there to say, Danny?"

"Plenty, Jen. I feel awful about the way we left things last Thanksgiving."

She nodded.

"I was so angry and bitter. I was practically out of my mind with all that had happened."

"Me too."

"You know how I felt about Kennedy, especially with us being there and seeing him killed before our eyes. For a long time afterward I couldn't think straight. I couldn't feel anything, except rage."

"I understand, Danny. You don't have to explain."

"Yes, I do, Jen. We broke up because I was so angry at God, and because you were convinced we were going in different directions and wanted different things out of life."

"That's all in the past, Danny. Why dredge it up now? We've both moved on with our lives."

"Have we?" He sat forward intently, his square knees pressing against the coffee table. "There's something you need to know, Jen."

She shook her head. "No, Danny, don't say it. I have no ill feelings toward you. In fact, I wish you every happiness." Distractedly she picked up the rose. Careful to avoid its thorns, she breathed in its sweet fragrance. It was perfectly formed, as beautiful as any she had ever seen, but it summoned raw, painful memories. Her mother had given her roses when she missed her graduation. Mrs. Kennedy had given her a rose just before tragedy struck. Now Danny was giving her a rose as he broke her heart and said his good-byes, leaving her alone forever.

"Jenny, just hear me out, okay?"

She lowered her gaze and ran her finger over a soft, velvet petal. If she could just get through these next few minutes, nothing else in life would be quite so hard. *Help me, Lord! Don't let me break down and cry in front of Danny!*

"Jen, I've spent these past six months on a spiritual odyssey, slowly reclaiming the faith of my childhood." He paused for a long moment, massaging his sturdy knuckles, first one hand, then the other. "It's taken me a long time to realize that the voice I was hearing in my head all these years wasn't my father's voice. It was my heavenly Father's."

His deep voice broke over slow, rising emotion. "Don't you see, Jen? I wasn't rebelling against the reverend; I was resisting God's call on my life. He wanted a Father-son relationship with me, a loving connection. And all I could see was my human father, who was absent for the first eight years of my life because he didn't even know he had gotten my mother pregnant." Danny's thickly lashed eyes met hers with an unnerving intensity, piercing her defenses. "I couldn't forgive my dad for being a minister and preaching at me when he himself had sinned and abandoned my mother and me."

"Your father has always regretted what he did," said Jenny quietly. "He's spent his life trying to make amends."

"I know that now, Jen. I realize my dad's human just like me, and I've forgiven him. But after Kennedy was killed, I blamed God the same way I blamed my father. It took me a long time to realize God isn't to blame for the wrongs in this world and in my own life. I understand now that God hates sin more than we do. He grieves right along with us. I wanted you to know He finally got through to me, Jen."

She touched the rose to her cheek and savored its softness, its delicate scent. Tears pressed hard against the back of her eyes. Why was Danny telling her all of this now when it was too late for them to be together? "I'm happy for you, Danny," she murmured, brushing away an unwanted tear, "but shouldn't you get home to Donna?"

He looked quizzically at her. "To Donna?"

"Yes, she came home with you, didn't she? On the train?"

Danny made a scoffing sound low in his throat. "No, Jen. She's back in Georgia planning her wedding."

"Oh? I thought you were planning it together."

"I tried to help her out some in Dallas, but most of the arrangements have to be made in Georgia."

Jenny nodded. "That makes sense. I suppose you'll be flying to Atlanta. Or will you take the train?"

"I don't know. What difference does it make?"

"None, I suppose." She held the rose, running her fingers over the stem, pressing the soft pad of her fingertip against a spiky thorn. She felt its sharpness pierce her skin the way the thorns had pricked her flesh in Dallas last November. She watched in silent fascination as a tiny bubble of crimson formed on her finger.

Danny saw the fleck of blood and jumped up in alarm. "Be careful, Jenny."

"It's nothing," she said solemnly. "It doesn't matter."

He sprang off the couch, darted around the coffee table, and knelt on one knee beside her chair. He took her small hand in his and gently kissed the blood from her finger. "I wouldn't have given you the rose if I thought you'd hurt yourself," he said, cradling her hand in his.

"It's okay," she assured him, her heart quickening at his closeness. "You can't have a rose without thorns."

He bent his face close to hers, anguish etched in his blue-green eyes. "Oh, Jenny. Jenny, I've missed you so much."

"I've missed you too," she murmured dreamily, entranced by his nearness.

His lips moved over her cheek, light as a hummingbird's wings. She savored the sweet peppermint warmth of his breath on her face. Memories of youthful fantasies and tender yearnings sprang unbidden to her mind. Danny's gentle kiss brought a heady, delicious euphoria . . . until Jenny remembered Donna.

"We can't," she whispered. "What about Donna?"

"Donna? Why do you keep talking about Donna?"

"How can you ask that, Danny? You're marrying her!"

Danny sat back on his heels and looked wide-eyed at her. "Where'd you get a crazy idea like that?"

"From the letter you wrote Bethany. That's all you could talk about—Donna's wedding. How you were helping her plan it. How you were looking forward to seeing her come down the aisle."

"It's all true," he said with mock seriousness. "I helped her plan her wedding. And I can't wait to see her come down the aisle. You've just got one fact wrong, Jen."

"What's that?" she asked warily.

He stifled a chuckle. "I'm not the groom. I'm the best man."

Jenny stared at him with a mixture of astonishment and suspicion. "I don't understand. Are you getting married or not?"

Danny stood and pulled her up, facing him. He held both her hands in his and swung them slightly. "I am getting married. At least, I hope so. But not to Donna. She's already taken."

"Taken?"

"By a very nice man from her hometown. Glen Hawthorne. Glen asked me to be his best man, so I'll be standing beside him when Donna comes down the aisle next month."

"You . . . you're not marrying her?"

Danny swung her arms wide. "No, you silly goose. If I marry anyone, it'll be you."

Jenny's thoughts were flying in every direction at once, like confetti in the wind. She couldn't pull them together to utter a coherent sentence. "But Bethany said . . . your letter . . . the surprise . . ."

"Honey, I wrote Bethany and Dad about Donna's wedding because Donna's the best friend a guy could have, but I never dreamed Bethany would think I was the bridegroom."

"We all thought . . . oh, Danny, then you don't . . . love her?"

Danny drew Jenny against him, his strong arms circling her, holding her so tight she nearly gasped. "Darling, you're the only one I love, the only girl I'll ever love. And God willing, you still love me too."

"I do," she whispered, "but I—I can't marry you. I gave everything to God, Danny. Even you. I promised I wouldn't take back anything that God doesn't give me."

Danny nuzzled her hair with his square jaw. "Well, I've talked to Him about you a whole lot lately, and I believe with all my heart He wants us together. So ask Him, Jenny. We'll sing for Him or find some other way to serve Him, but we'll be a team—the three of us."

With sweet abandon Jenny nestled her cheek against Danny's muscular chest and reveled in the feel of his strong arms around her. She felt safe and loved and protected. She felt the pleasure of God pouring down on her like summer sunshine, golden, warm, and beneficent. "Wait a minute," she said, looking up at Danny. "If Donna wasn't the surprise you were bringing home, then what was?"

His lips spread into an expansive grin. "I wondered when you were going to get around to that."

"Tell me," she urged. "What's the surprise?"

He fished for something in his back pocket and produced a small silver box. "This is for you, Jen. My surprise . . . if you'll accept it."

She took the tiny box and opened it with care. On a black velvet pillow sat a gold ring with an exquisite diamond. Tears welled in her eyes. "Oh, Danny!"

"I love you, Jen, with all my heart. Will you marry me?"

"Danny, you'll have to ask my Father."

"Papa Robert?"

"Oh, yes. Papa Robert too."

"Who else?" Danny paused and rolled his eyes heavenward. "Oh, I understand." He chuckled. "Well, like I said, I happen to have some pretty good connections with Him, Jen. He's the kind of Father who doesn't withhold anything good from His children."

Jenny looked deep into Danny's eyes, basking in his love. "You're right," she said softly. "He's the kind of Father who'll always be there for us, Danny, the way a father should."

Danny removed the ring and slipped it on the third finger of her left hand. "Will you marry me, my sweet Jenny?"

She gazed enchanted at the dazzling ring. "Yes, Danny," she answered with pure, rapturous bliss. The ring looked exquisite on her finger, as if it had always been there and would be there forever, a perfect token of their timeless love.

Look for the First Four Books in the Heartland Memories Series

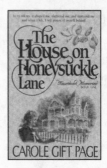

The House on Honeysuckle Lane (Book One)

It's 1932, and Annie Reed and her best friend, Cath Herrick, share dreams of the future at Annie's house on Honeysuckle Lane. But never could they have imagined how troubles brewing in the world around them would reach into their lives and change so much.

0-8407-6777-3 • Trade Paperback • 288 pages

Home to Willowbrook (Book Two)

When Catherine Herrick awakens from a coma after a car accident, she must rebuild her shattered life. As old memories come back, Catherine begins to learn hard lessons of acceptance and renewal. Set just after World War II, this is a compelling story of faith, mercy, and the power of love to heal wounded hearts.

0-8407-6778-1 • Trade Paperback • 252 pages

The Hope of Herrick House (Book Three)

When a devastating fire kills her mother and destroys her home, Bethany Rose Henry comes to live with her half-sister, Catherine Herrick. Resentful and frightened, Bethany contends with a new world as she gets to know the family she never knew she had. Soon she learns that her mother was murdered, and clues to the murderer point to a member of Catherine's family. Will Bethany speak up, or will she push everyone away, including the handsome young minister who has fallen in love with her?

0-8407-6780-3 • Trade Paperback • 288 pages

Storms Over Willowbrook (Book Four)

It's 1951 and Alice Marie Reed has finally become a success as host of a popular TV show. Then comes an urgent message summoning her to a Chicago hospital, bringing her face to face with her long-lost husband who deserted her so many years ago. When reunion turns to loss and an unexpected pregnancy complicates her life, Alice Marie realizes there is only one safe place for her in the world—her old home in Willowbrook and the family she has been estranged from for so long. There she meets a handsome stranger whose mysterious mission could cost her everything, even her life.

0-7852-7651-8 • Trade Paperback • 288 pages

ABOUT THE AUTHOR

CAROLE GIFT PAGE, an award-winning novelist, has authored forty books. A professional writer for more than twenty-eight years, she is a frequent speaker at conferences, schools, churches, and women's ministries. Carole has taught creative writing at Biola University and is the recipient of the C. S. Lewis Honor book award. She has also been nominated for several Gold Medallion awards and the Campus Life Book of the Year award.

She is the author of four other books in the Heartland Memories Series—*The House on Honeysuckle Lane, Home to Willowbrook, The Hope of Herrick House,* and *Storms Over Willowbrook*—and of *In Search of Her Own, Decidedly Married,* and *Rachel's Hope,* three romances from Harlequin's Steeple Hill line. Carole and her husband, Bill, have three children and live in Moreno Valley, California.

Excerpt from *A Locket for Maggie*
Book Six in the Heartland Memories Series

Any other year Maggie would have found the towering Christmas tree in the parlor comforting, reassuring, a beauty to behold with its silver garlands, silky angel hair, and bubble lights. Any other year. She fingered one crimson candle as silent bubbles percolated mysteriously up its narrow glass stem. "I love these," she told Jordan, averting her gaze, lest he read more in her face than she wanted him to see. Lightly she said, as if candles were all that mattered, "From the time I was a child I always felt a spurt of joy watching these lights bubble. I thought they were magic."

"I know," said Jordan. "I remember. I was there."

"Of course you were," she murmured. "You've always been there."

Even to Maggie her words sounded more accusing than affirming, as if she had said, *You were there yesterday, but tomorrow's another story.* She gazed again at the ornaments. It was more than memories they stirred; not memories; rather, feelings that Maggie couldn't articulate, even to Jordan; strong, heartfelt, urgent emotions, deep as the roots of the gnarled oak trees surrounding her parents' home—this timeworn Victorian mansion on Honeysuckle Lane where she had lived forever, where life was wonderfully, infuriatingly predictable. Try as she might, she could never get far from her roots.

The memories flooding over her today, the sudden sweep of feelings, were like that exactly. Their roots were deep, untouchable, unseen. One knew they were there, felt their presence, saw the result of their work—the sturdy tree with its limbs flowering everywhere—but one didn't see the roots.

With a sharp breath she turned at last and looked at Jordan, tears dancing in her eyes. *Please, God, don't let him see what's really there.*

"You're in a mood." Jordan was standing by the love seat, arms crossed over his crisp new navy uniform, his pilot "wings of gold" gleaming on his left-breast pocket. He was a tanned, strapping man, over six feet tall, with the hardy, stalwart face of a warrior—high forehead, straight, distinctive nose, generous chin. But he still had the jovial, mischievous eyes of a boy eager to please. Even now, a curious expression crossed his face, a mixture of love, wonder, and pride, as if he'd just climbed a mountain or won a race and was waiting for her to congratulate him. She couldn't, wouldn't. She was losing him.